THREE TIMES TABLE

Three Times Table

Sara Maitland

Chatto & Windus
LONDON

Published in 1990 by
Chatto & Windus Ltd
20 Vauxhall Bridge Road
London SW1V 2SA

A CIP catalogue record for this book is available from the British
Library.

ISBN 0 7011 3497 6

Typeset at The Spartan Press Ltd,
Lymington, Hants
Printed in Great Britain by
Mackays of Chatham plc,
Chatham, Kent

I would like to thank Donald Lee, who introduced me to gardening; Mildred
Lee, who introduced me to teenagers; Ros Hunt, who went on being interested; Richard Jones and the St Mary's Tenants' Association, whose garden I
have shamelessly plundered; Alan Mould, who really tried to help me understand maths and mathematicians; Rowan Williams, for more than his quotation; John Noble Wilford, whom I have never met, but who wrote *The
Riddle of the Dinosaur*, which has been my principal source book; Anne
McDermid *sine qua non*; Jonathan Burnham; Antonia Shooter; Janet
Batsleer; Matt Hoffman; Michelene Wandor; Emily Young, and the whole
staff of Hackney Borough, Parks and Recreation Department, who not only
answered endless questions but also manage against almost impossible odds
to make the parks and gardens around here so beautiful.

*For Adam Lee, who introduced me to
dinosaurs and other joys*

BOOK ONE

'But the dragons,' said Arren. 'Do they not do great evil? Are they innocent?'

'The dragons! The dragons are avaricious, insatiable, treacherous; without pity, without remorse. But are they evil? Who am I to judge the acts of dragons? They are wiser than men are. It is with them as with dreams, Arren. We men dream dreams, we work magic, we do good, we do evil. The dragons do not dream. They are dreams. They do not work magic: it is their substance, their being. They do not do: they are.'

'In Serilune,' said Arren, 'is the skin of Bar Oth, killed by Keor, Prince of Enlad, three hundred years ago. No dragons have ever come to Enlad since that day.'

'There is a desire in you,' said Sparrowhawk, 'to see dragons?'

'Yes.'

'Their blood is cold, and venomous. You must not look into their eyes. They are older than mankind.' He was silent a while and then went on, 'And though I came to forget or regret all I have ever done, yet I would remember that once I saw the dragons aloft on the wind at sunset above the western isles; and I would be content.'

Ursula le Guin.

One

The curator had had a tiring day.

A very tiring day.

Rachel Petherington was seventy-four years old and it had been a terribly tiring day.

She stood now, a moment's pause, at the top of the monumental sweep of staircase, under the shadow of her grandiose museum. Once she had found it ostentatious, typically Victorian, but now she loved it, and its outrageous vulgarity; she was soothed, reassured, although the traffic pouring past the foot of the staircase did not notice or care. Normally she would have slipped out of the door at the back – modern, convenient to her office and about half a mile nearer home – but today she needed that pause, that assured swagger; she needed all the outdated civic dignity that the ornate brickwork could give her; she needed that moment of standing framed in the massive doorway and looking out over the traffic through the plane trees. She needed to steady herself.

For a flicker of time the pause became a pose. She hitched her voluminous and shabby satchel further behind her back, out of sight, and stuck her hands deep into the pockets of her jacket. Even the noise of the traffic could not silence her mother's voice saying, 'Rachel, I do wish you wouldn't adopt those mannish postures,' and she grinned a defiance nearly sixty years old. There were no cameras; the pose was for her own invisible spirits to admire; for them to congratulate her on her courage and integrity. She could seek no other praise. She had not acted virtuously, only necessarily. There would be no congratulations, nor should there be.

Rachel Petherington had had the most tiring day in her long life, and standing here her back turned to the modern revolving door, looking out over the city, she wished she were dead.

The gardener had had a tiring day.

At precisely the same moment, several miles further east, Phoebe Petherington also paused at the top of a flight of stairs. A rather different flight this, at the top of an eleven-storey tower block in Hackney. A few moments before she had chained her bicycle to the gate of the dustbin store and, finding that the lift was not working, had started to climb the stairs.

The stairwell was not attractive, but the lift would not have been either; enough of the windows had been broken to allow the smell from what were obviously puddles of piss to be diluted and unoppressive, but the graffiti were aggressive and insulting, and were scrawled without grace or energy. The stairs went in nines, she had noted, nine steps then a flat turning, then nine steps and another turning; a rectilinear spiral. She had climbed nearly 400 steps and now she paused puffing, although she was unusually fit for her age. She tried to have righteous thoughts about how appalling it would be to make this climb with a baby and shopping, but self-mockery and panting interrupted them. Now, when she had recovered her breath, she would turn out of the stairwell and into the top corridor with its blank walls and green painted front doors and walk along to the window so that she could look out over her garden, although she did not know what comfort she could expect from it. She had had a tiring day.

A terribly tiring day.

She was thirty-seven years old. It had been the most tiring day of her life. And standing here her lungs heaving and her eyes closed, she was afraid that she would live.

The schoolgirl had had a tiring day, and she too paused for a moment on her walk across the park.

She had already passed the playground on the Bayswater side where she had, once upon a time, learned to swing herself with wildly waving legs, a joy that had been short-lived in her case. She had briefly been tempted to climb the iron palisade and try once more that older pleasure, now she had jettisoned more exotic joys, but she had hastened on, reluctant to be late.

She had passed between the Round Pond and Kensington Palace, and now paused at the top of the hill and looked down towards the gate. She could see Hermione waiting for her, her bright red jacket and black hair unmistakable in the paling sunshine. Such a short distance away. It was the first journey in her whole life that Maggie had made on foot and alone, and she felt the bleakness of being solitary.

She also noted with pleasure a new ability to look out at what was real. She noticed the people more than the leafing trees and greening grass. They seemed to her to have a precision, a novel solidness – *this* little pink nosed baby in *this* red-and-white striped buggy, wearing *this* navy blue padded suit with *these* candy pink stripes pushed by *this* woman with a brown wool coat open to the springtime. It reminded her of the first time she had worn her glasses: the fuzziness of mild myopia suddenly replaced with a sharp focus so that each hair on this passing old man's head seemed like a sturdy wire. But although she recognised that this would be some sort of compensation, that it was indeed for this precise clarity that she had made her choices in the dark of the night before, it did not seem somehow quite enough. So she paused.

Maggie Petherington was fifteen years old. She had endured the most tiring day of her short life, and standing here looking down on the road and her waiting friend she was afraid that she had grown up.

All three of them had guessed the evening before that this would be a tiring day, but, although they all lived in the same house and were as closely related as three women could be, none of them had mentioned this fact to any of the others.

There were at this precise moment probably eight million people in London alone, all of them somewhere and going somewhere else. And dogs and ideas and house plants and dreams and lead particles held in solution in exhaust fumes. More things than were imaginable were actually happening. For example, Rachel's mother, Margaret Hunter-Pearce, née MacDonald, turned in her grave – she had been restless there for fifty years.

The traffic lights at the top of Gloucester Road changed and the renewed sweep of the traffic distracted Hermione's attention so she did not see her friend Maggie pause above her.

The man who should have been mending the lift in the tower block suffered another attack of violent coughing as he lay in bed wondering how soon his wife would get home.

High over the glowing city Fenna puffed delicately from his vast nostrils, creating smoke rings so perfect that they made him laugh a deep dragon laugh.

The very top floweret of a hyacinth in the Community Association's little park, like a butterfly from a chrysalis, broke through its own laborious green bud and flexed its waxy wings in the sunshine; several specks of dust in the closed dinosaur exhibition hall in the museum drifted into the air and were transformed into a rose pink cloud by the late sunlight piercing through the stained glass upper windows.

Millions of years elsewhere a great diplodocus trailed its forty-foot tail across the swamp. St Margaret of Antioch, who never existed at all, finally climbed out of the dark belly of the dragon. Paracelsus, half crazy with the effort, wandered in his mediaeval herb garden struggling to think new thoughts in an old language. Deep inside itself the mutant cell took its own selfish route and with symmetrical elegance divided itself into two. Franz von Nopsca, the would-be King of Albania, carefully stirred the massive dose of barbiturates into his lover's tea and smiled. Tang Li in her palace in the Northern Province contemplated her bound feet and feared that she could never be a revolutionary – which made her so angry that she had her gardeners whipped for letting the water lilies go rusty at their fleshy edges. The concept of a quark inside the neutron of an atom probably agreed to consent to the uncertainty principle.

And yet really it was an evening of London at its sweetest and these three women paused just for a moment at the end of their tiring day.

All of these things were represented in their home. All three, for a start, had photographs of each other in their bedrooms.

Rachel kept her photographs under the glass of her neat dressing-table in her bedroom. She had three pictures of Phoebe, and the one least hidden by tidy clutter showed Phoebe at about four playing chess with her father; they were sitting on a low wall in a north Oxford garden, Martin looking both gentle and distinguished and Phoebe, with a face of perfect concentration and a neat white bow in her hair, solemnly reaching out for the white knight. The second, a small print of a formal portrait, showed Phoebe at about sixteen – almost but not quite a coming-out portrait, her grandmother's pearls discreetly tucked behind neat white blouse; an earnest and intelligent face, of character rather than beauty. The third photo, a more recent coloured snapshot, was also of Maggie and showed the two of them sitting beside a river eating a picnic – and with them, was a smiling man. At some point this picture had been neatly cut in two to separate the women from the man, but had since been stuck, equally neatly, back together. This man was not in fact Maggie's father, of whom there were no pictures in the house, but a Sino-American paleontologist, Rachel's old colleague and Maggie's beloved Uncle Wong. There was another picture of Maggie. It showed her juggling with four oranges in the kitchen, delighted, showing off and concentrating hard.

Hanging on the wall near Rachel's bedroom window there was a faded photograph of Tang Li, taken in her palace near Kalgan, standing beside a now unrecognisable Rachel, then aged about seven, both of them looking formal and, in that formality, oddly alike. And a cartoon of Nopsca, signed by himself and inscribed to Rachel's mother, was framed in her drawing room.

Phoebe's photographs were stuck under a perspex frame. There was one of Rachel showing her nearly half a century ago, brown and whipcord slender, wearing shorts and a soft sun-hat over her cropped hair and looking, it had to be acknowledged, magnificent. There were several pictures of Maggie, beginning with one of her naked and feeding at Phoebe's breast; but the one most prominently displayed showed Maggie aged about two in a buggy at a political demonstration. She was surrounded by a group of women and grinning wildly as she waved a balloon printed with a now indecipherable slogan. In none of these pictures was Maggie alone.

Phoebe also had a picture of her very beautiful grandmother, Margaret Hunter-Pearce, wearing the exceptionally ugly street clothes of 1912. A close examination of the picture showed that it was not an original, but a print of a photograph, which had clearly been cut out of a book. She was not alone either.

Beside Phoebe's bed, some of them open and left spine upwards, were several books, one entitled *Paracelsus: Magic into Science* by Henry Pachter. In Phoebe's sitting room a white hyacinth in a workmanlike flowerpot was just coming into full flower and the same sun that pierced the exhibition hall illuminated the motes of dust that danced in the air.

In Maggie's magical attic, pictures were stuck higgledy-piggledy onto a board; there was a picture cut-out of a magazine showing Rachel and herself in Rachel's museum: she had been littler then and was playing with a plastic model of Carnegie's diplodocus on Rachel's desk. Rachel was looking quite grand and quite fat sitting in her leather desk chair. There was also a picture of Phoebe climbing a rock face in the rain, though it was hard to tell it was Phoebe since she was wearing a woolly hat, looking in the other direction, and the camera lens had been blurred with rain: Maggie had taken this herself with the camera she had been given for her tenth birthday. Both these pictures were deeply obscured by other papers, stickers, advertisements, cartoons and a surprising number of sheets labelled Important List, or even Very Important List.

On almost the only other available section of vertical wall there was a paler patch, where there usually hung Maggie's eleventh-century

7

illumination of St Margaret of Antioch leading a dragon into a city on a golden chain. It was far too valuable a painting to hang there in a child's bedroom, and Rachel had only been able to give it to Maggie by pretending to Phoebe, who was woefully ignorant of such things, that it was an almost worthless Victorian copy. And although Fenna had been driven out of the room, his presence still hung over it with a soft smell not dissimilar from stale tobacco smoke.

The memory of the coughing electrician who should have been mending the lift in the tower block moved along hidden wires all over the house, for he had been the apprentice of the man who had done the rewiring thirteen years ago when Rachel had bought the house and divided it into the two self-contained but linked maisonettes where the three women now lived.

The house, even without its women in it, was filled with the ghosts they had made of each other, and with other shadows.

Photographs taken at this precise moment, on this February evening, would show Rachel Petherington (née Hunter-Pearce) pausing at the top of the steps of her museum, where she had honourably and with distinction filled the post of keeper of dinosaur fossils for many years; technically her job was now honorary, a dowager keeper, but it had genuinely not occurred to anyone even to consider that she might move out of her own office. The huge doors would make an impressive frame for a large woman with neatly pinned-up grey hair and an air of prosperous benevolence. But the self-conscious element in her pause, the suggestion of a pose, was of professional not personal vanity. She knew that Phoebe kept the ancient photograph of her in her room, but that was Phoebe's vanity, not hers. For herself, she had known what had come about one day several years ago when she had been reading a P. G. Wodehouse story. It contained a description of a woman who 'fitted into my biggest armchair as if it had been designed for her by someone who knew they were wearing armchairs tight about the hips that season.' Instead of laughing she had wept. She had, when young, always imagined that she would grow up into a magnificent old lady, tall and gaunt with a craggy but splendid bone structure and fingers like lizards' talons. She had been wrong about that too. Now she bought her clothes at Harrod's, because they did not have a separate 'Out Size Department'.

A photograph of Phoebe taken at the same instant would have been a snapshot. Her pause was mainly to gather her breath and she leaned against the wall puffing, unposed. Despite the puffing she was a strong woman and, despite the earliness of the year, deeply tanned – an unusual

8

mixture of just-back-from-skiing and the real weathering of outside work. Her dark hair was beautifully and smartly cut, but her fingernails were filthy. Looking at her it was hard to guess exactly what she did for a living, although the air of competence and self-assurance might make an observer curious. She had once, long ago and far away, been a promising young mathematician, but now she was a gardener, employed by Hackney Council with responsibility for the small community garden that lay at the foot of this tower block. The camera would have caught her at a rare moment of unselfconsciousness, head down and lungs heaving, an unusually tall woman approaching middle age with a great deal of physical grace, a craggy but splendid bone structure, and strong hands with fingers like lizards' talons.

The best photograph of Maggie now would have been a long shot, taken from the Round Pond side of the Broad Walk, almost as far back as the bandstand and looking towards the palace garden, a wide scene taking in the other people around her and the space of the park itself. Only this distance could properly catch that extraordinary grace and slenderness, almost a frailty, as though a wind might snatch her up and away forever, the peculiar beauty that made people look at her more closely and then wonder what it was that made them do it. Close up she seemed quite ordinary, a perfectly normal teenager, no more attractive than most and not helped by the odd clothes that were at that moment the height of fashion among her peer group: a very ragged and faded pair of blue jeans, a man's suit jacket several sizes too large, gaudily coloured socks and clumpy black lace-up shoes. It was a brilliant camouflage. For several years she had worked hard on the job of disguising herself as normal and now it fitted her as it never had before. In a close-up taken on this particular evening there would moreover have been a singularly unendearing look on her face; not so much of open misery, but of sulkiness, a mulish obstinate expression of one set mainly on enduring. Taken from a distance this expression would not have been visible; instead her sadness somehow separated her from the other passing people and would have offered to the camera an unexpected and touching sense of aloneness, a solitary hermit in teenage attire standing at the top of a hill.

9

Two

Photographs taken at the same time on the evening before would have given such a different impression, although that evening too had been sweet and pale. By this time all three of them had at least an idea of how tiring the night ahead was going to be. So they had sought pleasure and found it, all of them, in the company of their friends.

Rachel had spent the evening with Paul and Simon.

She had arranged this the previous Thursday, when she had been getting ready to leave her office and she was ashamed that she had not realised sooner that Monday night was going to be difficult; she was a woman who didn't like to be caught out by circumstances.

She knew she should have guessed from the unusual fact that she had not asked Clare to check any of the references and had had the paper typed by a woman in Gloucester, picked at careful random out of a copy of the *TLS*. She did not like this havey-cavey conduct, but she had not drawn the correct conclusions from it either, which irritated her later. Last Thursday morning the typescript had been returned – and very nicely done too, Rachel had thought, pleased: two neat copies and only a few very minor errors, almost inevitable from someone who had probably never typed up a scientific paper, let alone one in her field.

Being committed – more lovingly and more clearly than at any time since she was twenty-five – to scientific excellence, Rachel had read the paper with a detached pleasure: it was as calm and reasoned and sparkling with accuracy and detail as anything she had ever done before. It demonstrated with grace the remarkable breadth of her reading in the contemporary literature, and it was warmly generous to the contributions of previous scholars, even where she was obliged to contradict them. It did not mention Maggie or Fenna directly, because she had been afraid that this might confuse things and she had wanted there to be no possibility of mistake. But she had known, and so perhaps had they, and her love and fear infused the paper with an unusual brilliance.

Even as she had read it through she had the altruistic thought that she ought to show it to Clare, her dear and conscientious research student. ('It isn't fair,' they had complained for quarter of a century, 'she always gives jobs to the girls,' as though men didn't give jobs to the boys.) She felt, as she had often felt before, very sorry for Clare; who had a methodical mind and a plain dumpy face, little dress sense and no charm. If Clare had been a man she would have done very nicely in a mild sort of way, but without Rachel's sensitive patronage she would probably never have got this far. Clare's admiration and devotion irritated her though, and suddenly made her fell guilty as well. Clare would need now to distance herself from Rachel professionally; and she, Rachel, was going to have to help her, as she lacked the acumen or guile to do it for herself. Perhaps it would help her if Rachel invited her to co-sign the paper.

Rachel had sat there, feeling benevolent, almost smug, planning Clare's future and neatly correcting the minor typing errors. In her mind she drafted a letter to her old colleague and friend who edited a major US journal in animal paleontology. She had felt in control.

When she was just about ready to think of going home, there had been a knock on the door and without even thinking she had swept the neat pile of A4 sheets into a drawer with a gesture of panic and slammed it shut.

'Come in,' she called, panting, her hand still tight on the brass drawer handle. It was one of the janitors, come about a loose window clasp, and she felt her whole body heaving with relief. And then she had known instantly and shamefully that she had not made up her mind. That she had left every loophole possible, she still might not go through with it. She did not want to go through with it.

So immediately, swallowing her blushes, she had rung Paul and invited herself around to supper the next Monday, the evening before the Board Meeting.

'No, nothing special, should there be? Just that I haven't seen you and Simon for ages and someone's just cancelled something that night' – kind of true she told herself, she had cancelled her own peace of mind – 'What? No, please, just the two of you. It would be lovely if you could put up with an old lady. No, I didn't really say that . . . Bless you, about seven-thirty, then.' She had been almost weeping with relief.

She did not dare to be alone. She could not go home to an empty and frightening house; nor could she go home to her own charming and comfortable flat, because the two were the same. Even worse was the idea of spending the evening with Phoebe, because then Phoebe might see through the webs of normality that she had wound around herself and her dilemma. Phoebe was probably the only person in the whole world who would even have an inkling of how expensive this all was for her. Because of course it was damned expensive. No one could know how expensive, except possibly Phoebe, and she did not want Phoebe to know. She did not want Phoebe's pity, nor her scorn, nor to be grist for Phoebe's self-righteous theoretical mills. She had told Phoebe nothing and she hoped her daughter wouldn't find out. She could not afford Phoebe to know the weight of her dependence. Not yet. She would need Phoebe soon enough, when she was old and dying; she could not afford to use up her daughter's limited supply of tolerance and guilt.

Although ringing Paul had been instinctive, out of interest she surveyed the rest of her closer acquaintance, wondering what she would have done if Paul had been out or even away.

Bill was in America. She could ring him of course, but he would not see the problem the way she saw it. She was not up to having her inner being probed over an Atlantic cable. As a matter of fact she had never really been up to having her inner being probed, even face to face, by Bill. And this, she insisted to herself, was not a psychological problem, it was simply a professional one.

But she needed to keep away from her professional colleagues too. She knew well enough what she ought to do; but she knew that no one in the museum would want her to do it. Even Clare would rather have let her off the hook, and not just from professional ambition either, sadly. Clare would feel sorry for her, as she so often did for Clare and she did not think she could bear that. She neither wanted nor needed that compassionate tolerance, and that professional indulgence. They would all let her, they would even encourage her, to get away with it. That realisation made her sad. It hurt. She did not want to despise them. Martin, her late husband, would have despised them.

Actually Martin's acerbic pleasure in her renunciation of her original beliefs was exactly what she needed now. It was odd, but what she missed him for most nowadays were precisely the qualities that she had found most annoying when he was still alive. He had despised museum work, and would have been delighted to disparage her colleagues and encourage her to snub them. She reminded herself that he would probably disapprove of her new ideas even more than he had her old ones.

Exasperated, he would have slapped his hand against his forehead and then banged it down on her typescript and barked, 'For heaven's sake, Rachel, can't you manage your footnotes better than this?' He would not have given her the benefit of a single doubt, and would have dismissed all her fretfulness in a highly practical demand for his supper. She needed someone who had their priorities that clear.

She knew that the museum would have given her every benefit of the doubt and then some extra. It was a popular exhibit, it fitted in with modern ideas of museumology even better than it fitted in with outdated ideas of palaeontology. And they would not want to be made fools of, for which she could hardly blame them. Part of her fear, her reluctance, was as simple as that: she did not want to look a fool. Even her dear Clare – several months ago she had tried to probe Clare's reading of the new literature, by hinting in half-jokes that there might be something in the new theories, and even Clare had suggested that they leave it 'for now'. She had meant – Rachel now saw – until she, Rachel, was dead, or at least senile. She could not last forever. Much more dignified all round to give the demolition job to some bright young man whose professional greed would give a delicious savour to his task.

If she confessed to Clare, she would indeed be invited round to Clare's clean dull flat, where Clare would cook her a well-meaning supper – lamb chops and apple crumble, perhaps – and would pour over her all the daughterly affection that Phoebe so stubbornly withheld. But Rachel knew suddenly that she preferred Phoebe's astringency, so like Martin's, and the last thing she wanted now was kindness to a poor old lady, and the sympathetic reassurance that she really did not need to publish the paper at all. No one would expect it of her.

Paul would not be kind, he would be triumphant; he had, in a real sense, won on every count. Despite being younger, perhaps because of being younger, he had travelled faster and more bravely on the journey away from his intellectual beginnings. And he had, in his going, sowed the first seeds of her doubts.

When Paul, over supper, with a mischievous grin, his beautiful hands coiled round his wine glass, had first said, 'You're not going to like this, Rachel, but I'm coming round to Catastrophe Theory,' she had laughed at him. She had thought he was joking, teasing her as she teased him. They often laughed at each other, because under the teasing and the pleasant dinners lay a solid security. They still had that deep mutual respect that had led her, voluntarily and though it was not her field, to work with meticulous and Martin-trained patience through his thesis footnotes; and had led him to dedicate his first book to her as 'the most creative intelligence in our science'. So she had laughed at him then, gaily, and they had enjoyed – or rather she had enjoyed, perhaps he had been frightened or angry, she must ask him sometime – a merry giggle over the more outrageous suggestions of comets and meteors crashing through the universe.

Later, more seriously, in an academic context, he had raised the problem again.

'Rachel, the leaps do seem to be there. What are we going to do with them?'

She had pooh-poohed it all; dragged up in text-book form the inevitable deficiencies in the data. She had told him sharply, as though he were an undergraduate trying to be clever,

'For heaven's sake, Paul, we're Darwinians, aren't we? I thought the DNA chaps had resolved that one; there is something to mutate and it mutates. You don't need me to tell you that. Slowly and steadily. Where are you going next? Bakker's warm blooded *Deinonychi*? Sheldrake's morphogenetic fields?'

'Possibly yes to the first, and probably no to the second. I didn't say that anyway, I said some sudden and catastrophic intervention. Would that, perhaps, explain the data better? It needs explaining. That's all I said.'

She was about to sneer, when she heard Martin's own tones in her voice, and she blushed instead. After a pause she tried more gently, 'That's a post-Hiroshima solution, not a scientific one. You can't bear it, if you're going to be blotted out at a blow, you're not going to give the dinosaurs the gentle ending they deserved.'

'Come to that,' he said indignantly, 'perhaps gradualism is a nineteenth-century liberal bourgeois solution not a scientific one. If the huge monolith of the moneyed aristocracy is going to be slowly and subtly destroyed by the tiny but hardworking rodents of capitalism, then the poor dinosaurs must go the same way.'

Suddenly stung, she nearly rose to his bait, but caught herself in time and added, with a very sweet smile,

'They were nicer than us, Paul, much nicer, so they had a nicer ending.'

He had returned the smile and she had breathed out, but there was still an edginess in his voice when he said, 'Don't bring theology into this, Rachel; it doesn't suit you.'

Now though, it was his bookcase, not hers, that was full of theology.

He was still travelling. A long smooth trajectory from his extraordinary thin white hand on her door twenty years ago, to Simon and this Vicarage now. He would be glad of what was happening to her and he would never rub it in. What he would do instead was love and affirm her, not as a reward but because he would always love and affirm her whatever happened. He was the love of her life, and when he sat on his sofa with his arm casually along the cushion behind Simon's head, vicariously, strangely, it would please her. The first time they met, he had said to her over that long lunch, 'They told me you were the only Big Ideas Paleontologist in England. Now I've found my Big Ideas teacher.' It was a professional courtesy, a thank-you-for-your-time, but it was also true.

And here, the following Monday evening, was of course the exactly right place to be. She knew it the moment that Paul filled her usual heavy cut-glass tumbler of whisky and handed it to her with a smile. It had never occurred to her that he might be queer, not in all the first ten years she had known him. It was only when he had told her that he was in love with Simon that she learned that she fancied him – as well as loving and liking and working with him, she fancied him and she always had, right from the start. It was one of the reasons why their friendship worked; she had fancied him and he had never fancied her. Thank goodness she had not noticed, it would have been fatal.

Simon had done something almost miraculous for Paul. To an extra-ordinary degree Paul had suddenly come into focus, not for her but for himself. The loss of his overreaching desire to do great work had left him free to do good work. Not to lean on the data, but to look at it. He was lucky to have had Rachel to show him the way in, and he was lucky to have had Simon to set him free to move on. She smiled at him, in the simple trust that he would not push, would not comfort, would expect of her still and continually only that thing that was most important to her, that she should act with a complete respect for her professional standing. She was not in his view diminished by being wrong, she was enhanced by it.

She knew too that it was impossible for her to tell him about tomorrow, impossible for her to confess to him that it had even occurred to her not to publish, not to tell them. He was ferociously pure. She had not told him about the paper either; once she did, there would be no escape for her. It was the only thing she could do, she suspected, that would dent his love for her.

She did not even tell him how on her way from the office she had crept into the dinosaur hall and admired her own dinosaur. She had admired it and apologised to it and asked it for guidance. She really was going gaga.

Instead she drank their excellent whisky. Nothing rocked the smooth flow of humour and lightheartedness that she shared with Simon, who reminded her suddenly and surprisingly of Phoebe's friend Lisa, with whom she had similar affectionate bantering exchanges, though two people more superficially different would be hard to imagine. Under the banter they both respected her and they both liked her. Simon was cleverer though. And, praise be, a much better cook. Rachel seldom cooked herself, but she loved food; and went through to the kitchen with pleasurable anticipation. Simon served quickly and neatly, without fuss and, she had learned over the years, did not want or like too many comments, but she enjoyed it enormously. As he extracted a whole baked sea bass from the oven and ran a flat knife along its spine he deflected her admiration by asking,

'Have you decided on your dates for Italy, then? We've got a picture of the house now, and a wonderful view. I'll show you after supper.'

'Simon, it's sweet of you, but I'm not entirely convinced that you want me.'

They had invited her to come out and stay with them in the cottage they had booked, as they did each year. She had been touched by the invitation, and had discovered that she very much wanted to go. She found travelling for pleasure very difficult. Holidays were one of the things that Martin had always organised, and she had never learned the skill. She loved going to warm places and seeing new things, but she did not quite know how to do it on her own. She had not been abroad for several years now. But Simon, like Martin, seemed highly skilled; if she was staying with them it would be easy. She wanted to go so much it made her shy of pressing her luck.

'Wouldn't I be a boring old nuisance?' she added.

'Well, Rachel,' Paul said, 'we're only asking you because Simon feels he doesn't get enough penitential sacrifices when on holiday, and because I know you are stinking rich and will take us out to dinner in better places than we can afford.'

She looked up and caught his grin.

'Come on,' he said more severely. 'Don't do that to me or to yourself.'

'Actually,' Simon said, 'Paul is desperate for you to come. Most of our friends are either entirely wrapped up in their children or else, like me, obsessed by relics. Paul can't bear wandering round churches having to observe our bizarre devotions, and hear our well-informed highly cultivated comments on the history of ecclesiastical architecture.'

'Rubbish,' Paul interrupted. 'It's not that. It's you, and your utterly boring style of sightseeing. He walks round these exquisite places with his nose in Baedeker, so frightened of missing a twelfth-century ambo, or what have you, that he never actually looks at the whole structure.'

'How odd,' Rachel said, 'my husband was like that too. Sixteen travel guides and no eyes, I used to say.'

'Well I like that,' Simon retorted, turning his back to remove the potatoes from the oven, 'you two are the ones who are always telling me that if you don't see the detail properly you can't see the whole. The evolution of architectural style is no different from the evolution of mammoth tusks.'

'Yes, it is,' they said in one voice and smiled at each other.

'No, it isn't. Well, I suppose for architecture Lamarck works better than Darwin.'

'Wait a minute,' said Rachel.

'You're cheating,' said Paul, 'what on earth has Lamarck got to do with all this? Don't show off.'

Rachel said playfully, 'I don't know, Paul. Perhaps cathedrals do evolve by inheriting acquired characteristics.'

'I wasn't thinking of that,' Simon said, coming back to the table, 'I was thinking of evolution by aspiration, by desire. Crawling animals grow wings because they want to fly so much. Cathedrals reach higher and higher, stretch up like giraffes, in their desire for God.'

Rachel laughed and was about to say that Lamarck had never said that, it was a misunderstanding, but Simon went on, 'It makes so much more sense and comfort of things you see. Even rococo excrescences, or cancer growths, are just aspirations that didn't quite work, a failed struggle for wings, or other new organs.'

'Ah, metaphysics,' said Paul grinning. 'I thought we were talking about science.'

'Real scientists,' said Simon tauntingly, 'not life scientists like you, poor lambs, but real scientists are getting more and more metaphysical every day. Look at all that eastern-mysticism-meets-western-mathematics; the new physics as the door to heaven, eh? What does Heisenberg and his uncertainty principle do to your scientific model, Rachel? Or that sub-atomic time reversal stuff? Does the old man throw dice, and if so why shouldn't cathedrals aspire to their own evolution?'

They all laughed and in that moment of relaxation Rachel confessed, 'It's no good asking me about all that; you'd have to ask Phoebe.'

'Phoebe?' he sounded surprised; Simon didn't like Phoebe much.

Paul extracted a fish bone with indecent haste and said quickly, 'Surely you know Phoebe is a maths whizz?'

'Was,' said Rachel tersely.

'Is,' said Paul serenely, 'or at least enough of one to sort out that stuff for you, Si, but you'll get short shrift if you aren't careful. She takes it with a kind of bitter seriousness, like ex-catholics. And what's more,' he added, 'she has gone seeking spiritual enlightenment in the distant east.'

'Ages ago,' said Rachel crossly.

'How extraordinary,' said Simon, 'I never knew that. I thought she never thought about anything except the political status of female gardeners after the socialist revolution. I thought she was in love with the soil that nourished the noble workers.'

'Mock not, that thou be not mocked,' Paul said mockingly.

'And anyway,' said Rachel 'that's nonsense; she's just idle. She can be quick enough when she wants, but she lacks commitment. I don't think Phoebe is in love with anything or anyone.'

'How sad. Poor Phoebe,' and Simon sounded as though he meant it completely. Rachel saw him look at Paul and glow. The same glow as she felt when she looked at her dinosaur. How could they really expect her to destroy her beloved? It's not fair, she wanted to whine. Instead she smiled at them, and Paul asked how Maggie was.

How was Maggie?

Maggie. Her legs were so skinny that they filled you with fear for her on windy days. Her shoulder-blades were like wings, trapped under her shirts, mobile, fluent, fighting their restraint. Sometimes when Maggie spoke her silvery words of wisdom you could almost see the delicate flames emerge from her mouth and nostrils, not to burn but to illuminate. Phoebe had grown up to repudiate the hard clarity of science, butting her fierce and stubborn head against the edifice of logical thinking, of a reasoned and relaxed relationship between facts and conclusions. Phoebe called it 'masculine modes of thought' and rejected it conscientiously. It made her a cranky and trying young woman, frankly, Rachel thought, though Phoebe was her daughter and she went on loving her. But Phoebe had produced Maggie and Maggie was a bell of clarity. The truth was in her. So deeply and naturally that she did not have to fight it. The ancient and enduring truth, so that when she sang and danced, and walked and breathed, the light poured out of her and her shiny eyes were wide and deep.

Now that was love. She would not sacrifice Maggie to any principle or cause. She opened her mouth to tell Paul that Maggie was as always as nearly perfect as it was possible for a fifteen-year-old to be in the eyes of its stuffy and elderly grandmother, when she had a pressing terrifying sense that this was not true.

'I don't know, Paul. I worry about her. Phoebe doesn't like me to, so I try not to, but . . . but I think she has got stuck somehow. Something isn't right, and I don't know what. She's in . . .' Rachel wanted to say that Maggie was in trouble, but she did not have the nerve.

For once Paul did not give her time to collect the right words,

'Rachel, she's fifteen. Of course she's in trouble. It's not easy, being fifteen. Maggie, of almost anyone I know, will be all right. She's protected. Honestly. I tell you what, bring her to Umbria with you. She'll enjoy it. Swimming pool and all. She's fine.'

She wanted so much to believe it, that she did. She sank into the comfort they offered her.

And then suddenly, just when she was ready to leave and Simon had gone next door to call a taxi for her, Paul hugged her abruptly, almost roughly,

'I've got something for you,' he said, and reached into the inside pocket of his jacket, pulling out his wallet as though he were about to give her a tip. The idea made her grin. He handed her a bit of paper, folded in four. She opened it and read the quotation in his tiny immaculate writing written slap onto the middle of the page as he always did.

> This is the most miserable time of all. The hunch is stronger than the observation. The links between the hunch and the observation are clearly there, but at this stage people still think you are quite mad. They are as fearful as if you had cancer. The danger in cancer is to die; . . . and the danger in the scientific process – at least in this society – is the danger of having an idea which is wrong. It's equivalent to death.
>
> *An Imagined World.* June Goodfield

'Who's she?' Rachel asked.

'June Goodfield? A journalist I think, but the speaker's a biologist, or a biochemist, something. A woman.'

'I may cry,' she said.

She wanted to say, 'Paul, tomorrow I'm going to have to destroy it, order it to be taken down. Paul it's even worse than that. I don't know if I can, if I have the courage. I may cheat, lie, deceive; it's my dinosaur, my father's dinosaur, my life work, Paul. I wish I was dead.'

19

But she did not know how to say those things, so she just repeated, 'I may cry.'

'You'd better not,' he said, and held her gently against his soft wool shirt. His jacket smelled like her father's and she leaned against him like a child. It flashed through her mind that she had not been held so, by someone who would honestly try to take care of her, for far too long. She stayed there, rocked, enclosed, for a few seconds – a fat old woman and a queer, she tried to tell herself, but she felt only peace and safety.

'Thank you,' she said and gave him a kiss; and after that, almost inevitably, it took much too long for the taxi to arrive.

Phoebe had spent the evening with her oldest and still closest friend Lisa in a wine bar.

She had not planned it with Rachel's precision. That was not her way. She had stayed late at work, freshly aware of the new energy of the garden in the expanding spring. In the morning she had finished the disgusting task of cleaning slimy mould off the cement paths. The job had put her in a bad temper; the paths themselves were a constant and unhappy reminder that while she had control over her garden she did not have it over her budget. Three years ago when the garden had been only a long-deserted ex-building site she had sat with the borough surveyor and outlined a set of meandering stone-slab paths for the central section. The Community Association, reassured as to the potential smoothness and accessibility for the elderly, were happy with the design; the Parks and Recreation Department were happy with the design; she had known it would be beautiful. Now she had cement tracks which had cracked in the frost making them bumpy and irregular; they grew algae in winter making them treacherous and slippery; they looked ugly and they had to be cleaned in the early spring with a foul-smelling tar oil formulation which ruined her clothes and her sense of humour. She hated them so much that she did not even suffer her usual qualms when she applied a vicious residual herbicide.

After she had finished, and locked the weedkiller securely into the cupboard in her shed, it was after three o'clock. She thought fleetingly that she might slip off home a bit early. It was then that she realised she did not want to go home and be alone. Maggie had told her she was going out that evening. The flat would be empty and resonant. Downstairs Rachel might be lurking; Phoebe knew that she did not want to have to confront her mother and have those perceptive, bossy eyes fixed on her. Rachel saw too much and could be guaranteed to say the sensible sane thing, which was precisely what Phoebe did not want to hear.

Crossly she told herself that she still had at least two more hours to work and there was plenty that needed doing. She took vigorous shears to the heathers which were straggly from the winter, and then decided to prune the salix and dogwoods. She had new secateurs. Rachel had given them to her as a Christmas present and she had been touched then. Now they made the job a pleasure. Pruning was always satisfactory – a job she could start, do right and complete. *Cornus* especially, since so little judgement was required, she simply had to cut away everything, right down to the bottom. The piles of dark red and yellow sticks mounted cheerfully and her mood rose with them. If she was quick she could plant lily-of-the-valley this year, here between the shrubs. She leaned forward to inspect newly exposed soil around the shrubs, and the last of the thin sunshine stroked her back and kissed her naked neck. Quite suddenly she felt fit and well and gently pleased with herself.

Self-consciousness returned with the awareness that someone was watching her. She did not look round at once; she carried on steadily with her work, but now observing herself as a person observed. Finally, irritated, she straightened up and turned slowly. Lisa was sitting on one of the red shiny metal benches about fifteen feet behind her.

Her irritation turned into a smile. She covered the ground and embraced her friend with that odd looking upper-arm-only hug, with her wrists turning outwards, that people who are used to their hands being muddy learn to make graceful by practice.

'Lisa, what brings you out so far from chic West London? Can it be that you are seeking the wisdoms of the orient?'

They both laughed.

'I wanted to see you, Bea.'

'Good,' said Phoebe, and retreating from the hug, added in a fake cockney accent to tease Lisa, 'Cor, Miss, you do look posh.'

Fifteen years ago, somewhere in the middle of their running quarrel when Lisa had said she wanted to leave the house, wanted to get a proper job, Phoebe had said,

'And you'll have to wear a skirt to the office.'

Lisa had said, 'Don't be silly.'

Now the boot was on the other foot, indeed on both Phoebe's feet, and Lisa's beautiful swirly wool skirt and fashionable large jacket looked more appropriate to both of them than Phoebe's dirty overalls. But that quarrel had been over years ago.

Lisa said, 'What are you up to, then?'

Phoebe was about to say dismissively, 'Nothing interesting' when she decided that Lisa deserved better.

'I'm extending the herb garden. Shall I show you?'

She led Lisa over to a group of raised beds, divided by redwood planks. There was not, to the uninitiated eye, a great deal to see.

'Look, eight different kinds of mint. And that'll be comfrey – helps your bones set, should you need any.' Suddenly, she got excited and began to describe in great detail the division of gardening duties and therefore medical knowledge according to gender and class at various points in history.

Lisa listened, almost envious of Phoebe's fluency, and then laughed and said, 'Watch out, you'll turn into a witch.'

Phoebe smiled too, broke off with a self-mocking gesture, and pointed to a small clump of emerging leaves.

'That's dope. Finest marijuana. I'm growing it for the West Indian kids. The rastas need their ganga.'

'For God's sake, Phoebe, here, in a public park? Are you crazy?' Lisa sounded horrified.

Phoebe laughed, 'You're a nit, Lisa. Finest stinging nettles, more likely. Never try and tell me that high-salaried media ladies don't turn alarmingly respectable in middle age. But so do low-salaried borough employees. Anyway we never have enough sun to make it worth it; I'd need a greenhouse. Well, do you fancy a drink, then?'

'Not in the pub round here. I'm not dressed for it, as you noticed. Have you finished anyway? I can wait.' And after a little pause she added, 'It does look lovely; I'm happy to sit.'

This was generous, but true; Phoebe glanced around her garden. The croci and early daffodils were sparkling; the benches and toddlers' corner had been washed after the winter and the grass was beginning to grow again. The weeds had hardly started, and in the unexpected sunny weather the whole garden had an air of promising readiness. If Lisa hadn't asked so nicely, Phoebe would probably have insisted on another ten minutes while she piled her clippings into a barrow, but now she turned towards her shed, unbuttoning her overalls and pulling the top half down her arms.

'Where shall we go, then?'

'Morgans? And we could eat there later if we wanted.'

'Fine.'

In the shed Phoebe tugged her wellingtons off, and then leaned against the side of the shed and removed the bottom half of her overalls. In her socks, jeans and soft wool shirt she leaned over the sink to wash her hands.

Lisa had to keep dodging, between the tiny desk, the awkward stacks of tools and the doorway.

Phoebe, aware of her inconvenience, smiled and said, 'It's not much more crowded than your office.' She pulled off the rather muddy woollen cap she was wearing and her fringe flopped forward. She pulled on a delicate Fair Isle sweater, picked up a hairbrush from the desk and smoothed the curls on her neck. Finally she reached in the cupboard for her shoes and jacket and was suddenly transformed. The incongruity between her and Lisa disappeared and they both relaxed.

'I've got my bike. Shall we meet there?'

'Or we could drive up and I'll bring you back?'

'Fine.'

'We're meeting someone.'

'Oh?'

'And you are very sweetly going to do me a favour.'

'Oh God, who is it?'

'She's very young, and very bright.'

'And very cute, I expect.' Phoebe put on a fake leer.

'Bea, you have a filthy mind.'

'Rubbish, I've just known you too long. What role am I supposed to play in your seduction of this infant? What is truly amazing, given your susceptibility, is that you ever manage to make any money.'

'I only fancy women who are very talented.'

As she locked the gate Phoebe felt a flicker of fear, but she banished it firmly. She felt the reassurance of Lisa's company, a powerful spell to keep the witches away. Whatever Lisa wanted of her it would be harmless, and infinitely preferable to an empty house tonight.

In the wine bar, after they had bought a bottle of wine and found a table, Phoebe was less sure. Her pleasure faded and Lisa's energetic sharpness filled her with despondency. She contemplated the backs of her hands while Lisa searched for an ashtray and noted with irritation that she still had dirty fingernails. Then she looked up with a broad grin because Lisa was her friend, because she had had a good day and because she liked to be here with the cool wine glass in her hand.

'How's the dinosaur?' Lisa asked.

Phoebe grinned. 'Fine, as ever.'

Why the hell did Lisa always call her mother that? Why the hell did she always respond with that easy grin? How the hell could so many immediate and reflexive emotions be triggered by that one word. Only she, only she, not even Maggie, was allowed to criticise her mother. She of course could and did endlessly, tiresomely, even whiningly, but no one else. And she got little sympathy from her friends, almost all of whom, like Lisa, really liked, even loved Rachel. For them the humorous nickname was a reference not to Rachel's age, figure and antiquated morality, but a mark of respect for her profession, and public standing. And yet Phoebe knew that it was she, not Rachel, who kept, touched and acknowledging, the picture of Rachel in Africa; it was she who had cut out for Maggie the picture of Rachel and Maggie in the museum.

Lisa was her best friend. Her fingernails were dirty. The very mention of her mother filled her with inarticulate irritation and guilt. Her heart sank at what she had to do tomorrow. And she did not understand why she had not told Lisa, or rather she did understand and that made it worse. And after tomorrow . . . she could not even look at her fear – for herself, for Maggie, for Rachel – nor at her anger that she had to carry that fear, that responsibility. At the same time she was here and content to be here, cosseted by the warmth and comfort of so old and sturdy a friendship.

And still high above her heart she felt the dark joy of hidden, secret love. Until tomorrow. She wanted one more night of secrecy. She was not going to tell Lisa. In this moment of confusion she found she wanted, suddenly and surprisingly, her father. He was dead.

She poured herself another drink.

'God, I'm tired,' she said to Lisa, smiling sleepily. 'When is this paragon of all the graces going to appear?'

'Later. I wanted to see you first. I haven't had time with you properly for ages. How was the skiing?'

'Wonderful. Terrific snow, lots of sunshine, and a hotel where I didn't have to cook all week. No responsibilities and lots of sleep.'

'How was the sex?'

'He didn't come.'

'What? Why not?'

'His daughter got the measles.'

'Oh.'

There was a pause.

'Actually Lisa, it's over. Finished. Since Christmas, really.'

'Can I ask why?'

What could she say; because I don't love him enough, because he knows I don't love him enough. Not even enough for what we had. Because I'm in love and not with him. Because he thinks I'm insane.

Phoebe ran a sequence of possible answers through her head, and decided they were all too exhausting to contemplate. Lisa could not, would not understand, and partly she would not and could not understand because Phoebe was not telling her the whole story. And that, in Lisa's eyes, was practically a capital offence.

She said, 'Not tonight, all right?'

They smiled at each other across the slightly wobbly table, because they were old friends, and because they knew the preciousness of that old friendship and they would try to preserve it at considerable cost.

Lisa reached out a quick hand and patted Phoebe's wrist.

Phoebe filled the gap, asking with a lazy smile, 'So what is this tiny favour I'm meant to be doing you? As though I didn't know. She's just bought a darling basement flat in Kentish Town or Victoria Park and would I very sweetly design her a tasteful, easy-care garden, with water interest, and a piece of abstract sculpture, at half the price she ought to be paying for such high-quality professional advice. And she will be dead impressed, not just by the garden itself but also with you for knowing such unlikely but useful women.'

'You are such a bitch,' Lisa said laughing. 'Actually it's nothing like that. Maybe it's me doing you the favour this time. And be nice to her, she's rather serious-minded. I'll be nice to you too, I'll get another bottle of wine.'

'Plenty in this one.'

'Before she gets here. Anyway you'll drink it between you.'

Lisa got up and went back to the bar. Phoebe watched her affectionately, almost envious of all that energy and optimism. She felt tired and anxious again now she was no longer being fed directly by Lisa's animation, her passion for life. She recognised something protective in her attitude to Lisa at this moment; she wanted to protect all that joy from fear, from danger, from contamination. Or was it herself and her new love that she was protecting, protecting from Lisa's disapproval and scorn? Once more she stamped firmly on the impulse to ask Lisa for help.

She was relieved indeed when Lisa returned, a bottle and extra glass on one hand, and her other arm round a young woman.

'Bea, this is Annie.'

'Hello.'

'Annie is going to make you into a movie star.'

'What?'

'Hang on,' said Annie, 'Let me sit down first.'

She was not that young, Phoebe thought, probably at least thirty; she was pretty though, and, like Lisa, glamorous. Phoebe remembered again that her fingernails were dirty and that she was tired. She reached out a hand, took the glass from Lisa's hand, and poured the remains of the first bottle into all three glasses. She pushed her bag off the spare chair, and watched the other two sit down.

Phoebe and Annie made appropriate social noises at each other. Lisa, Phoebe noted with some irritation, was looking smug.

'So why is Annie going to make me into a movie star?' Phoebe asked Lisa.

But Annie rather emphatically answered for herself.

'I'm making a little series of TV documentaries. For this new women's magazine programme thing that Channel 4 are doing next year. About women in manual trades. Rosie the Welder business. Lisa and I were chatting and we thought that a garden seemed a good idea, pretty visuals, a change from the factory, you know.'

'A woman jump jockey would be better.' Phoebe felt her heart sinking, 'you could have great shots and all that blood and guts stuff.'

'It's been done. And the commissioning editor would like a gardener better, wider appeal. Anyhow that's not the whole point. I really wanted someone a bit more middle-class, someone who believes in it in theory and who can articulate some sort of feminism around the whole issue.'

'Me? Lisa must be going round the bend. Lisa, what in god's name have you been telling this poor woman?'

Lisa grinned a little sheepishly.

Blast you, Phoebe thought. She recognised yet another round in Lisa's five-year campaign to get her, Phoebe, to do something other than garden. Lisa thought it indulgent and wasteful. At the same time Lisa knew that Phoebe would never let her down in public, with a young woman who did not share their long history.

Lisa said, 'I never said you did it only from high-principled socialist motivations. I did say you were someone who had stayed with the late and unlamented hippy thing.'

'Worse. I'm not a hippy and you know it. Lisa, honestly . . .'

'I'll rephrase that. I meant that you were about the only person I knew that I could say had stuck with our childhood dreams. The seagreen Incorruptible. That you didn't sell out.'

'No one offered to buy. I'd sell out in a flash if the price was right. For a Lotus and a month's skiing every year. Just not for a VW and a flat in Putney.'

26

Lisa drove a VW and lived in Putney. The two of them grinned at each other. Annie looked slightly nervous.

'Anyhow,' she interrupted, 'you do do it, so you must believe in it.'

'I do it because it earns my living. What do you think I should do? I don't have a degree. There aren't a lot of fascinating jobs available to someone like me, you know.'

'Well, Bea' Lisa said, 'you don't have to do it for Hackney Borough do you? You could make more money for less work if you set yourself up as a nice yuppy garden designer. Look at all the bright young things who have just bought darling basement flats in Kentish Town or Victoria Park, who would pay through the nose for you to design them tasteful, easy-care gardens, with water interest, and a piece of abstract sculpture.'

'Touché, you sod.' She could not help but admire Lisa's nerve. 'I'll tell you, Annie, regardless of our mutual friend's supportive respect for my noble life style, there are two very good reasons why I don't set up as a consultant. One is VAT, which I couldn't cope with, and the other is bedding plants.'

'Bedding plants?'

'Yes, I have a deep and unnatural passion for bedding plants. Begonias, french marigolds, even dahlias. Especially wall-flowers and tall tulips in neat rows, colour blocked. No trendies want bedding plants; they want shrubs and old roses. No one wants bedding plants except old-fashioned councils, in old-fashioned parks. I have very vulgar tastes in flowers. I like large lawns, in lovely neat stripes, and I adore floribundas. So you see, I have to work for Hackney Council.'

She grinned, pleased with herself. The witty answer turneth aside wrath, she told herself.

'The truth is,' she added, 'that unlike most of you I'm entirely devoid of natural ambition. It's a job. It's a pretty easy job and it makes my body beautiful which saves me the money you all have to spend on weights and gyms and jogging shoes. No heroism, no nobility, no commitment.'

Instantly she wished she had not used the word 'commitment'. Once she had had commitment, commitment and passion, but Phoebe knew she had broken the connection.

On the dreary early spring day that her father had died Phoebe had not been paying attention. Or rather, she had been paying perfect attention, but not to him; not to important things like life and death and justice. She had been paying almost perfect attention, as perfect as a teenager can pay, to some minor questions of topology. Towards the end of a ten-day struggle there was a sudden burning clarity: she could see and grasp the patterned complex elegance of the numbers, not as abstracts but as shapely forms, hard, brilliant.

A few years before this she had worried that she could never be a mathematician because of this sense of the shape of a problem, this completely concrete hard *thing* that strings of numbers looped and patterned in her mind. It was meant to be abstract, it was meant to be pure. But by now she knew enough mathematicians to know that most of them shared this sense with her, that when the shapes . . . patterns . . . there was not a proper word, nor should there be . . . but that focused solid hardness in the head started to appear, that was when one was working well.

She had been a lucky child. Remarkably lucky: her school had done its best, but her teacher had taught sums not maths. She had been a nice woman, and immensely fond and proud of Phoebe, but also vaguely irritated – probably aware that she was not up to the job, and not sure that the job was worth being up to. She had not been at all amused when a haughty teenaged Phoebe had interrupted a question from one of her classmates – 'But, Miss Fields, what's it all *for*?' – with the arrogant announcement that as soon as it was for *anything* it wasn't maths.

The very young Phoebe had quickly consigned Miss Fields to the same category that she consigned her mother to – women who would take any intellectual idea and try to use it; who thought that communicating was the same as thinking. Her mother, and Phoebe had writhed in shame at the thought, worked in a museum; you couldn't expect her to understand anything.

But her father had understood; Martin, with a charming pride, had found for her not just mathematicians, but philosophers and musicians to teach her. He had, from another discipline, sought out the secrets of hers, knowing what he did not know, humble and loving. She had spent her adolescence in the company of eminent old men; eminent old men who received her respect as their due and enjoyed teaching the brilliant daughter of their colleague. Her father arranged special tutorials for her with his friends and wrote several letters to the headmistress of her comprehensive about its deficiencies. Sometimes she did not go to school for weeks; if her mother had not insisted she probably would not have gone at all. Her father would have let her pursue her enthusiasms and her studies in the best and richest way. He knew and continually reassured her that she was special.

Martin had for her that tender pride that some men have specifically for their clever daughters. Where a son's achievements may be a challenge, a daughter is never going to take over. A daughter who plays first-class chess at the age of ten reflects a glow on her academic father, a glow which few schoolteachers or other adults will even want to steal or claim. Phoebe belonged to him and to him alone, and he never thought of her as a woman, but as his child.

Once he and she had gone to tea with an old friend of his and the two of them had sat in the shabby college room and laughed together about why women never made good scientists. The other man joked about writing a scientific monologue on the subject; and had suddenly looked up, remembered Phoebe's presence, and hastened to say cheerily,

'Not you, of course, Phoebe, you're different; we're only talking about statistical norms.'

But she had not needed comforting, she hardly heard them; she had known all along that what they were saying didn't apply to her, but to other women, women like her mother.

Years later she learned a new shame. She had shamelessly betrayed her mother's love to win her father's pride. At some point in her late childhood she had realised that a number of her parents' friends and professional colleagues treated Rachel with a serious, benign respect, but the adolescent Phoebe could find no way to explain this. She had no one to ask, so she let the matter go. Her father, who admired her, despised her mother's work: her mother was a museum curator, busy with the needs of spotty schoolchildren. Phoebe never had spots, and from the age of about ten never thought of herself as a schoolchild. She knew her mother was more famous than her father, but she was not interested in fame. To her arrogant eighteen-year-old mind, it was impure for people outside your discipline truly to understand what you were doing.

The language of analogy was a deficient tongue: in musical appreciation class they had been asked to say what pieces of classical music had 'reminded' them of, or had 'made them think of'. It was a silly game that Phoebe was no more willing to play than she was to play tennis, or learn to dance. Music was its own language, it was simply not *about* horses galloping on sand dunes. She hated late nineteenth-century mood music which tried to do that; she stuck to Bach and Mozart and knew that people did not like to play with her because they felt her interpretation was soulless; she tended to think that theirs was mindless.

She was Athena, sprung entire from the head of her father, goddess of the arts, of order and civil decorum, who preferred Odysseus for his wily intelligence, and guarded him in the face of the passions of lesser gods, who despised the bovine virtues and physical prowess of other heroes. But all that was the language of analogy, of anthropomorphism, and she would not then admit that she ever used it.

So on the dreary spring morning when her father died, Phoebe had not been paying any attention. She had been looking at some consummately elegant graphs. She had read some of René Thom's ideas about Catastrophe Theory, Topological Mathematics' brand new baby. She had begun to understand the excitement they were generating; that here perhaps was a way of recording, quantifying, what maths had never been able to express before: a way of plotting the leap of change. Now, here with the graphs in front of her she could, perhaps, now, here, realise, make real, make shapely, absorb, contain, almost . . .

If she had allowed herself then the language of analogy which she can use now because she no longer hears the singing of the spheres, which had deafened her, she would have had a language for her excitement. A language for what was shaping up to become a moment of conversion, her journey on the Damascene road. At that moment in her university room she knew she was on the point of faith. She had a momentary and demanding vision that this would be truth and joy; that this, this knowledge, this mathematical code, could explain beauty – could explain how it is inevitable that when moonbeams fall on moving water there will and must always be twinned sparkles on the waves, twinned reflections of the single source.

Labouring towards the end of the most exciting journey of her life, she had a distant view of the promised land. She could be, at least for the instant, certain that this Catastrophe Theory could be used to mark the point, demonstrate the process, explain the inexplicable moment of life; of how a cell moves towards division, swells, ripens, inclines towards a point, along a smooth and steady path, easily plottable, even its gathering speed in terms of acceleration and mass and density, but the instant, the exact instant of division is a leap, a collapse and re-formation of the mathematical material. And she can, she could, be able, she might be able, to understand, to see. She knew she could not see, but that she could learn to see if only nothing, nothing at all, is allowed to come in, nothing but the pattern of numbers that will make it into sense.

Maths is for her at this moment the language of ecstasy; the tongue of hypostatic union. Mathematicians are the chosen people, they dwell safely in the promised land where the messy universe cannot obtrude, cannot force its intolerable realities. This is not simply because numbers are abstracts, are ideals – love and beauty are abstract too – but because inside the perfect world where nothing is allowed to interrupt, numbers prove Plato wrong. They are themselves the Ideal forms of themselves, there is no outer, higher, subliminal, pure essence of number from which numbers are but an emanation. They are.

So that when there was a knock at her door, and a voice that refused to be waved away, that would not take no answer for an answer, that was more insistent, though less welcome, than the shining shapes of her problem, told her that her tutor wanted her now, her first impulse was of intense and arrogant fury – how dare he, how dare he interrupt her now?

The fury terrified her. That she felt no grief, but only anger, petrified her. Darkling, all the shadows of the words she had refused ever to hear shrouded her – that real women could not be mathematicians; that if she was a mathematician then she was not a real woman. Real women wept for daddies when they died. Real women loved people, not abstruse and meaningless theories. Real women rushed to their fathers' graves; desired nothing in the world but to give their fathers the last service of their love.

And still the rage remained. Perhaps, she thought later, she would have been better off if she had been ruthless. If she had closed her eyes to her dead father and returned to her desk unmoved. She saw that quality of ruthlessness in others and was always to admire it. It had been the most memorable quality of Maggie's father; it had attracted her later to Marx – that he had let his children die of starvation so that he could write his books. And when feminism had been born in her life she had delighted because for the first time she saw that ruthlessness in women – saw women who, unlike her, put aside all the demands to follow their own stars to their own mangers in Bethlehem.

But she could not. She did not. She could neither free herself from the anger, nor follow it to its natural conclusion. She had loved him and he was dead. Suddenly she was split entirely and irrevocably in two; divided, she was incapable of any passionate feeling, unable to be either furious or desolate, she replaced both with irritation.

That irritation sustained her on the cranky and trying train journey from Cambridge to Oxford. Over those cold lonely hours the irritation reached out to embrace Rachel as well as Martin. Why should Rachel need her? Why should she be needed? Surely it did not take that many people to arrange a decent funeral?

She arrived cold and tired on Oxford station in the late afternoon.

There were no taxis and she walked up along the river, growing tireder and colder. When she arrived she found that her mother was not there, was still pursuing her own and less important work in London, while she, Phoebe, had been obliged, had been forced, to abandon hers. Her main impulse when she asked where her father was, and went up the stairs to his bedroom was to give him a piece of her mind, throw her intolerable six-hour-old irritability in his face. Who the hell did he think he was?

But he was dead. She had never seen a dead person before. Nothing had prepared her for that: for that exact way in which he was completely himself – Martin Petherington, Fellow of St Elizabeth's College Oxford, paleontologist, member of the Royal Geographical Society's general council, husband of Rachel Petherington, née Hunter-Pearce, and father of . . . and her father, her daddy, daddy, daddy, dada, da – and yet at the same time he was completely, totally and forever absent from himself. And from her.

And her pent-up confusion, now ocean deep and mountain high, lashed back on her, overwhelming, drowning, breaking her, so that she had to grope down the corridor and into the bathroom to be sick; retching up her own inadequacy, her own selfishness and the im-possibility of maths ever reaching a description, a pattern, an elegance, to describe this final catastrophe. The pure intensity of the morning, the self-centred joy was spewed out along with her bile and flushed down the old-fashioned vitreous enamel bowl. He was dead and gone and she had been so wrapped up in herself that she had dared to be angry. There was only one place that it was possible to direct that anger, and the guilt for the anger, and the desolate knowledge that she, she had failed him; and that was towards the one thing she loved better than she loved him. And there, hanging over the loo, she made a vow. At a level deep beneath consciousness, shivering, juddering with shock and cold and misery, she vowed that she would renounce the glory of the morning, that she would do no more maths, ever again.

Of course she had not believed that mathematics would take her seriously, take her at her word, would block its beauty off from her. After the funeral she had gone back to her university unaware that she had changed. On the contrary she had behaved in an exemplary fashion. She had pulled herself together, gathering all the pieces off the bathroom floor, flushing away her vomit, washing her face and combing her hair.

She had gone downstairs and assisted those who had taken on the task in the business of trying to find her mother. And when Rachel finally returned, she greeted her with a seemly and daughterly affection; going out into the garden and embracing her, breaking the news to her herself. Her father's friends would have envied him his neat composed daughter who was such a support and succour to his wife in her bereavement. It was extraordinary that a child so intelligent and so, it had to be said, oddly educated, should be so mature and sensible at a time like this.

Rachel and she were abundantly sensible. Phoebe watched the two of them, mother and daughter, going sensibly through the process of death. They had been in harmonious agreement about a quiet cremation and a memorial service in his college afterwards. They had been in full accord that expressions like 'suddenly at home' and 'dearly beloved husband and father' were vulgar, but that on the other hand a proper announcement in *The Times* was called for.

Martin had, not surprisingly, left everything in excellent readiness for his demise and this helped them – there were no excitements about wills or the deceased's intentions. The only person to create any drama at all was Mrs Crale, the daily, who wanted immense quantities of sympathy for the nasty shock she had received, for the burden of responsibility she had carried so calmly at the time, and for the loss of her dear, dear man. Martin had, with total accuracy, left her a personal bequest large enough to surprise her and not large enough to embarrass her.

She urged her mother to buy a decent hat for the memorial service. She wrote, in a neat hand, a large number of replies to condolence letters, agreeing once again with Rachel that it was pretentious to put notes in the Personal Columns regretting one's inability to reply, and that it was ill-mannered to make no response. She was a little upset that Martin did not get an obituary in the national press, but she realised that he had, after all, had the misfortune of dying on the same day as a major Commonwealth Prime Minister. One night she wished briefly that her father had seen fit to leave her something personal, some gift, some recognition of her personality in his will, like his chess set; but Rachel thought of that herself – 'I know Daddy would have wanted you to take it' – so there was nothing to be unhappy about.

Having impeccably performed all these duties, and mulishly set herself against her filial duty of crying at the service, she went back to Cambridge thinking that everything would go on as before.

And then it did not.

It was as simple as that.

She could not do her work. It was total. The patterns and shapes no longer wove their enchantments for her. They were solid, rejecting, static. And because she could not do her work she found she could not do anything else either: she was suddenly cut off from all delight and pleasure and engagement and feeling. She simply could not.

Her irritation returned. She could not touch again that bright hot fury, but she was irritable. She scratched irritably at the half-formed scab in her gut. All this was her father's fault. He should not have died. And then, knowing that there was no reasonable way she could hold this against him, she started to find other causes. It was his fault that she had no friends; he had never wanted her to have friends, he had wanted to keep her for himself. He had wanted to turn her into a little infant prodigy for his amusement, for his delight. He had never wanted her to be a woman, only his thing, his valuable thing to show off to his friends.

And in her irritation she attacked her mother too; her mother who had done nothing to save her from this devouring father. Her mother had betrayed her, had encouraged her father to eat her up just so that she would be let off behaving like a real mother and could get on with her stupid, silly, petty unimportant little job.

As it was boring to stay in bed all day, and impossible to read or think or play the cello or chess, she had to find something else to do. It was the summer of 1968. She smoked a good deal of dope, although she did not like it; she drank a great deal although it made her sick and that reminded her of the bathroom the day her father died, and she fucked a lot. She could remember practically nothing of the next year, except the complete unbearableness of it all.

The connection had been broken. Rejected, she had never dared attempt to love again. She had cut herself off from a pure sort of energy and would just have to live without it.

In the language of analogy, which this now, today, older and wiser Phoebe will use, despite knowing that analogy cannot be pressed, she could say that she had thrown a pearl away richer than all her tribe. She threw maths away in a stupid and foolish moment and it damaged her. She had destroyed her own centre and set herself spinning off into the world, which is glorious and golden but in which she is without gravity. She spins not as a gyroscope centred and sensible, but as the sub-nuclear particles spin: randomly, uncertainly.

She had come over the years to realise, very inarticulately, that somehow, in abandoning maths and virtue, in abandoning that early and resilient commitment she had abandoned also the capacity to form commitment.

Recently she had found herself remembering more and more that passionate engagement in her late teens. She had been in love with those elegant abstracts. She had been unfaithful to a very demanding lover. She would not be forgiven. She could not go back. Though she was tempted sometimes to try, she knew that it was impossible. It was not maths she wanted back, anyway, it was passion and commitment. Now in her late thirties she was ripe for conversion and too well-educated to find anything worth being converted to.

So she fell in love, quite unexpectedly, and fell in love with all the things she hated most in herself.

She bumped back into the warm present and poured another glass of wine. She was cross with Lisa. Lisa ought to have known all this stuff after nearly twenty years of friendship. Lisa ought to have realised in her turn that Phoebe was never going to commit herself to anything, not even her own work, with the sort of idealistic enthusiasm that Lisa could bring to even the most mundane of projects, and wanted her to show now, so that she, Lisa, could project her own merits onto this boring and silly young woman. What was more, Lisa did know it, and Phoebe, from all those years of practice, knew what Lisa was up to. It was not only a part of Lisa's seduction technique, it was also another of Lisa's many and variegated attempts to get her, Phoebe, to take herself seriously.

'Annie,' Lisa said now, almost sternly, 'you must not believe a word Bea says to you. She's not as silly as she pretends to be.'

'Be that as it may, my friend, I'm certainly not silly enough to present myself to Annie's camera as a committed middle-class socialist of high and noble virtue. Even if I had the time, which I don't.'

'Oppressed by domesticity, Bea?'

But Phoebe was not prepared to bare her soul in front of Annie.

'You know how it is,' and she hated herself for sounding pathetic.

'Actually, I don't.' Lisa looked at Phoebe with great affection, and then said to Annie, 'One of the things you have to understand about Bea is that she was one of the few people who genuinely suited the anti-materialism and detatchment of the early seventies. She has a naturally solitary soul, so that communal life was easy for her. She is the least domesticated person in the world, and yet here she is with more of a house and more of a family than anyone else I know. And it all happened by accident, it's not surprising that it makes her grouchy.'

'Knock it off, Lisa,' Phoebe said, but she was touched. There were things that Lisa really did understand perfectly.

But Annie was getting bored by their implied intimacy which excluded

35

her from the conversation. She said, 'Perhaps, Bea, I could come and see your garden anyway. Then we could discuss it ourselves, without Madam here wanting to organise the whole thing.' She touched Lisa's shoulder, focusing attention back on herself.

'Like the rest of the public, you're always welcome.'

Phoebe knew she sounded ungracious, but she knew too that Annie would not come. The whole thing had been an elaborate set-up so that Lisa and Annie could spend an evening together.

She found though, quite suddenly, that she did not mind. She did love Lisa enormously, and it was precisely because of Lisa's qualities of engagement and determination. She was more than happy to assist Lisa. She bought another bottle of wine, gave Annie a witty account of her years as a posh middle-class student at horticultural college, and how she had annoyed both the instructors and her fellow students and then turned the conversation to gossip.

They drank. They laughed. The rest of the evening was good – a reassuring touching of the web that they had all spun together over many years, of friendships and shared interests and ideas. 'What on earth,' Phoebe asked herself, 'could be more precious than this?' And for a few last hours she banished the shadow of her lover, and the fears of the next day.

Maggie had planned to spend the evening on her own, but she had ended up spending it with her friends.

She felt she ought to practise, if she was going to live the way other people live. She planned the journey in advance, carefully and in detail, a complicated combination of Tubes and buses, designed to test her endurance to its limits.

She hated travelling on the Tube. It made her panic, and she did it very seldom. But she hardened herself to the task, walked down Queensway, past the ice rink where she had been taken as a little child. Momentarily she was tempted to abandon her rigorous plans and walk in, pay her money and skate. She skated well: skating had been one of the very few forms of entertainment for the young of which both her mother and her grandmother approved, and consequently she had often asked to go, to have lessons. She was deterred not just by courage and will, but by the shame of having to hire a grotty pair of skates, with battered ankles and frayed laces. She knew that if she went home to find her own neat black ones she would not dare come out again.

The Central Line was the worst, which was why she had chosen it. At this stage in the evening Maggie was clearer and more decided about the next few hours than either of her grown-ups. She had steeled herself. But even so, as she went down the escalator, the dread came upon her. It was not the depth, nor the darkness.

She was not afraid of the dark because when she was very little Maggie had had Fenna's lair as her playground. She had gone down into the dragon's lair and found it bright, a darkness ablaze. Fenna had drawn her into the great cave, into the darkness that was absolute, where no light came, and yet there were the colours. Not sun colours but night colours, muted colours whose beauty was darkness: dull reds and shades of rust, ochre, orange, burned sienna, all the colours of shadow, and great grey cliffs. There were roofs high, far higher above than cathedrals and more extraordinarily wrought; and here and there were the tight clusters of crystals, the heart of the hoard.

All this was wrought by the power of water; water working with darkness to shape caves that would never be seen. She could not forget it. Later, in school, they had once been asked to consider the question of whether a tree falling in a forest would make a sound if there was no one and nothing to hear it. She had replied at once that of course it would, because it would hear itself, just as it had grown itself, and just as the secret caves were shaped and embellished even when there was no one to see them. It had been an odd-look thing to say: she had learned to avoid the odd-look things.

It was not the depth, nor the darkness that scared her. It was the other people.

She hated it. On the platform she stood tight against the wall, feeling it crouch and hover over her. Her hands were sweating and slapped flat against the tiles. At least it was better on her own since she did not have to cover her fear up, did not have to add to it the greater fear that her mother or her friends would notice. She shut her eyes. She could feel people all around her. Only seven or eight paces away the great cliff and the rails waited greedily for her. Her hands and ears listened for the distant vibration, the noises in the dark that would tell her the train was coming. She wanted to scream.

'I'll get used to it' she told herself, 'I will; I'll have to.'

She knew that the metal monster would come roaring out of the tunnel, and that the least slip would be fatal. Someone might jostle her; someone might notice her, might know she was here, different, frightened.

She was getting confused. These moments of confusion were increasing. It was one of the reasons why it had to stop. Here, underground and swallowed up in the crowd, Fenna could not keep his dangerous eye on her. Here she knew with clarity that it had to stop.

So she forced herself onto the train when it arrived, forced herself to hang, jaunty and soignée, from the strap. She accepted with a carefully composed grin the look of admiration from the business-suited young man who could scarcely fail to observe how well-fitting her jeans were and how long her legs as she danced to the rhythm of the train. Her black canvas boots had luminous green laces; she could glow in the dark.

The change at Tottenham Court Road was the worst. The maze was full of noise and rush; and now they were under the very heart of the city, its huge weight compressed her. There were people all around her and more people, more people than she could imagine, pounding along over her head. She had to stop once between the platforms and struggle for breath.

She might have died there if it had not been for a young woman playing the flute. She heard the notes before she saw the player, and they created a tunnel of quiet within the larger turbulent tunnel – she could walk down the passage of music towards its source. The player had long straight hair and a completely blank expression. She played as though she had been in the privacy of her own room, as though she, like the tree in the forest, the water in the cave, would make the same music whether anyone heard or not. Her separateness gave Maggie the strength to find the right platform, to wait out the inevitable delays on the Northern Line, to let three trains running rush on to Edgware without sucking her in and forcing her to change her plans.

She felt proud of herself. Apart from a brief spasm of terror when the train failed to stop at Mornington Crescent and then delayed an unreasonable amount of time at Camden Town, she was almost able to forget the whole horror.

None the less, arriving at Highgate, and seeing the trees around the station, was a relief. It reminded her of the picture that Rachel had given her, of that other Margaret leading the dragon back into the city, docile, tamed. Could Fenna perhaps be so tamed, patterned into story?

She had underestimated the distance between the Archway Road and the Heath, but it was quieter and she was soothed by the slowly changing character of the streets; Jackson Lane had a raucous energy about it, but after she turned left into Southwood Lane, crossed Highgate High Street and started down West Hill and Merton Lane there was a gentle elegance which matched the rural street names. At home, back in Bayswater, they did not go in for Lanes much. Her mind slipped from her high quest and returned to more normal channels, like the simple thrill of having escaped her adults' supervision and whether or not she could afford a new green lampshade for her room.

It was cool on the Heath, and the ponds were splashed with evening sunshine as she walked across the causeway between them. Away up on her right was the women's pond, where her mother used to take her in the hot summers when she was younger. There had been a ferocious warden there who had tried to conduct swimming tests, insisting on the dangers of the waters. Her mother and her friends had called her The Dragon and Maggie had giggled, not at their joke but at the very idea. She had enjoyed it, but had not been for ages because her friends would not want to go to places where there were no boys. This summer, perhaps, she would feel like that too. It had been fun.

She planned to walk right across the Heath and down to Hampstead on the other side. The light was fading and the evening further advanced than she had expected, but she felt no sense of danger, only a small malicious delight because her mother would be livid if she were to see her there. Her mother, whom she knew for a fact had travelled alone all the way across Asia and back, got in a dark fury if Maggie was out alone in London. It did not make sense. It was one of the things that most annoyed Maggie: the unfairness of it. Phoebe preached independence and strode about the dangerous East End, where according to most reports muggers and rapists lurked on every corner and drug-crazed loonies pounced out from under tower blocks every time you turned your head. Not that she was allowed to say such things to Phoebe, who would give her tiresome lectures on snobbishness. Phoebe always got angry and she never got worried. Rachel sometimes tried to explain that they were the same thing, with different masks on, and anyway she did not want her mother fussing over her endlessly like some people's mothers did. But Phoebe ought to be fair. Of course her mother did not know that she was absolutely protected. Tomorrow, when she was no longer so protected, would she understand her mother's fears for her and walk carefully in the daylight and the lamplight?

Suddenly she felt worn out. She abandoned her mental tussle with Phoebe and came back to the task in front of her. She could not do it. She could not. Out there in the real world it was all too complicated. She did not want to have to deal with it. She did not have to. She could stay as she was. She felt exhausted. She told herself it had been too long a walk, but she knew it was not true. Her mind sought its habitual refuge, in the overwhelming delights of Fenna's fury and forgiveness. She had to drag herself away forcibly. For weeks she had struggled to keep all such dangerous thoughts hidden from Fenna. She did not know how much, if anything, he knew about what she was planning.

Then suddenly she was at the top of the hill and London lay below her getting dressed for the night, laying aside its working clothes and stringing its neck with garlands of pearls and diamonds; costuming itself for her amusement. On Parliament Hill there were two young men walking their dog and an old drunk asleep on a bench. She spun round lightly taking the sweep of it with pleasure; behind her was a meadow of cropped grass, and in front of her was the City. Away to her left she could see a man with two small children flying a kite, in the last of the light. She realised there was a wind, and knew that the wind would blow clouds out of the west before morning and they would be lace-edged with moonlight later on.

It was such a lovely evening, the light fading down with a soft elegance, and the sense of striding above London, lightly over the grass, was at least the shadow of flying. She came down at last through Parliament Hill Gardens and saw inside the houses ordinary life and electric lights going on. It was that time when, all over the gloaming and lovely city, good moods expand and work is dropped casually and slinks away for a few hours. In well-regulated homes children are read stories and put to bed, food is cooked, and drinks poured. People come back together, happily or otherwise; and which of the two scarcely matters.

Maggie realised, quite abruptly, that she had got the whole thing entirely wrong. She ought not to be on her own. Indeed, she must not be on her own. The very reason why she was going to destroy her whole life, cast it into the burning night and see what phoenix might give birth to itself out of the embers, was because she knew that it was not good for a person to be completely alone. Imperatively, right now, she had to be with other people.

So immediately she lifted off, dodging the low branches on that pretty tree-lined street, and seeking a flight path in the darkening air. Her purposeful course took her over South End Green at a reasonable height and as the hill rose again the other side she swept across the modern roof of the Royal Free Hospital.

Years of practice had given her a graceful style, although Fenna still teased her gently about the ugliness of flight without wings. He told her that it reminded him of the Superman Movies and she should wear Y-fronts over her jeans for the full effect. Secretly Maggie had been impressed by Superman, though she was scathing about the scene at the end when Superman had reversed the spinning of the world, which had made her laugh. She had been to the film on her own though, and was pleased afterwards by her unconscious wisdom, because she had been severely tempted to pass comments on the flying sequence, and especially the bit where Superman had held Lois Lane within the sweep of his cape and had flown her. It reminded her too poignantly of the first time Fenna had taught her to fly.

She flew now with competence and efficiency over the streets to the west of Haverstock Hill. It was not until she was well over Primrose Hill that she took delight in her flight and just for the joy of it she executed a delicate and precise triple somersault, straight-legged and in slow motion, which set the birds in the spider's web aviary of the Zoo squawking and screeching their envy. The Zoo at night had long been a favourite playground and she almost diverted now to visit old friends and say farewell, but the needy impulse which had driven her to flight remained and she turned away south and west across Regent's Park, and the spangled necklace of the Marylebone Road. It was dark now and her confidence increased; she hovered watching with pleasure the magical movement of the car lights, a river of fire, below her.

The glass roofs of Paddington Station, with their slim convoluted wrought iron supports always pleased her, and she roller-coasted their icy ridges, up-and-down swoopings, like a little child at a playground. She giggled. Through the thick plates she could see the movements of the station, muted as though all the people were under water, while the trains heaved and wriggled like trapped worms pinned in by the platforms.

Further west still she saw her own street from above, looking little and scruffy, and through the skylight of her room came a golden glow. She hoped she would get home before Phoebe discovered that she had left her lights on all day. Then, skimming over the bazaar atmosphere of Westbourne Grove and the posh dignity of Pembridge Villas, she came to Ladbroke Grove. The churchyard always made a safe and discreet landing place and she came down gently beside the north wall of St John's. Further up Ladbroke Grove, under the motorway, the streets would be noisy and joyous, but she could not land there because it was in a parish dedicated to St Michael, where dragon skills have no sway and his bright and cruel sword would burn her flesh. St John was gentler about such things, and the spire of his church made a good fixed marker for all flying in this district.

Maggie's green shoe-laces were glowing brightly as she trotted down the hill, and turned into the elegant crescent where Joanna lived. Twenty minutes after leaving the Heath, she was ringing on the doorbell and greeting her friend's mother pleasantly. She received a warm smile in return; her friends' parents tended to approve of Maggie: she had nice manners – instilled by Rachel; a lack of coy shyness – instilled by Phoebe; and a sort of seriousness which made her seem safe and responsible.

'Maggie, how nice, how are you? We haven't seen you for ages. What have you been up to?'

Maggie felt less enthusiastic; she found this mother rather trying. Joanna's mother was the sort who loved having her daughter's friends around her house, which was why they often met there: there was always plenty of Coca Cola, space and tolerance of loud music. But Maggie could almost hear the woman saying to her own friends, 'Of course Joanna's chums confide in me; I'm like a big sister to them.' And she described herself and Joanna as 'best friends'.

Maggie once told Phoebe this, and Phoebe had laughed and said, 'Poor woman, doesn't she have any proper friends of her own? What's the matter with her? Arrested development?' That part of Maggie which had wanted Phoebe to respond with a declaration of similar intimacy and closeness had been hurt, but another part had known exactly what her mother meant. Now she could seldom look at Joanna's mother without thinking 'arrested development', and wanting to giggle.

'Maggie's here, darling,' the woman called up the stairs, and then to Maggie, 'Quite a gang of you here tonight. Go on up, you know the way.'

Within moments Maggie was sitting comfortably in the clutter of her friend Joanna's room with a can of Coke. Amy, Hermione and Clare were scattered casually on the furniture and floor. Joanna was sitting at her desk. For a moment, entering from the cold night air, Maggie watched them from outside. She should have waited longer in the churchyard and got herself properly grounded, but in her eagerness to be there she had forgotten.

Maggie watched and listened to them, carefully taking in the lessons they offered her on how to be ordinary. She knew the time had come, despite the pain, despite the loss, the time had come when she must leave the courts of childhood and the great dancing secret of the dragon world. There was a choice and it had to be made now. Soon perhaps it would be too late. But she watched not with jealousy, but with curiosity and affection.

They were a mixed bunch of bright teenagers. The struggle between

Phoebe and Rachel over Maggie's education had resulted, as always, in a compromise, which Maggie had learned to understand. She went to one of the elite all girls' comprehensive schools, preserving both Phoebe's honour and Rachel's zeal for excellence.

All five of them were now acquiring a consciousness of these things and a well-developed code for labelling themselves and others, part joke and part self-definition. There were 'Carolines', trainee Sloane Rangers with houses in the country, of whom they did not know many but could identify with ease. There were 'Trendies' who smoked, both cigarettes and hash, and wore designer jeans and went dancing in night clubs even though they were under-age. There were 'Normans', mysteriously named after their putative boyfriends who were simply out of it, but who might also and simultaneously be 'T-bars'. It had taken Maggie a long time to work that one out, but they were swots whose mothers had once made them wear Clarks sandals, which had marked their personalities indelibly. There were also 'Sharons', who smoked cigarettes but not hash and wore stone-washed denim skirts too short and too tight. And there was 'Them'; they didn't need to find a name for themselves but under pressure from outsiders called themselves 'The Independents', or occasionally 'The Intellectuals', not overtly boasting, but as a joke from Adrian Mole: 'My trouble is I'm an intellectual, but I'm not very clever.'

When, a couple of years ago, the need for a disguise had forced itself upon Maggie she had sought the group out quite consciously. They were the only people among her peers who treasured moments of oddness, valued them as part of the value of the group. She had watched and inserted herself among them with considerable craft. But that was no longer true, now she loved them and needed them and depended on them. They were her friends, and she wanted to be like them, which was why she watched so carefully, and also why she tried not to exceed the invisible margins of permitted oddity.

They had made some flimsy attempts to justify them all being there on a weekday evening. Everyone except Maggie had brought their book bags, and they had even taken their books out of them. Joanna had a fairly earnest arrangement of books and papers on her desk, but in fact they were fooling around. Hermione was trying on Amy's new jacket, shrugging her wild black hair curls loose from the collar. She strutted a few paces and laughed.

'I think it looks better on Amy,' she said giggling. They all giggled. Amy was six inches taller and twenty-five pounds heavier than Hermione. The jacket hung four inches below her wrists and she did a little gorilla dance.

'I think I'll do my Empathy Project on the Pygmies. It'll be easier – I'm a midget and I'm black. Better than old Syon House, anyway.'

'Don't even talk about it!'

They all moan and groan, the shadow of the summer's exams lounging over them.

Maggie, who had in fact, like the rest of them, rather enjoyed the field trip to Syon House, and the attempts to understand a different kind of people, none the less said, 'You should hear my grandmother on the subject of the Empathy Project. She says its unscholarly, artificial and none of us learn any historical sensibility.'

Joanna said, 'Apparently there's some school on the South Coast where the teachers won't teach it – and I wouldn't mind being there. Anything to have Ms Kay refusing to teach me.'

'Girls, girls, girls. Your parents sent you here because they believe in excellence, excellence, excellence for women. The way this class is carrying on you'll find yourselves packing shelves at Sainsburys, Sainsburys, Sainsburys.' It was a plausible imitation of their history teacher.

'I told her,' said Hermione, 'that my mother would see that as social advancement, since she packed shelves at Tescos. Ms Kay went all pink and sweaty because she was afraid she had been racist. Then she remembered my father was a fancy doctor and got all muddled up. Then she went ranting on about women's opportunities and girls only schools.'

'Silly bag. Bloody feminism. I bet she's a vegetarian.'

'I'm a feminist, I think,' said Clare.

'I don't mind being one. It's just going on and on and on about it.'

'I'm not,' said Amy, and in serio-comic tones added, 'I need a man.' She turned round wrapping her arms across her back and fondling her own shoulders.

They all laughed and danced, their own exuberance and vanity overwhelming them. They all longed for love and giggled about it. Clare had a boyfriend whom they call her 'main squeeze' – laying on thick Caribbean accents, idiotically different from any of their own voices. They discussed sex in the abstract, endlessly, but seldom revealed personal details. They fretted about money, but never about poverty. They had infinite ambitions and unexpressed fears. Maggie wanted to be like them.

And eventually Joanna's mother came in and reminded them gently, smilingly, about last buses and homework. It was time to go. They flapped hands against each others' shoulders and performed their own ritual parting gestures which included faked head-butts and Egyptian-style walks. Maggie drew a deep breath and knew that her hour had come. She walked with Amy down to the corner of Ladbroke Grove where they parted, and she climbed up the gentle slope towards her churchyard for the last time.

Three

And later, Rachel came home in a taxi.

And later, Phoebe came home on her bike.

And later, Maggie flew home.

They all arrived at the same time. Maggie, of course, was careful, landing circumspectly around the corner, under the great shadows of the plane tree that was well used to her comings and goings, and parted its branches to allow her a steady, gentle descent. So that as she turned into her street Phoebe saw Maggie sauntering down the road, and waved at her with pleasure. Maggie's spirits soared as she realised that the lies she had told her mother when she had planned to walk alone on the Heath had been turned into truth – she was indeed just coming home from visiting her friends. Relief made her puppy-like, lollopy, and she threw herself on her mother with enthusiasm, embracing her, bouncing around. They exchanged soft hugs and with the two of them lifting the bike up the few steps to the house, it was almost effortless.

At that very moment Rachel's taxi drove up and she lumbered out into the street below them. She had her own front door, down the area steps, and she usually used it, but there was also a connecting door inside the ground floor, and they paused – Rachel down on the pavement and her offspring on the steps above her – deciding in which of the many available ways they were going to enter their home. For once the pause was without tension.

The house welcomed them.

Maggie remembered no other home. She had come there when she was two years young, thirteen years ago, after one more winter of croup and snivels, one more winter of Phoebe resisting the sweet steady pressure from her mother and her daughter. She had come to comfort and health from a disintegrating and unhappy household. Maggie did not remember those things – she never gave the house a thought. It was simply and always there. It was home. It was her home.

Phoebe had come there first travel-stained and weary. Phoebe had come defeated; had come not from some other home, but from the road. But the house had made her welcome; the house, and, on her best days she had to admit, Rachel's subtle generosity. It had been, simply, a good sensible idea. She had grown comfortable there, put down roots, and then found she had become used to it and in that sense, at least, fond of it.

It was only in the last couple of years that the whole place had become a strain. The house seemed to demand more and more from her. First it had been Rachel's house, then their shared home; both of those had been acceptable. Now in reality it had become her house, her responsibility. Rachel did more than allow this, she carefully encouraged it; but Rachel had grown up always believing that there was someone else, somewhere else whose job it was to keep things going, make things comfortable. The years between her husband dying and her daughter moving in with her had been not just uncomfortable for her, but unnatural. As she resigned her responsibilities it did not feel to her that she was being lazy or unfair, more that things were returning to normal.

Phoebe knew she had failed to fight Rachel on this, as on so many issues. It was her own fault, as she herself would have acknowledged. She had taken the house over, put energy into it, created Maggie's room at the top, introduced house plants, shaped the garden, chosen more pleasing furniture and taken out bank loans to do so. Without noticing she had become the mistress of the house. But she had no desire to be that, no desire to be the grown-up looking after the two little girls.

She had become the mother. She had not started out as the mother; she had never chosen to be the mother. These two women, Rachel and Maggie so differently, so craftily, had sneaked into her life, her flesh, parasites of love. She wanted to escape and could imagine no escape.

The house, sensing the danger of her betrayal in its sturdy foundations, had fought back with outrageous demands – a deft damp patch in the cellar, vague wobbles in the window frames, discreet collapses in the décor, a minor jinx in the wiring – all requiring her attention and the investment of her time and energy. It was a big house; it craved a full-time mistress with its charming banisters collecting dust and its delightful Victorian tiles showing every twenty-four hours of neglect. Even the distance that Phoebe had to travel to work was tiring. Resisting her mother's determination to have more 'help' forced Phoebe to work harder at it so that she could justify her stubborn refusal to consent. The house and Rachel and Maggie conspired together to make her be not only a worker but a housewife as well.

At the same time as spiting her the house had wooed her too; Lisa was wrong in believing that she was entirely impervious to its charms. It had extended itself to her ever more warmly, wrapping itself around her, offering her privacy and large light windows, elegant spaces and practised comforts, unaffordable otherwise on her salary. Rachel was well there and so was Maggie. All the alternatives were both exhausting and cruel, the house told her. The house was fighting skilfully against her possible rebellion, and the house would win.

Phoebe knew that she was stuck with it all now; that her defeat had been more absolute than she could have imagined. She was stuck with it all and for the sake of a house, for the sake of two women she had never chosen as her friends, she would repudiate her new lover: would settle for cosy domesticity instead of dangerous passion. The house was the symbol of her defeat and so she loved it reluctantly and with a frequently sulky lack of grace. She despised her own whining and that did nothing to improve her temper.

For Rachel, climbing out of her taxi, thinking 'home again' was the easiest. She had chosen this home, and this family to be at home with. But it was not only that, the very word home for Rachel brought comfortably to mind the happy home of her childhood, nestled into the Suffolk plain, lazy, warm, rich with the patina of her mother's creative love for it. There had been a magic dissolution between inside and outside; long french windows opening onto crazy-paved garden, and garden leading out to lawn and lawn melting into field with cows. A ha-ha, marking the invisible break, enormous to a child, down down into the dip, long white stockings and the danger of never being able to climb out again – hidden from the house – and the great breathy cows looking over the edge, huge from this underneath angle and smelling warmly of grass. The brick was gentle with age, mutating through the seasons, absorbing sunshine, warm against snow, glowing against summer evenings.

Her father returning – where from? Where did he go? Anxiety at Father's departure, forgotten but lurking, the long newspaper lists after Paschendale, Ypres and the Somme, the stabbing terror at the unexpected doorbell, the sight of the telegram boy no source of joy, but of sharp intake of breath, while the child Rachel was still on the breast, not yet remembering. So now, though Father comes and goes safely, his return is still a moment of excitement pure and nervous, a moment of passionate desire from which she will never be free. Nor would she want to be. A very early memory is of him returning and her anticipation, and Mother's anticipation, and the long drawing room aglow with flowers, and dinner ordered and Mother dressing and Father coming, Father coming, Father coming.

Suddenly, it is too much: the beauty of the house and the beauty of her mother not to be separated and after he comes it will be her bedtime and he will belong to Mother, only to Mother in the long drawing room and up the front stairs where the carpet is slightly worn but very lovely, and it will be too late for him to come to the nursery. She has to do something that will break the spell, something that is not of her mother – the poem learned, the posy placed by his shaving table – something that is hers, hers and his alone. She hears the car, broomfing over the bridge below the drive. Quickly, quickly, a wild urgency seizing her for she must go down, must be there beside her mother to greet him, who is and always will be the returning hero, the wide blue ribbon of her white frock tight around her stomach. Despair suddenly, for her mother is so beautiful and here in her own house most perfectly beautiful, and crossing the hallway there is the basket brought up by the man in the week, waiting for Father, and she takes up a stone from on top of it, and hands behind her back joins her mother on the front doorstep just as his car rounds the great beech tree and clatters up.

Mother first of course, soft kisses, warmth and joy flow out of them both and they look so lovely, lovely, lovely in the fine sunny afternoon. Then her turn, 'How's my poppet? What has been happening?'

'Father,' she says, bold and crafty, 'we have some new fossils', and she holds out to him calm-handed, serious, the stone she had snatched up. She cannot remember what it was now – how odd: so crucial a moment in her life and she cannot now remember what it was that she excited and enticed him with. Something small enough to hold hidden in her hand anyway. He looks at it, solemnly to please her, probably, and then abruptly sharp-eyed, eager, turning it over in his huge paw. Suddenly delight comes over him; he hands the stone to mother almost without noticing her, as he might hand his coat to a servant, never rude but quite unnoticing, and he seizes her in his arms and swings her, up up up and around.

He is laughing delightedly, he is praising her extravagantly, he is loving her, her, her. The evening sparkles as she whirls in his arms, his tweedy savour is close to her. Father and fossils and exploding whirling sparkling joy, she is perfectly happy. Of course she will grow up to be a famous

49

paleontologist. She practises the word in bed at night, and when later, though she should be asleep, she hears them murmering sweetly in the long drawing room, far from feeling envious of Mother, she is grateful to her, grateful to her for keeping him safe and happy in this beautiful house so that she can grow up as quickly as possible and become a fossil hunter.

So it is still impossible to get out of a taxi and think 'home' and not know all these things concretely, even here on her front doorstep at the very final end of the long road, of the journey begun then, in innocence and certainty, pursued across three continents, for nearly three-quarters of a century, and still she was illuminated, even now at this point of disaster, by that joyful beginning. 'Home' for her was strong magic, and this house caught all the echoes of that strong love and casual centredness. It welcomed her now, tired and sad though she was.

Not just the house, but her darling Maggie welcomed her. Jumping down the steps, leaving Phoebe with the bicycle half in and half out of the front door, she threw her arms round her grandmother's neck and hugged her. Maggie wanted everything to be perfect tonight, everything to be of childhood and to be easy. So immediately after hugging her grandmother she leaped up the steps again and continued to help her mother with the bike. Her sudden reversion to childish enthusiasm made both the older women smile and, unthinking almost, Rachel came up the steps and through the upper front door. They stood, pleased with each other and a pleasing trinity to any watching night insect. Then Rachel closed the door and Phoebe propped the bike up in the corridor and Maggie danced lightly between them for a moment. There was one door off the hallway and a flight of stairs. The door opened directly into Rachel's bedroom: this had been handy when Maggie was little, although it was peculiar now. By tradition it was never locked, unless Phoebe was having a party, a throwback to an ancient and embarrassing evening soon after they had all moved in.

Rachel was tired now. Full of Paul and the evening and the work of tomorrow, delighted at Maggie's welcome, glad that there had been this moment of seeing Phoebe, of family and togetherness, she said 'good-night' and went into her bedroom, shutting her door behind her.

The two younger women went on upstairs and turned into the kitchen. It was a mess. They shared an unspoken relief that Rachel had not come up with them, as she might have done, so that they would have had to sense her disapproval. Their own confusions about this would have made them irritated with each other. They were grateful to have been spared that.

'Yes, Mummy, it's my turn,' sighed Maggie.

Phoebe grinned, affectionate and pleased suddenly with this young woman who was her daughter.

'Did you have a good evening?'

'OK. Not thrilling. Where have you been?'

'With Lisa. Some friend of hers wanted me to be in her movie.'

'Holy shit.'

'Maggie!'

'Sorry.'

Maggie felt a sulk form around her eyebrows, since no one she knew swore as much as Phoebe did, but she ordered it away quickly before it could creep down past her eyes, along her nose and onto her mouth: Phoebe never recognised her sulks until one of them lurched itself impertinently onto her lips, and tonight Maggie wanted none of that.

'Sorry. I meant good gracious me, of course. But why? And, are you going to do it?'

'I shouldn't think so. She wanted me to be a noble heroine tilling the soil of Hackney in the service of the people.'

'Oh, forget it then. You haven't got the right accent. If you ask me it's one of Lisa's schemes for your yuppification.'

'Is it that obvious?'

'Of course it is. You won't escape, you know. You'll end up as a learned professor of the history of gardening or something in some grisly northern town like Keele.'

'Oh shit,' said Phoebe, recognising the possibility all too clearly. Then realising what she had said, flushed irritably.

But Maggie's courage was high; instead of feeling cross, she laughed. The two of them giggled a little; the age gap, the responsibility gap, the expectation gap dissolving; good will flowing between them, in the fluidities of Maggie's age, and of Phoebe's sense of identity.

But of their determinations about the day ahead, that they keep sealed from each other.

'I'm going to bed,' said Phoebe, at last. 'If you aren't going to clear up in here, at least don't make it any worse.'

Suddenly she was worn down with tiredness, with fear held at bay and the complexities of everything. Maggie took an alarming new lurch towards adulthood, looking at her mother by the kitchen door,

'Are you OK, Mummy?' she asked.

It was not a new question, but there was a whole new context. She realised abruptly that she would have to carry a weight of responsibility and care and love, if not now, then soon. Her mother would get old like her grandmother and she would have to take care of her.

'Yes, of course,' and Phoebe, seeing in Maggie's eyes the new heaviness she knew too well herself, and unable to cope with that, edged quickly out of the room.

Maggie sat down at the kitchen table, a last delay before going up to her room and lifting the roof away in careful segments like peeling a banana. All her courage and strength would be called for and Fenna would be furious. Slowly, reluctantly, she reached into the fridge and extracted a half-full bottle of Coke.

'You don't have to do it, you don't have to do it, you don't have to do it,' she repeated dully to herself.

But she did have to. Now, before it was too late.

The Coke was flat, tasting flatly of old cigarette ash, and 'Oh shit', she thought, before emptying the black liquid down the sink and turning the light off.

BOOK TWO

We have already begun to see how this returning of memory is very far from being a congenial and painless process . . . because the self at any given moment is a made *self: it is not a solid, independent machine for deciding and acting efficiently or rationally in response to stimuli, but is itself a process, fluid and elusive, whose present range of possible responses is part of a developing story. The self is – one might say – what the past is doing now. It is continuity; and so it is necessarily memory – continuity seen as the shape of a unique story, my story which I now own, acknowledge, as mine. To be a self is to own such a story: to act as a self is to act out of the awareness of this resource of a particular past.*

Rowan Williams

One

So now it was night-time, and each of the three women had gone to her own room, stacked up like layers of sediment, geological formations each laid down in different eras. The oldest at the bottom. Rachel down on the ground floor of the house, touching the bedrock almost, she was the bedrock, in her flesh and her brain was the foundation of this world. She was not just the oldest, but the core, the source. The basement, though, was underneath her, as her mother was underneath them all. Two storeys above her Phoebe had her room, and high above them both, nearest to the sun and the rain, still being shaped by these external forces, was Maggie in her attic.

Rachel left her daughter and granddaughter and went through the door into her own bedroom. She felt comforted. It was a room of grace and order; like the rest of her flat, it was furnished with selected items from the Suffolk home of her childhood – now a hotel, now a house where she could never go again.

When she entered the room Rachel immediately leant against the door-jamb, took off her shoes, and dropped them, but after three stockinged footsteps turned round, picked them up again, and carried them to the wardrobe.

Standing there she removed her wool dress – front fastenings, side-zip. She had always shopped thoughtfully since the humiliating evening when she had discovered herself too weary to reach up and over for a long back zip, and had had to go upstairs and ask Phoebe to help her. Two days later Phoebe had brought her home a neat sink cord, with a fastening like a dog lead; an ingenious device to assist the frail elderly. It had almost made her cry. She could never bring herself to use it. Now thinking of that, as she undid the buttons, she was caught out by a vivid memory of Martin.

Almost she turned towards the mirror on her dressing-table expecting to see his face as he came up behind her to fasten the top hook of her dress; a tender regular moment of domesticity. He would fiddle with the collar and then, so often, would kiss her neck or caress her shoulders, but what she remembered now was his fascination, childlike, with her three-angled mirror. There were arrangements of its related surfaces that enabled one, with care, to see the mirror-image of the mirror-image – one's real face as the rest of the world saw it. Suddenly caught there, his fine bony nose supporting absurdly small round glasses, her smaller nose bearing the greater weight of her big ones, their heads on the same level, their mouths smiling in surprised satisfaction at the complicated image before them. A comforting image of domestic security.

She thought tenderly of him, and then was annoyed with herself. She could not now afford such sentimentality. In self-defence she tried to think about how much he would have enjoyed her present dilemma. A deliberate, wilful, mean thought.

'Damn you,' she told his dead shades.

Then she sat down on the chair beside the fireplace to remove her tights and the long-legged all-in-one undergarment that would, thirty years ago, have made her laugh. Not just vanity she often told herself, also tidiness. But she was not fooled. She did not like being bulky and old.

In her nightie and dressing-gown she went to the bathroom. She could never enter the bathroom without smiling. Once she had read that the difference between old and new money could be seen in the bathrooms: the old upper-classes kept them Spartan. Hers was. Tonight though, she wondered if life would be easier without irony and self-mockery. Even so she would be uncomfortable and embarrassed by a thick carpet and designer tiles. That at least was something they had in common; she and Phoebe and Maggie, all for different reasons, could giggle together in department stores over heart-shaped baths and gold taps. 'At least,' she thought crossly, 'I don't need false teeth.'

She knew perfectly well she was conscious of all these things because she did not really want to think about the important things. Or perhaps these tiny and measurable declines into old age were the really important things, not the dreadful and impossible mess she had made of her life, not scientific honour and professional conduct. Back in her bedroom she picked up the P. D. James novel she was reading and climbed into bed, but even as she opened it she knew she would not read it. She had to make up her mind. Or, rather, she had to make up her heart.

Tomorrow, at the Board Meeting, she ought to ask the board to take down the reconstruction which had made her name. Such a simple little thing. Her own, her very own, late Cretaceous carnivorous dinosaur, which she had excavated herself and reconstructed from her own fossils, reconstructed with 'an imaginative intuition amounting to genius', as the Old Man himself had said. The dinosaur named after her father, which had proved her bold and flashy theories, and which had stood as a central exhibit in the museum to the delight of schoolchildren and the admiration of her colleagues for thirty years. She ought to tell them to take it down, tear it apart and throw it away.

Because she had been wrong.

She had been wrong when everyone had said she was wrong, and she had still been wrong when everyone had said she was right.

'No, Rachel,' she told herself sternly, letting the novel fall back onto her lap, 'it is best to be honest; to be honest there has never been a time when everyone has said you were right.'

Even at best there had only been a time when what she had said had been generally accepted, had been in the mainstream. And that had been more because of the discovery of DNA than because of her work. DNA had given the pure Darwinian evolutionists a wonderful boost; it had given them a mechanism to explain gradualist evolution. DNA and Jungian anthropology and Darwinism had seemed to mesh together. The whole model had appeared to work. The overall shape of the answer to the mysteries had been clear, even if the details were not all precise.

And then along came the jumps, the great leaps in the fossil record. Or as Paul had put it,

'Rachel, the leaps do seem to be there. What are we going to do with them?'

She had resisted the leaps, and their inevitable consequence – Catastrophe Theory. Not a steady careful emergence; a delicate overlapping of species; a subtle interconnection of environment, climate, food-chains, mutations, adaptations and survivals. But a cosmic crash, accidental, inexplicable, random chance smashing into the patterns, distorting and restructuring them. Big Bang thinking not just for cosmologists and pacifists, but for nice orderly evolutionists as well. Catastrophe Theory, not proven, but increasingly accepted. All those brash Americans and their bounding energy.

And even that did not matter too much; she could cope with new information. It wasn't in that sense that she had been so fundamentally wrong anyway. It had been somewhere much more important: she had manipulated her data to her own emotional ends. It was that that made her life a failure. That and her arrogant determination to steal power from the soul and give it to science.

She had been wrong and she did not like it. Particularly she did not like the fact that, as a half-way competent life scientist, she ought to have been able to see. It was the seeing that mattered. It was the thing she had prided herself on most, her stock-in-trade, the first necessity for a field fossil hunter. And that was what she had wanted to be; that was how she had wanted to be seen. It was her sole claim to fame.

'Dear God,' she thought, sitting up abruptly, that reminded her: she must take care to live long enough for poor dear Maxwell to alter her obituary. She had better write to him; she would hate him to be embarrassed, and he was so old and gaga now that he was bound to miss the literature. They were all old and gaga now. She was too, probably. She ought to have retired. She was too old for the effort of making acting righteously feel as though it were enough.

Because, simply, it was not enough. She had given up too much for her dinosaur. She had not meant to, she had not set out to do anything so complicated. The paths in seemed always joyful and simple, but like a lobster pot, you went in easy and did not know until too late the impossibility of return. For women there was never anyone to hold the thread when they went into the labyrinth. Ambition it was called, but no one ever thought that they were being ambitious: they were just getting on with it, making today's choices, short term and just for now, for the enormous excitement of an idea, a find, a discovery, just for fun. No one told you when you were young and ambitious that all ambition was greed, and that all greed had to be paid for. Or it did if you were a woman, a woman who wanted to be any sort of scientist and . . .

. . . and oh, damn Martin.

'Damn you,' she said aloud.

She was too old now for understanding and forgiveness, which naturally had always been her job and never his. All the explanations – the War, and late fatherhood, and even the simple fact of being an ambitious man with a more successful – no, no, a cleverer, more competent, better-at-the-job: she was also too old to lie about it – a more intelligent wife – didn't help and didn't matter. Just damn you, because you could have been more generous, because you promised me you would be, you promised me that you wanted a colleague not a housewife, that work was the centre of love and you did not keep your word. You lied to me. So, damn you.

Rachel dealt in truth now because she had to. She was seventy-four years old, her husband had been dead for twenty years, and it was still his fault that she had been forced to this point of pain. His fault that she had come at last to this place where just holding on to a slim margin of dignity and professional integrity had to be enough. Because there was nothing else. Because he had taken everything away from her and left her with nothing but this.

But how could she dare to damn him, when there was Maggie carrying his genes, visible in her nose and the turning of her too thin neck? Crossly, Rachel pushed at the book on her lap until it fell off the bed and lay spine upwards, with the pages bent. She refused to feel guilty. Just now, tonight, her needs were greater than Maggie's. So damn him.

She reached out an arm and turned her bedside light off.

She was not afraid of the dark, because when she was very little Rachel had had the tobacco-scented hollow of her father's shoulder as her place of refuge. If when she was small she had been frightened, her cries had brought him to her bedside. Tucking against him, safe from all imaginable dangers, he had told her stories which carried her out of the reaches of the darkness of this world's night.

Out there, he told her, far beyond the power of earth's gravity and swinging through space, the lonely, upright, blasted planet, Mercury, whirls at unimaginable speeds in its attempt to outrun the savage pull of the sun. On Mercury, he murmured, while sleep returned to her, each night lasts as long as each year, the winter dusk moving to a spring evening, a midsummer midnight, an autumnal dawn and on to a winter morning. On Mercury, Rachel learned, it was truly dark: there were no clouds to be befrilled by the moonlight, and no moonlight to befrill them. On Mercury in dark of night the temperature fell to $-170C$, and its craters offered no comfort or shelter. Mercury travelled not in a smooth round orbit, but in progressive ellipses, forming rosette patterns in the sky. At the perihelion, Mercury's desperate flight from the sun becomes so frantic that it travels faster than it revolves; the sun wavers, no longer travelling across Mercury's sky from East to West, but falling back, West to East. Out at the aphelion, furthest from the sun, its panic subsides and the sun can catch up again, pulling the poor tiny planet back towards the burning, passionate, destroying embrace for which its gravitational pull yearns.

Secure in her father's arms, the child Rachel came to know that the steady, cloud-strewn darkness of her own homeland need hold no terrors for her. She could sleep safely on this gentler planet, which spun so smoothly and regularly, while new mountains grew slowly in the depths of the ocean, and her father rocked her in his arms.

Without remembering why, Rachel still remembered best in the dark. So now, still sitting upright, she set her will to exploration.

She had married Martin in 1935. She had been twenty-one and had just taken her brilliant degree. To remember Martin then, without everything that came after, was difficult, was extremely difficult. To remember herself then was even more difficult. What she could remember, because it was unforgettable, was the fizzy sweetness of being in love, when she had woken early in her bed so as not to miss a second of a day which had such joy and excitement in it. And for her it was a special treat to be in love because she had believed it could never happen to her, that she wasn't the sort for it, that she was 'too clever', and not beautiful like her mother.

Yet surely she had not loved Martin just because he had loved her, just on some impulse of gratitude and surprise. She could not tolerate the idea of such narcissistic conduct in herself. There must have been something else, there must have been. Something in him, only in him, which she had recognised and wanted. She needed to believe that he had changed, not that she had been stupid and blind. She liked to imagine that it was the War that had changed him, the dark time in the Camp that he would never talk about.

After all, her father had liked Martin. Her father, who had not been a man given to easy likings, had both enjoyed and encouraged Martin.

'Of course, you're too young. But if you want to, you'd better marry him. I can talk to him. He's a good man. He'll take you to Africa, he tells me. Lucky you.'

And her mother . . . she had always understood her mother to have been simply deeply relieved that all this education had not protected her only daughter from womanliness. But now, in the light of the new data, she realised that she did not have the first idea what her mother had really been like, and she had never bothered to find out. Her mother's beauty had scared her, and she had invented a mother with whom she could cope, a mother who was allowed perfection in her own sphere, but no access at all to the world of courage and intelligence and adventure, which she Rachel had chosen as her own.

But when she tried to think about the Martin whom she had married she felt stuck. They had not grown up together. His friends were not her friends. There was no one to talk to about him. Sometimes she envied Phoebe that casual chatty intimacy that women seemed to have nowadays. She had no women friends like that.

She had asked Bill directly once, because Bill was a man who invited such queries. Bill was her friend now, but years before that he had been Martin's friend: he had been a bright and charming Rhodes Scholar, at the same college as Martin. After Oxford he had gone home to Boston, but they had exchanged Christmas cards and the casual paraphernalia of male friendship. When Bill had contacted her after her book was published, it had seemed socially comfortable, easy, that she should become friends with one of her husband's oldest friends.

The summer after Martin died she had accepted an invitation to go on holiday with Bill and his wife in their sailing boat, in the gulf of St Lawrence, a trip of extraordinary gentleness; constructed by Bill in his affection to console her for her bereavement. During that succession of hot lazy days and enormous fish meals, it had been appropriate to ask Bill then about Martin; they had spent much of the holiday gently recalling their own pasts, and Martin's. In that context she had been able to say,

'That must have been about the time I first met Martin? Bill, do you remember him well? I find it terribly difficult to remember how he was then. Do you think the war affected him very badly?'

Unfortunately it had not worked. Bill had not heard the right need in her question. He had said reassuringly, very Bill-like,

'Rachel, don't worry about that. You'd be surprised how common memory losses are immediately after bereavement. Time will give him back to you, all refurbished and polished up.'

She had laughed then, teasing him. 'Oh Bill, all those years poised over the couch sucking out the innards of innocent and unhappy people, and pouring in comfort instead. It's become a professional reflex with you. Like me unable to sit on this boat without noticing the sandstone sedimental strata on that island over there.'

But after that she could not use Bill to pursue Martin any further, because of an embarrassing shyness. The trouble with the inscrutable and infinitely wise Bill, eminent Jungian analyst and loving friend, was that he tended to see more and name more than she necessarily wanted. It limited their friendship, her fear that he would pierce her with his tender affection.

Rachel had very little sympathy for neurosis, for clinical psychoanalysis. In thirty-five years the depths of her friendship for Bill had not overcome the inner voice of her mother saying 'Morbid self-indulgence, dear' and 'Pull yourself together' and 'If you haven't got anything better to do with your time than brood, dear child, you need more exercise. Run down to the garden and do some weeding.'

Rachel knew perfectly well how eminent and respected Bill was, how major his contribution had been, but it was in the area of anthropology, of the reconstruction of mythology, the seeking for the signs and stories in the heart of the dreams that she admired her friend. The other, the couchwork as she called it, made her giggle slightly inside, girlish, defensive as though Bill might peer into her.

She wished, as she lay there, damning Martin, that she had been braver in her researches. She needed to be reassured that it had been a reasonable, proper and seemly choice when she had so passionately needed to marry him all those years ago.

She had married him anyway. There need not have been any hurry, but she had wanted to go excavating. Martin had been offered an expedition, in southern Africa. He would be away at least two years. How could she bear not to go? Not to be with him for two years, and not to be digging where he was digging. It was probably the expedition that swayed her father, persuaded him to give his consent. A fossil hunt was something he understood. More than understood – delighted in.

Rachel's father, Major David Hunter-Pearce, was not a great or profound paleontologist; he was one of the last of the Victorian *grands amateurs*. He loved three things with passion: he loved his Suffolk home and his wife, somehow packaged together, just as all these years later Rachel still packaged them. He loved his only child. And he loved field paleontology. He was a real fossil hunter and had dug in obscure corners of every continent. He was respected for his eye, his money, his hard-working energy, his good humour and his almost military skills in organising and administering and provisioning field expeditions. He was perhaps the one person who could understand why his daughter, who ought to spend the winter dancing, now her protracted education was finally finished, wanted to go excavating with a rather poor and already balding academic.

She wanted to go excavating with Martin, hammers in their hands and ideas in their heads. They would of course have to be married or else she could not go. She had tried, quite recently to explain this to Phoebe and Phoebe had roared with laughter, not very kindly laughter. Phoebe had no sense of history, unfortunately.

David Hunter-Pearce financed Rachel's place in the expedition as his wedding present to her. It was by no means her first field trip; in practical terms she was probably the most seasoned member of Martin's expedition, although they made very little use of her wide experience. Her father had been on the Central Asiatic Expedition in 1923; he had taken her and her mother with him as far as Kalgan. So she had spent the end of her first decade in that strange and colourful city up-country from Beijing.

There her mother had poured immaculate afternoon-tea seated at a camp table, and there the wind from the desert of Mongolia was held back by the great and ancient wall that snaked across the wild lands of the innermost continent. She had stood high on that wall in her neat black stockings and looked northwards into the vast vacuity which had spawned the Mongol hordes. The wind sweeping in from the waste lands beyond the wall now spawned promises and rumours of a still more hidden secret: the dream and the reality of fossils, of dinosaur memories, and of the origins of man. Perched there, still as spindly as Maggie was now, Rachel became conscious for the first time of the thrill of real field work. Ten years later, promising, hopeful, and in love, she needed to go on Martin's expedition with him. Her father could understand that.

So her father financed her and they got married ten days before their ship sailed. She was described as Martin's assistant and secretary in the expedition reports, but she had known herself to be his companion, his colleague and his friend. It was from that charmed and charming field trip that the photograph in Phoebe's bedroom came. No wonder she had looked magnificent; she had been magnificent. Africa had opened its arms like a warm mother, though doubtless Phoebe would say that was racist, and heaped her sweetness up on them. Sunshine and good luck and a wilderness still almost untouched and friendship and an unexpected abundance of Upper Jurassic and Lower Cretaceous dinosaur fossils and wonderful sex.

Martin had been so kind and generous and eager to teach and share: mentor, tutor, and lover as well. And, although she had not said it then or since, best of all had been the growing certainty that this was what she did, this finding and understanding of fossils. She was easily at home and exceptionally talented: an odd combination of learning and then seeing, guessing and then confirming, and proving both learning and sight with the utter physicality of digging and extracting. She had been made for this. Warmed by Martin's benignity and seniority, she could escape the veiled insinuations of some of the young men on the team and concentrate on learning her job. She had been filled and overflowing with joy.

They should have known that a shadow had fallen over the world and the diluvian rain clouds were gathering, but they had not cared. They had turned their backs on a troubled Europe and plunged into a superficially untroubled Africa, not bothered by the things that should have bothered them. The guilt had come later, but she could not now pretend that it had been otherwise.

Professionally it had felt like a time of unbounded optimism. The archaeologists were pushing backwards and the paleontologists and geologists were pushing forward and there seemed good grounds to believe that they would meet in the middle somewhere, probably in Central Asia or Western Africa, and it all seemed more exciting and more important than the fate of Abyssinia, or Spain, or even central Europe. And when you leaned forward to examine newly dug ground, the sun stroked your back and kissed your naked neck. Who could fail to be pleased with herself?

They had two seasons in Africa; the first technically financed by Martin's university, and the second, in reality, by her father. This was something that she and Martin chose not to talk about. He gave them money himself and he raised it from his friends – not from the academic scientific community, but more from his old world-wandering acquaintance, who read John Buchan and ruled the Empire. He presented their dig not in terms of scientific development, but as adventure, as one of the last great explorations.

Both Martin and Rachel in their blithe innocence rather despised him for this. Martin did not like it at all. He did not want to be his father-in-law's paid fossil collector. He was a scientist, not a hired field-hand, working for some rich English gentleman. He wanted a serious academic career. Palaeontology was a new science; it had to be done properly. Like many of his contemporaries he was concerned about the professional standing of the subject. They needed serious university posts, and serious university funding.

Rachel soon discovered that while she liked the early stories of her profession, Martin did not. It irritated him somehow, for instance, that Mantell's first iguanadont tooth, which had led to the realisation of the whole nature of vanished species, species which had to be saurian whatever the Parisian experts were trying to say, had been found not on some well-structured dig, but casually, accidentally, by the wife of a country doctor. Rachel had a better grasp of her own history, although she was not able to articulate this for a long time to come. She had been in China with Andrews, she had been in Patagonia, in Java, on digs which had produced significant discoveries, but had all been put together in gentlemen's clubs for the hell of it.

She was also a woman, although she did not articulate this either, at that point. A woman and a lady and the only child of a rich man. She didn't need, as Martin did, the appurtenances of professionalism. Moreover she knew that whatever his motives, her father and his generation were not frivolous. They were not just dilettantes.

Nor did Martin refuse the money. The second year's dig was perhaps even more tightly disciplined, more carefully chronicled, because of Martin's fear of amateurism; and that did neither of them any harm. Rachel thought she shared his feelings; she thought the time had come to laugh at the old-fashioned collectomania, where any fossils were as interesting as any others, so long as there were lots of them. She knew that indeed they had to be firm and scientific about the whole thing.

But she loved her father and she loved being there on the dig. She was more worldly than her husband; she knew that they would not get any other funding than what her father's affectionate enthusiasm could provide. Sometimes she felt angry with Martin, because he would do nothing to help his father-in-law. She could not see how, if the work was good, it could possibly be discredited by trying to describe it to an informed and intelligent patron in the sort of terms that would assist him in raising more money.

She wrote her father long and rich letters, describing their work and finds in detail. But she also told him about life in the encampment and the aggressively abrupt evenings and the enormous stars. She wrote to him about how scary hippos are when seen from canoes; and how their heads rise up out of the water looking like enormous old rubber boots. She wrote about tribal dances, and the soft throbbing drums of late evening, and about a friend she made in the camp, who in faltering English tried to tell her the ancient stories of his people, tales of monsters and witchcraft and huge devouring spirits of the night. She told him about Elephant Ivory – a magical tree whose fruits must pass through the digestive system of elephants before they become fertile.

She wrote to him weekly, even when she had no means of posting the letters, and sent them in great bundles when the occasions arose. She wrote precisely and carefully about the things that she knew would amuse him, and amuse his prosperous cronies as they fretted on about the decline of empire and the general decadence of the younger generation. These letters were acts of love for the two people she loved most in the whole world, her father and her husband. Only later did she realise how much the letters had done for her own capacity to write, to look, to seek the larger context.

But the writing still seemed peripheral to the work. To the moments when, standing beside Martin, she would watch him attentively as he inspected newly broken ground, or turned over small rock pieces, his eyes widening. To the painstaking rewarding labour of chipping away surrounding sediment to reveal the delicate bones which had lain undisturbed for over two hundred million years. To the more muscular messy task of swathing the newly exposed fossils in plaster of Paris and moving them to the camp. To the moments when, the lamp light making their whole tent glow across the veldt, they would draw up careful notes on the day's toil, transforming it into an ordered shape. Later they would turn to each other's arms and the great dark palace of their mosquito-netted bed.

So they had two seasons of rich and exciting digging. For two years she hardly spoke to another woman except at occasional and artificial dinner parties laid on by the white farming community who found the paleontologists hilarious, but enjoyed their company. For two years the sun shone, and isolated from the rest of the world she lived like a boy, a child, in the camp. For two years she rested out the rains in the small up-country hotel, where Martin taught her how to draw the exquisitely accurate field sketches of which they were both so proud. She was happy, she was in love, and she was working and learning hard.

They returned to a cold and changed England that they could not really understand, to find that ancient loyalties had shifted and that what seemed strange to them had become daily fare to old friends. They found it difficult to reconnect and were pushed still more closely into each other's arms. Politically, along with their friends, they opposed appeasement, but in the secret corners of their hearts they did not: they did not want a war, they wanted to spend time with their fossils. They wanted time to work and catalogue and assess, to contemplate and to publish. They wanted contact with their German colleagues, the best paleontologists in the world. They told themselves that the community of scientists should be international and above petty political boundaries; but they had to close their eyes, and refuse to see the evidence. So they were confused by the world and excited only by each other. None the less with considerable solemnity and self-satisfaction, with unspoken murmurs of look-at-me-and-my-fine-sacrifice, Martin had joined up in 1939, and she had been alone. 'Take care of our bones,' he said on Waterloo Station, and disappeared.

Almost immediately she took a museum job in London; she would not normally have had such an opportunity and she knew it, but there were not many women paleontologists around. Later the job became the more dramatic, but less scholarly, one of preparing the entire major collection for evacuation. It turned out to be a reserved occupation.

She did try at first to keep in contact with what was happening around her. The Suffolk house had been requisitioned, and her father, in a furious temper because the government could find no use for him, stomped off to

Scotland to sulk for the duration in the draughty castle of some distant relative. She found that in just two years she had become quite unlike any of her old college friends, who were either married and wrestling with children, ration coupons and the struggle to pretend everything was normal, or were brisk and business-like in smart military uniforms, trotting through London on their way to or from the really important centres of action. From the perspective of a woman of her background London was deserted. And, above all, no one understood or was interested in her work. It, more than anything else, cut her off. She was childless and fit, why had she not joined up, or at least gone to work in some real job? She grew sensitive to the implied disapproval all around her. What was she doing? Just messing about with old bones while other people furthered the War Effort.

She spent most of the war alone, missing Martin terribly, missing sex and companionship and real work. It seldom seemed worth the effort of dodging air raids to go back to the flat and be alone there. So she moved a mattress into the basement of the museum, which at least made her feel adventurous and suffering, and effectively lived there, strange and temporary in a cave under the world, while hell flickered above her and its distant rumbles disturbed her dreams.

For the first time in her life she started reading widely – history and anthropology first, and later psychology, the Greek classics and mythology. Finally addicted, she read novels, children's stories, folk literature, anything and everything she could lay her hands on. And in between this animated reading and doing her job, she looked endlessly, lovingly, tenderly and hopefully at the beautiful, scholarly drawings that Martin had done of their fossils. They were the nearest thing she had to him and to her own work and they gave her back the feel of an Africa so distant and strange and wonderful that she knew sadly she would never go there again.

And while London burned and she mourned, she conceived her idea. A curious amalgam in a curious time; part Jung, part Franz von Nopcsa, part Africa and part inspiration. In 1943 Martin was captured. She wrote the book for him, reaching out to him in prison, in the cold place where he could not touch fossils or her, and she had to tell him stories across the dark, across the dark which was ablaze with the fires of hell; where fire fell from the sky and smoke rose up to meet it.

The book was called *Fossil Remains and Dragon Lore* and was subtitled 'a scientific fairy story'. Like all her later writing, the book was conspicuous for both its breadth and its precision. It was readable. She gave her readers a sense of adventure by treating paleontology historically; explaining dinosaurs and ideas about the pre-mammalian world by describing how the science's nineteenth-century founding fathers had proceeded and developed. But she also leapt disciplinary boundaries, explaining Darwin – on whose knee her own father had once sat – and gradual evolutionary development. She retold the ancient stories, Chinese and African as well as European – Beowulf and St George and The Book of Changes – and reassured the reader that everything could be explained. That science ruled, and the eons of great night-terrors were over. Even dragons, she concluded, were not the products of imagination, they were deep race memories of the dinosaurs. She demonstrated that even primal myth could be placed safely in the hands of the natural sciences.

It was a hopeful, forward-looking idea. Underpinning the book was a clear and careful analysis of her own and other people's fossils: a lovely and coherent demonstration of Darwinian gradualism, and the steady movement towards higher forms. Over millions of years changes that seemed bizarre, improbable, unimaginable, were as smooth, gentle, purposive and elegant as the growth of a golden daffodil from a dead-looking bulb.

It was an idea for the post-war era, for the New Britain; an idea which fitted into the dreams of a new life of science and technology which was going to arise out of the ashes of a broken world. It was one of the first really accessible books on what paleontology had been trying to do for a hundred years. And although it was scholarly and innovative, it moved beyond text-book publications. It stepped aside from the élitism of a profession which was still trying to claim its scientific credentials – not because she had felt a populist mission, but because she had been too young and too professionally privileged to experience that struggle, because she had been lucky and beloved.

The book was published in 1947 and to her genuine surprise proved immensely popular. Fellow paleontologists were amused and impressed, or challenged and stimulated. Her father was delighted.

Martin was furious.

He expressed his fury in coldness and in his determination to get her pregnant.

He had come home in 1946. She had been so happy to see him. Like all POW wives, and especially those whose men had been in the East, she knew her man had had a bad time, that it might be difficult. Love, they were told, would conquer all. Of course he needed a home life, and attention, and love; now was not the time to tell him about her work, about what she had been up to while he had been missing all the fun. She resigned her job with scarcely a regret – she had not deserved it anyway, and she knew it. She wanted to be in Oxford with him.

When she showed him her typescript she tried not to mind that it took him a surprisingly long time to read it; after all he had his own stuff to catch up on. After all it was only apprentice work. After all he was the real scientist; she was just his admiring student. She had dedicated the book to him. He treated it, rightly no doubt, as a matter of not much account – an interesting idea possibly, though rather over-stretched. He pointed out some minor technical errors. He also corrected her punctuation, but she ignored that. He never discussed her central thesis. And, she noticed, he always said 'my fossils' not 'our fossils' as he worked on the important task of cataloguing them, pushing aside all her preliminary work.

'Casaubon,' she thought one night, and was ashamed of herself.

It was not until after the book was published that she realised how angry he was. She still tried not to acknowledge the reality – it was not until the book was successful that he had really been angry.

'I wish to God,' he said one day, 'that you hadn't dedicated that thing to me; it's so embarrassing.'

When he did not get the job in York that he had wanted he said, 'I do wish you'd seen fit to use your maiden name for your so-called professional publications – I'm afraid they may have got me confused with your visionary ramblings.'

'Look,' she said, 'I'm just a populist, a communicator; it's the real academics whose work matters.'

She never told him that she had been invited to apply for the job herself and had refused because she knew that he wanted it. It was not fair on him and his colleagues that they had had to go and fight a war while she had done their work and had time to do her own too. She told herself that he didn't mean to hurt her feelings; it was only a perfectly natural disappointment at not getting the job, which had gone to some bright young American who had never had to suffer as he had suffered.

'You're better off in Oxford, you won't have all those departmental headaches,' she told him comfortingly, 'You'll have more time to publish academically.'

But it was Rachel who was publishing academically, steadily. She had to defend her idea, which argued for a later extermination of carnivorous dinosaurs than was generally held; she had to describe her sources and

69

compare new finds. Quite apart from her book she had a modest but real reputation in late dinosaur studies.

In 1948 the Russian expedition to Mongolia through Ulan Bator discovered the 'The Dragons' Tomb' – an extraordinary collection of late dinosaur remains. Early on they sent her some technical notes, and some queries about how she would interpret some of their data.

When she first saw the material, tumbling out of its huge brown envelope onto the dining-room table at breakfast she was so thrilled that she wanted to leap up, run round the room and yell,

'Eggs! Martin, eggs! They've found eggs, nests, baby dinosaurs. Hurrah.'

But she looked up and the enthusiasm died on her lips. Just in time; he hated to be disturbed at breakfast. He had lost weight in the Far East, his neck skin drooped, and his nose seemed larger than ever. He would never talk about the concentration camp, but she knew that things had happened to him there which made her enthusiasm seem petty. All those years of suffering, while she had become famous, using his research. She decided not to bother him now with the Russian material.

Later she took the notes to her father, although his memory was not as good as it should be any more. She danced her excited glee for him in his new flat in London, and they had a happy time working through it.

'I told them back in Kalgan in '25 . . .'

'1923, Daddy,' she said gently.

'All right then, I told them in '23 that we should go further north. Russians, huh.'

'You didn't do badly then, did you?'

'No, we didn't, did we? Mind you, Andrews: he could sniff out fossils at twenty miles, he had the nose for it. We wouldn't have had to have gone much further north.' He rambled on happily about long-ago expeditions, but came back to the present and her notes with pleasure. 'Well Rachel, so now the Bolshies need your help, do they? I hope they know your capitalist father took you to Mongolia while they were still serfs. Guillotine material you are, my love. *A la lanterne* stuff, if they only knew. Let me see what you say to them, won't you? This pelvic whatnot here, does it remind you of some of those Montana thingies they were talking about before the war?'

But when she left he kissed her and said, 'I'm proud of you, Rachel. Pretty soon you'll have been worth the raising.'

'Get on with you,' she said affectionately, teasing. 'It's yourself you're really proud of.'

But to Martin, when she finally admitted to him that she had been sent some field notes from Ulan Bator, she said, 'Of course they only sent it because Daddy was with Andrews. But it's quite exciting stuff. Since we've got hold of it, do you want to have a look? I'd be grateful for a hand with it.'

He took the material and read it, but when she pressed him for his opinion on part of her response, he said, 'I'm sorry, Rachel, I really haven't got the time. I've got some rather important lectures to prepare.'

Once, in the middle of the night, she woke up from a deep sleep with the horrid conviction that he had told people in his department that he had seen the field notes from Ulan Bator without telling them that they had been sent to *her*. She hated herself. She had no right to be so mean and suspicious. And anyway she had used his fossil material in her book.

When he read the highly flattering letter that had accompanied the notes from Russia, she said hastily, 'They can't actually have read my book; it's not professional enough. It must be the association with dragons in the title.'

But he stopped bringing his visiting colleagues home to meet her and he started insisting on the baby.

Well, of course she wanted a baby. She wanted Martin's baby. Before the war it had been him saying, 'Wait, wait, there's no hurry,' and 'We've got so much work to do together.'

Now they had a house and he had a secure job. So why was she so frightened? No, no; frightened was not the right word. But there was plenty of time, and she had been invited to go to the United States. Of course Martin had been through the war; and of course he was older than she was. She wasn't that young either, though. She began to sense a prejudice: scientific women weren't truly womanly, didn't want children, were self-centred, shouldn't get married. All the things she had believed before she met Martin. Surely it was not true. Of course she wanted to have a baby. Perhaps she was not being fair to her husband.

Apart from the business about her book everything was wonderful between them. Perhaps he was just being kind, perhaps there really was something badly flawed in the book and he was too sweet to tell her. Of course it had been oversold. It was just lucky timing. If she wasn't always working perhaps it would be more fun for both of them. She did love him so much.

In 1951 her father died. Within eight weeks she was pregnant.

She thought she was bound to have a son who would look like her father. Instead she had Phoebe, who from birth onwards looked exactly like Martin.

Martin was totally delighted about his daughter. Throughout Rachel's pregnancy he had been increasingly tender and thoughtful: he would come home in the evening bringing her flowers, books, gifts for the unborn child. He wrapped her in gentleness and pleasure. Although she missed his lovemaking she understood that his reluctance came from delicacy not disgust and appreciated the thought if not the reality. But his goodwill towards her was as nothing compared with his joyful glee after Phoebe was born. She had thought that he too might expect a son, but from the moment he arrived at her hospital bedside and announced that he had already been to the nursery to view his new-born daughter, Rachel realised she had been wrong. A girl-child was the very thing for him. He was glowing with pride and love.

For a few years they were extraordinarily happy, locked together each evening and delighted by their own cleverness and domestic affection. It was almost like a paler, more serene repetition of Africa. Except of course that the work was left out. Martin increasingly wanted to leave his in the office when he came home at night.

'Boring work,' he'd say, throwing down his shabby book-bag unopened on the hall table. 'I have to do it all day. Now I want to spend time with my beautiful girls.'

Touched by his devotion she tried to keep her work out of their shared time together as well. Although often she would have liked to consult him, discuss her writing projects with him, or meet his colleagues, she felt that it would be mean and ungrateful to suggest it.

He was an affectionate and attentive parent. Phoebe would sit on his lap, her little chubby legs banging against his long bony ones, and absorb the outside world through him. He was proud and diligent, teaching her to read before she was four, and taking her for long weekend walks in the park, unembarrassed by the pram and, later on, unbored by the repetitious tasks of toddlerdom – feeding ducks and learning to ride a scooter. Rachel admired him enormously because she too often found Phoebe boring and herself short-tempered.

She did not like this new self and did not understand it. Because Phoebe was a very easy baby and complete delight, and because she was influenced too by modern psychology, she did not employ a nanny, and so had all the pleasure of Phoebe's growing. She saw Martin's delightful conscientiousness, but knew she could not share it, and felt guilty. But as Phoebe grew older and she had less and less worktime of her own she felt obscurely frustrated and dissatisfied.

She did write another book, based mainly on her father's travel notes and photographs, but it was not a serious palaeontological work; more a personal account of a nineteenth-century amateur natural historian. It was quite successful and, once he realised that it did not interfere with Phoebe's life, Martin enjoyed both the book and the short burst of publicity that it gave her.

She began to feel that it really did not matter that she had so little time for her more significant professional labours, because she had run out of steam a bit. What she needed, desperately needed, was some proof. She needed one, just one, suitable dinosaur, later, not even a lot later, than anything they yet had. She was sure it was there, waiting for her; all the evidence suggested that it was bound to be there. Indeed the profession was coming round to her way of thinking, they all now wanted it to be there; once they had grasped the notion they tended, those who liked grand theories, to like hers. It made them important for one thing, though she had not seen that then; it kept attention focused on them, rather than on the climatologists, or the origins-of-man people, who were grabbing the limelight, the influential positions, the publishing space, the best jobs.

She wanted to go and look for it. Too frustrating to wait for someone else. She wanted field work to refresh her mind. She wanted the stimulation of travel and the reality of a spade and hammer in her hands. Martin wanted her to stay at home with Phoebe. Martin was suddenly extraordinarily well-read in child psychology for someone who had been so scathing about its use in her own work.

'I could take her with me.'

'Too dangerous.'

'Don't be silly.'

'I'd miss her too much,' he said. 'I'd miss you too.'

'Come with us,' she said, sudden memories of the warmth of the sun and his kisses on her neck.

But he had forgotten. 'I've got too much work to do; real work.'

Once when she tried to suggest even a brief dig, he'd snapped, 'I've got neither the time nor the patience to hang around some god-forsaken dust hole, trying to keep some uppity camp boys under control while you try and bend scientific fact to match your crazy theories.'

'Martin,' she had pleaded, 'if you're so sure I'm that wrong, can't you show me where.'

'Oh God,' he said, 'if you can't see the problems for yourself, what on earth is the point?'

After that she did not talk about it any more. On the rare occasions that her work came up he simply looked distant and a few hours later he would complain about the state of the house or the inadequacies of her cooking, but now at least she could understand what upset him so much. She knew how it would hurt her if he had a theory that she was sure was wrong, and he clung to it and would not listen to her. She knew too, of course, that if the atmosphere between them was bad, then it was bound to affect Phoebe, so of course he would want to avoid fights and arguments. And she did love him very much, and they were so happy apart from this one little thing. So she learned to cook better, studying it with the serious intensity she used to bring to her fossils.

Then in 1959 he was offered an expedition of his own. He was pleased and sunny and laughed and said that it just showed that careful, conscientious, scholarly work paid off in the end. He seemed to have forgotten how much he would miss Phoebe and her. Rachel decided that she would go too. She knew he was not enthusiastic about taking her with him, but she decided not to care about that. When they were there, when they were back in Africa, he would remember the first time, remember how good it had been; he would remember how good she was at field work, and how good she was in bed. She convinced herself it would restore their original relationship and that they would be happy.

She thought the whole project through and played her cards with care. At cunningly planned dinner parties she let it be known that she and the child were going with him. She put him in a position where he would look silly, petty and needlessly fearful if he refused point blank to take her. She managed to have herself enrolled as the expedition's Secretary. She persuaded him that small children were not impossible on field trips; that indeed she had been with her parents several times, when she was even younger than Phoebe was. She hated herself for all the manipulation and she hated him for imposing the necessity of manipulation upon her. She felt guilty, but she could barely suppress her excitement at the thought of once again doing what she did best, digging up new fossils, being a field paleontologist.

And then, when she had out-manoeuvred him, when she had shamed herself and him by her professional greed, when the trunks were almost packed and the course of malaria pills half-taken, she received a telegram from the States; a great long telegram such as only Americans would send, and it was followed by frantic telephone calls and upheavals of a kind that she, Rachel, did not like. Telegram and phone calls were both from the same young man, a young Sino-American paleontologist.

He wanted her to come, he wanted her now, he could raise the finance. He thought he had found what she was looking for, perhaps he had found her evidence, and would she please, please, please, come at once and dig with him? Could she come now and have a look, there in the wilds of Wyoming.

'Of course I couldn't,' she said laughing down the phone at his enthusiasm, 'I'm just about to leave for Africa.'

'It's not in Africa,' he told her, 'It's not in Africa, it's here. Come on, Mrs Petherington, you must want to find lovely late dinosaurs even more than me.'

'Dig it up and send me the drawings,' she said, still laughing.

So he had to confess that he had already told his financing trust that she was coming. He had committed her, without even asking, in order to get the grant.

'If you won't come, it won't happen. I won't be able to raise the money. I'll be in terrible, shameful disgrace with the Yale Carnegie trustees. I haven't the seniority to raise the money elsewhere. Mrs Petherington, I need you, I need you like no woman has ever been needed before. We have to dig this summer. Do you know what those wicked winds are like out there? God knows what will be eroded away forever if we don't dig this summer.'

It was that simple; it was now or never.

'Give me twenty-four hours,' she said, 'I'll ring you back in twenty-four hours.'

She spent the hours not thinking about Martin, not thinking about what this would mean to him and his carefully laid plans, but ringing round the world, checking out the young man.

'Tim Wong?' an old colleague in Boston told her, 'Well he's crazy and he's young, but he digs well; he finds stuff, he has the nose for it.'

Later she realised it had been that one phrase that persuaded her. It was an expression of her father's. 'So and so,' he would say, grinning, 'yes, we'd like him in on this one; he finds fossils, he has the nose for it.'

She booked the flight for herself and Phoebe before she even told Martin. Underneath all her excitement and rushing around, it lay like a heavy weight on her stomach. She was afraid of him and afraid of her own fear. She practised openings,

'Darling, the most extraordinary thing has happened . . .'

'Darling, you're not going to like this but try and be pleased for me . . .'

'Martin, you know how much I love you . . .'

They did not help much. She cooked him delicious supper. That did not help much either.

'Darling,' she said, 'I've decided against coming to Africa.' Did she imagine the tiny flicker of what might have been relief on his face, before he said affectionately,

'It's a bit late for that, isn't it, Rachel? How will I manage without the most high-powered Secretary any paleontological expedition has ever been lucky enough to get? What's the matter then, worried about Phoebe?'

'No,' she said and drew a deep breath, 'the Yale Carnegie Trust have invited me to dig in Wyoming this summer. They're finding some very late stuff, they think, and they want me to be there when they excavate.'

'And when did this extraordinary offer come up? You didn't have to accept. Didn't you even think of discussing it with me?'

Part of her wanted to scream that he had accepted his expedition without consulting her; he had presented it to her and known she would be pleased; that he was selfish and cruel. But Rachel seldom did things like that. She said instead, with a well-constructed wry smile,

'Martin, be honest; which would you rather do – be a camp follower and secretary, or have a dig of your own?'

But he pushed his chair away from the table, flung his napkin down and walked out of the dining-room.

The next day, he asked her in tones of biting calm, 'Who is this Wong then, that you'll run half-way round the world for him? That you'll insult the Royal Geographical Society and play ducks and drakes with a detailed, carefully planned, scientific expedition?'

Her heart leapt for a moment. He was jealous. She put her arms around him and for a brief moment they both relaxed.

'I've never set eyes on him in my life. He's very young, and they say he is very sharp. He was in Montana with that dig last year that you lectured about. He was a pupil of Harry Schlauer's, and Harry thinks he's good.'

After a pause she said, 'Martin, darling, I want this so much, honestly. Please. But I won't go if it means that you'll be unhappy about it. If it means that much to you.' She hated herself for pleading, and for lying: she realised quite vividly at that moment that she would go anyway, even if it meant the end of their marriage. But now she had begged, it was easier for him. A little stiffly he returned her hug.

Five days later she and Phoebe waved him off from Southampton, and eleven days after that the two of them flew to New York via Rekjavik on the first leg of their journey to the mid-west.

She had a wonderful nine weeks.

They arrived at the camp twenty miles west of Sheridan, Wyoming, late one evening after what seemed like eons spent travelling; travelling not just everlastingly westward like the first explorers, but also backward in time, back from the civilised urbanity of Oxford, through the brash newness of New York and on across the rolling prairies with Phoebe anticipating a run-in with dangerous Red Indians, while Rachel felt less and less able to reassure her that this would not happen. When they finally arrived, jolting up a poor un-tarmacked road in a large truck Rachel was more smitten by the astonishing beauty of the place than by anything more scientific. The sun had already set behind the Big Horn Mountains which rose spectacularly just to the west of the site; but the sky was still violet-mauve and eastward the land sloped away away until far beyond sight it reached the Great Plains. In between, where she now stood, was a rough wilderness of grassland, pitted and tuffetted with rock formations, where the everflowing water and the everblowing wind had scraped away eighty million years of sedimentary rock and exposed the ancient grey-brown mudstone on which earlier life forms had walked free and unselfconscious.

In the days that followed all her certainties about digging were confirmed, but now she was no longer a bright shining baby, brought all this way by her affectionate husband. Now she was the senior member of the expedition. They respected her. They treated her magnificently. This was not like Africa twenty years before, pitching camp and making do. There was electric light, and cooking and even a refrigerator for the endless beer that the diggers seemed to need. Although the men all slept in a neat row of tents they had provided a caravan for Rachel and Phoebe, to which she could retire each evening and from which she could emerge in the morning, coming down the two steep steps and finding the entire team waiting at attention as it were for her orders.

Tim Wong, who quickly became Phoebe's Uncle Wong, was charming. He was so pleased to have her, so delighted with her, with himself, with the dig, he overflowed with joy and it lightened them all. Rachel perceived quickly that he did not have a brilliant mind, but instead a brilliant personality. Although he was shorter than she was by some inches and his mop of black hair made her think wickedly of one of Phoebe's dolls, his driving enthusiasm and his wild excitement reminded her in some ways more of her father than any other paleontologist had ever done. But he treated her with a direct admiration, almost a veneration, and in his glow of pride at working with her she realised how much she had been starved of straightforward intellectual respect in the last few years.

And far more importantly, she found her dinosaur. She wanted it so badly and despite everything she found it, or enough of it anyway: a good part of the skull and several vertebrae in good condition, plus some not very easy fragments of major bones. Not articulated, not properly *in situ*, but late, late, late, and exactly what she had predicted.

Now twenty-five years later, propped up in her bed and searching her soul, she knew that she had wanted it too much. She should have known that you must not want too much, that you must not be greedy, that greed distorts judgement. But she had said, privately and in public, for ten years that she would find it, and she had found it. She would have liked some teeth as well, of course, but no one gets everything: she had enough.

She would remember the joy of the first hour that she had known it was there for the rest of her life. She had been alone with the digging team, working over some clearly stratified new ground. That morning Tim Wong had taken the smaller truck and Phoebe north into Montana to see the site of Custer's last stand. The two of them had driven off in the pale dawn; Phoebe snuggled, still a little sleepy, against her Uncle Wong and Rachel had seen them go with a great flood of pleasure at her own company and gratitude to this cheerful young man who was clearly giving himself as much of a treat as he was giving her daughter.

She had enjoyed being alone for once. When the men stopped work for lunch she had stayed at the diggings in the bright hot sunshine, brushing gently, almost abstractly at the surface with the long soft brooms they were using, and then, there, like magic, was the unmistakable shape of a long jaw. Too large to be anything else at this digging level. She knew, she absolutely knew. And at the same time she was crafty, cautious, hesitant. Like a virgin on her wedding night. She was forty-five years old and in love again. She had worked, with hammer, notebook, and tiny little brush, solidly all afternoon and when the light began to fade she asked them to rig up a cable so she could go on. She could feel their excitement, for she had never done any such thing before; but when in the far distance she heard the first rumble of the truck engine, she stood up quickly.

'Canvas,' she said, almost imperious in her haste, 'and take the light away. We won't show him till its day light. Nobody tell him, we'll give him a surprise.'

His surprise and delight were part of the magic of the expedition. He was wholeheartedly enthusiastic, he seemed to harbour no resentments that it was she not he who had found it. He had wanted *her* to find it, the whole expedition had wanted her to find it. Each morning she would leave the caravan and walk over to the site, and then the men would follow behind her, watch her closely while she looked over the work. Even as she tried to scrutinise the digging face she would feel their keenness on her back, along with the sun. She strongly suspected that Tim Wong had exaggerated her status and skill, but it did not matter now because she had indeed brought home the goods.

Once they were at the fine-work stage there was an extraordinary intimacy between her and Tim as with chisels and brushes, inch by inch, they laid bare the hidden monster. She had not experienced that sort of professional comradeship for years; not since her father died, not since the African expedition. With her glasses on and her hammer in her hand, something in her was restored and she wrote long entertaining letters to Martin in Africa and she missed him.

She and Tim extracted her dinosaur together in a closeness tighter than lovers, and when she flew West again with the lovingly prepared photographs and her own detailed notes she thought that she would be happy forever. Not many people get to discover a brand new species of dinosaur in their lives.

She got back to Oxford six months before Martin did and she hardly cared; with Phoebe back in school she worked night and day, fixed on her fossil notes as she had been in the museum during the war. She knew, and by the strange osmosis that exists within small academic disciplines, everyone else began to know too, that she had found something radically exciting.

Two years and two important papers later, she had produced her brilliant reconstruction of a previously unknown, late Cretaceous carnivorous dinosaur, named after her father, but better known in the museum and in the literature as the 'Dragon Type', which was generally agreed to prove the theory she had first suggested twelve years before. Natural science laid claims through her work to a whole new territory and everyone, except Martin, was delighted.

When Martin realised what had happened she knew it was the end. He would never forgive her. It made her fragments matter more, not less.

She had never gone on another field trip – there was Phoebe's education to be thought of. Gradually, without specifically planning it, she moved out of pure research, and finally when Phoebe was old enough, she took a museum job again. The new skills of museumology, the presentation of material so as to delight and edify, seemed to so many of the people around her a much more suitable area for her to work in. Women with children, it was implied, were naturally more suited to education than to hard science. She really did not mind. The museum was properly proud to have her: it was an eminent and relatively well-paid job, and one that she found pleased her more and more – perhaps after all she really had been primarily a communicator, a populariser of the important work that real academics did.

Also it eased the tensions between Martin and herself, and they managed to get along pretty well. They never recovered the spirit of camaraderie on which she had thought the marriage would be based, but, outside work, they found shared interests – they played bridge, bought a puppy, travelled. When he died in 1968, she was sad for quite a long while.

On the dreary early spring day that Martin died she had not been paying attention. Honesty obliged her to admit that she had not paid proper attention to him for years. She had mechanised him, even mechanised the job of acting lovingly towards him. She had never felt from him that peculiarly touching ill-temper that had driven her, several times a week, to visit her father in his old age. But life with him had a necessary daily domestic comfort; looking after him was like watering the plants, cooking meals, or keeping up with the professional literature.

After he was dead she often wondered if she ought to have noticed, but he hadn't been old, not seventy yet. He had been too young for her to be ready for him to die. It had been a perfectly usual morning. She had got up as usual, prepared his breakfast, left him a note about the supposed visit from the electrician; she also left Mrs Crale a note about lunch and then took the bus as usual to the railway station, and the train as usual to Paddington, and the tube as usual to the museum. The commuting was tiresome, but she prided herself on it.

Later that morning, she had learned afterwards, Martin had got up, dressed, eaten his breakfast, gone out to buy his *Times* and retired with it into his study, saying a pleasant and normal good morning to Mrs Crale *en route*. Sometime before lunch, the first few clues of the crossword filled in, he had simply died of a heart attack.

Martin was still sitting neatly and cleanly in his chair when Mrs Crale finally went in to see what was happening. Mrs Crale had of course delayed entering his sanctum far longer than anyone sane would have done, as she had a profound conviction in the importance of Martin's work, which made it nearly impossible for her to clean his study, or call him to the telephone when he was in there. Rachel found that respect one of the more irritating aspects of her relationship with Mrs Crale, but – not surprisingly – Martin liked her, liked her enough indeed to remember to remind Rachel not only to get her a Christmas present, but one for her birthdays as well. Mrs Crale and Martin would laugh at senseless jokes and, so it seemed to Rachel, bound together in amused superiority at her domestic deficiencies. Martin, if he had to be found in so undignified a posture as death, would almost certainly have been glad that it was Mrs Crale who discovered him. Rachel tried to cling to this in the long nights of guilt that followed his demise.

Mrs Crale had been calm, efficient and on the spot. Rachel, however, could not be found. They – Mrs Crale and the doctor she had called – spent a large part of the rest of the day trying to locate her, but she was not to be found. By the time she got home, on a later train than usual, everyone in the world except her seemed to know of her husband's death. Even Phoebe had been summoned from Cambridge; his college knew, her museum, as it subsequently turned out, knew . . . had she not been both weary and sad it would have almost amused her, that she arrived into an unexpected role and was unable to take it up. She had been obliged to offer comfort and thanks to those who had almost literally borne the burden of the day, whose shock and distress by the time of her arrival had already been mediated into grief.

She had not been paying attention because she had been working.

She kept telling herself this. She had not been having an illicit affair; she had not been shopping; she had not been having a long gossipy lunch. She had been working. Work was the important thing. It was not strictly true – or rather it was strictly true, but it was not the whole truth. The day that Martin died was the day she met Paul.

Life was rottenly unfair, unscientific sometimes; was it this endless irony perhaps that sowed the first seeds of doubt in her mind? She shifted uncomfortably in her bed and finally acknowledged that she was going neither to sleep nor to read, she was going to have to make up her mind, and questions like that were, even now, even twenty years later, too terrible to contemplate. Now at least she knew to her comfort that the fact that Martin had died while she lunched with a very young research student and discussed paleontology, had made it possible for her to pursue Paul into the realms of friendship and love in ways that might not have happened otherwise.

She had arrived that day at her office, intent on spending a morning looking at some photographs and drawings sent her for comment from America. There was a quality in Rachel's capacity to look that was rare. It was, she suspected, her primary scientific gift. To look blankly at the evidence, to look and look and look, without presupposition, without internal comment. She was frequently amazed at the difficulties some of her colleagues seemed to have with this process of looking. It was the beginning and the end, as far as she was concerned. You had to look everywhere of course and it was not always easy, but you had to look without knowing what you think you will find.

Not that she had done so, damn it, not that she had done so. That was the dark centre of her failure: she who had taught, and practised and prided herself on looking, failed to accept until far too late just how much she had looked in order to find. This was greed and no good would come of it, as her mother would have said.

But back then, in those days, she had still believed, not even with particular pride, but simply as a point of fact, that she knew how to look at something and that is what she was doing, probably at the very moment when her husband finally and forever stopped looking at anything at all.

She had been sitting at her desk looking. There had been a knock at the door, jolting and irritating. There were uses, especially to a woman in a man's world, of that disciplined and steady training in good manners drummed into her by her mother. Rachel was not only seldom ruffled, she was also practically never rude. An infinitesimal pause always came swooping down between her irritation and her response to the source of it. She knew that it let her get away with hell sometimes: the fact that she could do whatever she needed to do politely, could appear so humble and moderate and gracious in that world of over-inflated male egos. So she did not snap at the door, or pretend that she had not heard, and truly, as it turned out, virtue was for once rewarded and the reward was Paul.

'Come in,' she called and a long thin hand slid round the door, followed by a long thin person, very young and very lovely.

'Am I interrupting? They sent me to see you and I should have written first, but I was in London and took the risk; it's a long way from Aberdeen.'

'St Andrew's?' He was a paleontologist, not a journalist, a museum man, a publisher or anything else. She knew.

'Professor Crowther sent me.'

'That's a good start,' she said smiling. Later they were to discover that both of them cordially disliked Paul's professor.

'I'm not really a dinosaur person; mammals. But I have to know more, and they all say you are the only Big Ideas paleontologist in Britain.'

'Good Lord.'

They both smiled. How could she not have been delighted?

He was doing his thesis on giantism in tertiary mammals.

'Is that why you need a Big Ideas person?'

'No,' he said and laughed.

'Eohippus?'

'Not actually; the other way round – simopithecus and the poor old Baluchitheria. Getting bigger makes sense.'

'It didn't for my beasts, for the dinosaurs.'

'No, I know. Getting bigger makes sense, but getting smaller works better. Now, why is that?'

Then he began to talk about his work and she was absorbed. With part of her mind she hunted through her internal filing systems, noting the available data from Carnegie's diplodocus down to . . . hadn't she recently seen a rather interesting paper about Diprotodon and antipodean marsupial development? With another part of her mind she tried to look at the young man, blankly, as she had tried to look at the photographs earlier; testing him, deciding his worth. She liked what she saw. What could she do for him?

He did not want her specialisation, she could sense that; he had come to her for background, for wide-ranging theory.

'You'll have to go the States,' she told him.

'No.'

'Don't be so prejudiced. All the Big Ideas people are there; here we're doing the little bits, the looking and assesssing, you know that.'

'Know it and want it,' he said firmly.

And later he said, 'Now I've found my Big Ideas teacher.'

She took him out to lunch and they could not stop talking; they did not stop talking for three and a half hours, taking it in turn to shovel down their food while the other spoke. He ate more than she did, and she talked more than he did. He was only five years older than Phoebe. She did not think then, though she was to come to think later, that he could have been her son. What she did think, with delight, was that she, who had never had a chance before, to hand on what her father had given her, had found in one package – one charming and delicate package – both a student and a colleague, a friend.

Which was why she had not been paying any attention when Martin had died.

She was sorry about it afterwards and was quite sad for several years. She was surprised and even quite touched at herself by how much she missed him. Partly she was sorry that she had not been available to him at the one moment in her life when she really should have been a wife, not a paleontologist. Deeper still, though, she knew shamefacedly that she was glad that the first of the increasingly frantic telephone calls had not arrived until she had a coat on and was on her feet. She had not answered the phone, and secretly she was pleased she hadn't. She would have become for Paul, in that moment, something other than the best Big Ideas paleontologist in Britain and they might never have found their way back to that joyful lunch-time.

Even so she was lonely after Martin died. In order to make the marriage work she had narrowed down the part of herself that she gave him; made it a skinnier little thing, that did not include work, and so did not include something that was essential to herself. But within that smaller range they had been happy; he had made her life work smoothly, given it contours and meaning. He had been her leisure space and she did not know how to enjoy herself without him.

In the lonely hours of self-exculpation when she wandered nowadays, twenty years after his death, through Phoebe's empty flat, prying, probing and, ashamed, deeply ashamed, but still driven, looking, searching, for something that she needed once the fear came upon her: oh, then it was easy to blame it all on Martin, and stand there in Phoebe's bedroom, or lie here sleepless in her own bed and damn him. It was easy to say that it was his fault, all his fault, that he had promised her generosity, promised her space and freedom and work and he had broken his promise. It was easy for her to say to herself, that it was all his fault that she had become so obsessively, and unprofessionally proud of her dinosaur. But she had been proud of her dinosaur, painfully proud of her dinosaur, because it had been so expensive for her. It had to be good, it had to be. She needed so much to prove that the world of science was stronger and more real, more important than the world of the heart, of love and of joy.

But there were things that she could not blame on Martin. Soon after he had died another truth had started to obtrude. It wasn't just to Martin that she had not paid proper attention. She had not paid proper attention to Phoebe either. Phoebe had never asked for attention; she had been a sweet and lovely baby, easy to care for. Then an intense earnest child, Martin's child in so many ways. Martin's daughter. But her daughter too, and when her husband had died she had not paid proper attention to their daughter.

She had always been proud of Phoebe of course, but in quite a distant manner. She had liked to think that Phoebe would, as she had done, go further than most women go as a scientist. And at some point in the future Phoebe would understand how much that had been a gift from her pioneering mother and be grateful.

Looking back she knew that she had been proudest of Phoebe perhaps when Phoebe had won the primary school chess tournament. Phoebe was ten, and had been taught by her father in the home that she Rachel had made for them. It had made a point of the relationship. It confirmed something about women's capabilities. It reflected well on her, and her choices. She had been immensely proud of Phoebe.

Pride was not enough: she had not been paying attention. Phoebe had come home, summoned from Cambridge, and had been calm and efficient and organised throughout the funeral arrangements; orderly, supportive, affectionate to her mother. Meanwhile she, Rachel, had seen herself as the bereaved one, had been fascinated by her own emotions, of sorrow and guilt and irritation that Martin was once again demanding that she leave her work and attend to him. She had a pile of work accumulating on her desk, and her new student, Paul, waiting for her attention. She had accepted Phoebe's calm at face value because she had not been paying attention and because, somewhere deep down she had not wanted to bother.

Three months after the funeral she had gone off for her holiday, sailing with Bill and Talia, and feeling that she had earned it. Smugly convinced that she had accomplished widowhood with some grace, she felt she deserved the wisdom and affection of Bill, and the bright sunlight scattered over diverse rock faces and deep waters. She had been happy for three weeks. Then she had flown to New York, had seen Tim Wong and basked again in her international status. She had attended a symposium, had fed herself on the energy of America and the slightly complacent superiority which so much of their work gave her. Somewhere in that time she had, surely she had, scribbled off the habitual postcards to Phoebe, as she most certainly had to other friends and acquaintances. She was always courteous with such niceties. When she got home Phoebe had disappeared.

Astonishingly it hadn't worried her.

Well perhaps not astonishingly. It was the long vac. Phoebe had to be somewhere, Rachel was a liberal parent, no news was good news; she did not expect Phoebe to give her a minute by minute account of her doings. But retrospectively she really had suffered curiously little curiosity. It was not until October, when she got a phone call from Phoebe's college asking where she was, that she had started to be concerned. It was not until she had gone through the embarrassment of saying that she hadn't a clue, that she assumed Phoebe was in Cambridge; it was not until she heard the mild reproof of the tutor's surprise, that she realised that normal people did know where their eighteen-year-old daughters were, and if they didn't, they would be frantic about it.

Once she turned her mind to it, it was not impossible to find out where her daughter had been. Phoebe had gone to Greece with some friends for a holiday. Rachel went, after some thought, to Cambridge to talk to the friends. She was horrified by them. Not immediately; at first she associated the dirt and peculiar clothing with their being mathematicians. Given the dowdy ordinariness of Phoebe's usual sartorial effects, she was later to be amused by her own instant prejudices about the eccentricities of mathematicians. It was gently, but inexorably, borne in on her that these were not mathematicians, or rather if they were it was not this that led to their undefinable air of gaudy squalor. They were hippies.

In her pleasant north Oxford house, her protected journeys to and from her museum, her shopping forays into Summertown, her visits to friends in soothing groves of academe and literate flats in Chelsea, she had heard of hippies. She had seen them, both roaming in the streets, and cavorting on the television. She had never given them so much as a moment of consideration, not even to form the thought, 'Thank God Phoebe isn't like that.' It had simply never occurred to her.

These unexpected friends of Phoebe's seemed to speak a foreign language. They treated her with a lazy contempt. They did not seem to care about her worry or about Phoebe's whereabouts. They were very unattractive young people.

She had tried hard to talk to them.

'Yeah,' they agreed vaguely, Phoebe had gone to Greece with them. It had been cool, Bea had liked it and decided not to come home. They didn't know where she was now, probably on the road. It wasn't their business, they said, and implied it wasn't Rachel's either.

Rachel felt an escalating panic, and she had no practice in panic. The conversation went nowhere. Her eyes fixed themselves on the dingy greyish hue of one of the girl's neck, visible through a gap in her ragged hair. About the point that she was ready to give up in despair, this creature said,

'Hey, Lady, you Bea's Mum? I got a letter for you.'

She dropped her pile of books at Rachel's feet and wandered off.

Rachel was enraged. Her sense of responsibility forced her to stay in the middle of the quad guarding the pile of scruffy books. Her rage increased when she noticed that the top book on the pile was by Hegel. She had to contain that rage for what seemed an unreasonably protracted length of time. By the time the young woman finally did reappear Rachel felt sick with anger. So much so that she was unable to stop herself launching into a lecture of good manners, but the girl looked at her with disdain.

'Stay cool, lady, you've been pretty laid back yourself, you know. It's been three months. You could have come before.'

Her rage, huge and powerful, was suspended in mid-air; a huge wave standing high over her head. She felt as though her breath had been violently snatched from her as the wave crashed down on her own head. She felt sick with guilt and nausea, drowning in her own fury.

She took the rather crumpled envelope and fled to the reassurance of a smart tea room, where the girls wore pretty, colourful, full-length smocks, which did not entirely hide the fact that they too were greyish behind the ears. Their accents and the casualness with which they dished up her coffee led her to realise that they were probably students.

> Dear Mother,
>   I know this will probably come as a bit of a surprise to you, but I just don't feel up to telling it to you face to face and having to cope with your intellectual barrage and well-turned arguments. I'm not going back to Cambridge next term, or ever. There doesn't seem any point in Maths now, not with the war in Vietnam and the complete corruption of the whole system. What good has all that academic crap ever done you or Daddy? I am not sure what I'm planning to do, but guess I'll travel around a bit. See you sometime,
>   love and peace, Bea.

Rachel had never, in her entire life called Phoebe 'Bea'.

She sat a long time over her coffee, calming herself down and thinking what she should do. She was forced finally to face the fact that there was nothing that she could do, except perhaps pay a hefty cheque into Phoebe's bank account so that her daughter would not actually starve. Apart from that she would just have to wait.

She waited for three years before she so much as heard from Phoebe again.

Those three years were perhaps the most difficult of Rachel's whole life. They reminded her sometimes of the war years, when she too had been alone. Life was dominated by the same wearisome and complicated treks between work and home, the same focusing on work as the one thing that will guarantee salvation. But then had not been the same at all.

87

Then she had been young and enthusiastic and optimistic. Then she had been waiting, with love, for Martin to come home to her, waiting in the conviction that he would come and all of life would be ahead of them, a time of happy dreams and clear-minded work. Then she had been conceiving and writing her book, chasing her ideas, and growing, growing.

Now she was declining. She started to find that she increased her age in her imagination, 'Now, I'm nearly sixty . . .' she would think, although she was not nearly sixty, not really. But she would never have another Big Idea, and indeed there was no space for her to have one in. She was working hard and she knew that it was good useful work, consolidating, expanding, re-shaping. Her professional reputation was good. She was invited, and travelled to give, a significant number of lectures; twice indeed to give key-notes lectures, overviews, at important conferences. But that in itself was sinister, she felt.

She missed Martin and was angry with herself for missing him. She had always thought that he did nothing in their shared home, but now with autumn turning the garden into a soggy mess, and spring turning it into an over-exuberant wilderness, she realised that he had faithfully weeded, ordered plants, dead-headed the roses, kept the paths cleared. Inside he had paid the bills, organised the house-maintenance, kept Mrs Crale sweet-tempered, and he had been there when she came home in the evenings. She did not know how to plan a holiday: Martin had done that, and they had travelled in the last few years pleasantly together. Now she longed for the warm sun, the long Mediterranean meals they had shared together in Umbria and Crete and southern Turkey, and she did not know how to go about it. During the daytimes, she was busy and sociable; she had work and friendships and lots of things to do, but at night she was sad and she was lonely. She thought of Phoebe frequently, but usually with irritation and bitterness. She found the endless commuting bored her and increasingly tired her. She became for the first time in her life frightened, not of death, but of growing old.

When her father had grown old she had found for him a renewal of devotion, which had surprised her. After the war was over he had sold the mellow house in Suffolk, as though without his wife it had no meaning. She had seen the bitterness and coldness come over his contemporaries as one by one they had had to leave their inherited acres or worse, had clung to them, cold and leaking, and complaining. But he had gone with an unexpected grace; he had accepted – bless his sensitivity – without a murmur of complaint that she and Martin were not going to inhabit his family home and raise a brood of grandchildren for him. He had moved, quietly and efficiently, into a flat in South Kensington.

Rachel had visited him there, at least once each week. He had been not a chore, but a joy. Even his bad temper, which was frequently impressive and occasionally reduced him to throwing things – though mainly, she noted with some amusement and some concern, at Pinny, his devoted housekeeper, rather than at his daughter – seemed touching rather than offensive. There he lived with considerable dignity and, she thought, happiness. Luckily his mind stayed oddly sharp until the very end. Sharp and open. She had feared after the war that the Labour Government, for which she had voted, but secretly, as far as he was concerned, would drive him to apoplexy and inarticulate fury. But even here there remained something aristocratic about him, something that she realised Martin would never have; he had a sense that everything would go on, that they would be all right in the end, that Britishness was not a national characteristic, but a state of virtue. He did not agree with the Welfare State, but his view seemed to be that the wealthy had failed to live up to their responsibilities, so the poor could hardly be blamed for demanding an alternative. He had always thought Churchill a crass old man, suitable for wartime fervour, but not for peace.

Her father had loved her book and her eminence, the breadth of her imagination. He cackled away over some of the more extreme parts of it and told her scurrilous stories about Baron von Nopsca, with whom, he implied, she had a natural affinity. Martin, who visited dutifully with her when he was in London, turned out to be both appalled by the comparison, and in profound agreement with it.

'Crazy old bugger,' her father would recall Nopsca, but with affection. They had been friends before the war – the war remained always for her father the First World War, 'The Great War' on more formal occasions. He didn't seem to hold Nopsca's activities as a spy for the Austro-Hungarian empire against him – for her father, patriotism was an inevitable and natural thing.

'I'm not like Nopsca,' she would assert indignantly.

Although in a way, it was flattering. Baron Franz von Nopsca had been the most provocative palaeontologist of his generation; he had also been entirely crazy; alternating bold thoughts about the evolution of new species with bizarre plans to become King of Albania.

'I'm a scientist, not a raving lunatic. In fact,' she said boldly, more anxious to please her father than worried about upsetting her husband, 'I'm a better scientist than either of you two. You want to leave out half the data – all the imagination, and the myths and the tricky bits. You are sentimental: I'm the good scientist, the real mechanist who uses all the data. Nopsca indeed.'

'Hmmm,' her father would say grinning, 'but, Rachel, you have to remember, his ideas on early flight may have been crazed, but they got people looking at it again, really looking at it, everyone had just let it go. And classification. Classification he was right about. He just had fun while he did it. I miss him. I miss him in this cold time. It's a compliment.'

'Well, wait till I blow my brains out and kill Martin with some arsenic tea, like Nopsca did. Then you can say how much you miss me too.'

And his smile was a smile of infinite sweetness, he put up his thin, ancient, elegant hand and touched her cheek. She had to sit near him because he did not hear very well, and she could smell the tobacco – tweediness of his jacket, and slide through three decades in a swirling second.

'You won't get away from adventures by pretending you don't want them,' he had said, and her heart had over-flowed with tenderness; affection, respect, love, tenderness.

In those dark years after Martin died, she thought often about her father's old age and she was afraid. She knew he had earned her tenderness by his generosity, but she had not been generous towards Phoebe. She had not even paid proper attention to Phoebe, and Phoebe had disappeared and perhaps she too would have to die, alone and neglected like Martin had, even more alone and neglected than Martin had. Who would look after her when she was old like that? And as important as tenderness, as care, was recognition: looking and under-standing. She knew she had never looked at Phoebe with that loving concentration with which her father had regarded her.

It was because of that recognition that she had enjoyed her visits to her father. Now she feared that there would be no one to visit her. Phoebe had gone. She missed Phoebe, too. She missed her and worried about her and about herself.

Her husband was dead and her daughter vanished. Her work was stale and her life exhausting. She was capable enough of looking at the wholeness of this and seeing that she must make changes.

She thought she would move house. She had never truly liked the Oxford house: it was a sign of her defeat. She remembered when Martin had come home from the Far East and she, knowing he was coming, had made happy plans to find a house in London. A small house, pretty and cosy, which would take practically no care and would be situated in a neighbourly street. They could live there and go down to Suffolk at week-ends. Then, when Martin had decided that he wanted to go back to Oxford, she had not particularly minded. That was where Martin's job was, and although Cambridge would have been more convenient for Suffolk, Oxford was a city she knew and liked. Of course she would be happy there; Martin had come home and she would be happy anywhere.

But Martin had come home wanting a proper family. He wanted a wife and some babies. He did not expect her to go on working. And he wanted a proper house. A proper house in Oxford turned out to mean an overlarge Victorian edifice, in north Oxford, a villa masquerading as a mansion. She was a snob about that house. Quite recently she had heard Phoebe and some friends laughing over the differences between Sloane Rangers and Yuppies:

'I think,' said some clear voice, 'that yuppies have bigger houses in town than the one they have in the country, and Sloanes have bigger houses in the country than they do in town.' Rachel had smiled appreciatively, recognising herself, or at least her image of herself.

But back then, in the years immediately after Martin came home, he had said, 'For heaven's sake, Rachel, people will think I can't afford to keep you properly.'

In a heated moment she had said, 'Well, you can't. If we're going to buy one of these things, it will be with my money, and you know it.'

After that, seeing the pain and hurt in his eyes, she had had to spend more than she wanted to on buying his house to keep her in. Money that she had thought would be the seed money for their next expedition.

She had never made over a penny of her capital to Martin and he never asked her to. She sometimes wondered what had passed between him and her father during the interview in her father's study when she and Martin announced their engagement. They both knew it was her money, but they bought the house in his name. And she was a repellent little snob for reminding herself, never mention reminding him. It was not his fault that she was richer than he was. She was disgusted at herself. But her disgust did not make her like the house.

Then, in the years after Martin died, she wanted to sell it. She wanted to move to London, where her friends were, where her museum was and where she could at last have the sort of house that she had always wanted. But she was too tired. She was too tired and too busy with the travelling and her work. Without Martin's energy and direction that she felt she hardly knew how to set about buying a house.

There was another thing; a whisper in the night that scared her with its stupidity. This was not just her house, it was also Phoebe's house, it was the home of Phoebe's childhood. Her own happiest dreams, from which she woke smiling at dawn, were dreams of the home of her childhood. The home of one's childhood will aways tug one back again. If she sold Phoebe's home while Phoebe was not there, Phoebe might never come home again. She had no reason to believe that Phoebe was bound to the house by a mysterious invisible cord, any more than she herself was, but, superstitiously, she could not take the risk. This sense of being trapped by Phoebe's irresponsible and stupid behaviour, this sense of being at Phoebe's mercy while Phoebe had no mercy on her, made her feel angry and punitive; and that made her feel guilty and ashamed; and that made her feel lonely and unloved.

They were three difficult and painful years for Rachel, the years after Martin's death, when Phoebe had disappeared. She took them fairly philosophically, and was not aware then or later how depressed she had become.

Rachel had imagined that when Phoebe returned she would be draped in once gaudy, now faded and filthy tatters from some country over the sea where clear thinking did not count, and carrying with her a vague and sleazy flavour of some Indian bazaar. Her hair would be long, lank and unwashed and her expression would be totally washed out. She would be weary, exhausted, penitent and half-starved. Rachel watched the flower children in the streets; she listened covertly, on buses and in shops, to their disarticulated speech; she spied on them in the conversation of her friends and bought their strangely printed, unreadable magazines. Whenever they made her angry, which they frequently did, she would remember Phoebe, reconstruct her emotions and feel pity and concern as well. She found the heavy political types faintly more attractive than the drug-smeared ones. She consequently feared the worst.

But when Phoebe did come back it was at a moment when she was least expecting it, when she had, as usual, not been paying attention. She came in from work one delightful early summer evening and found her daughter sitting on the front door step in a set of workmen's overalls. Her hair was cut short, and her sleeves rolled back to reveal tanned strong arms. It had to be said that she looked wonderfully well, and reasonably clean. In fact, at that moment she looked more like the young Rachel, the splendid Rachel of the photograph that was, years later, to adorn Phoebe's bedroom wall, than she was ever to do again. They were exactly the same age: that Rachel and this Phoebe. Somehow Rachel knew it, and with it knew wisdom. Her first surge of feeling was fractured in half – part of her wanted to say, 'Darling, you're home,' and snatch Phoebe up in a hug to overwhelm all the loneliness in the world; and part wanted to yell, 'And where the hell do you think you've been, you selfish little trollop?' In the space between there grew the only perfect and appropriate response possible if the two of them were ever to go on together, anywhere.

'Hello,' said Rachel. 'Why are you sitting on the step? Have you lost your key?'

And Phoebe laughed a great sweet laugh, and stood up and embraced her mother and said, 'Yes, somewhere in the Hindu Cush. So I hope you've got yours.'

And as she smiled, Rachel knew that something magnificent had happened to Phoebe. Phoebe had grown, not only grown-up but out. The thin, slightly solemn child whom Rachel had clung on to in her imagination for too many years was only half, only a quarter, of a possible Phoebe, Phoebe who had evolved, developed organically, somewhere, somehow, since her departure. So that afterwards, even when they got on each other's nerves, even when they fought and sulked and were vindictive and mean to each other, Rachel always knew somewhere and somehow that the going away had been good for Phoebe, had been important and necessary. Though of course she never said so.

She fished her key out of her satchel and the two of them went into the house, and Phoebe seemed to inhale it, and Rachel was instantly glad that her feeling had been right and that she had not sold the house before Phoebe had come home.

That was about the end of the good times for that round. By the end of the evening Rachel felt, with irritation and bafflement and anger, that Phoebe had come home only to taunt her mother, to punish her for some unnamed crime.

'I want a fair trial, I want to put a case for the defence, I want to be assumed innocent until proven guilty,' she cried in her heart. At the same moment she also thought, 'Who does she think she is?' and responded with stubborn firmness not to a twenty-two-year-old woman whom she hadn't seen for three years, but to a naughty, recalcitrant child who just won't do what it is told.

Phoebe had no intention of going back to college. Phoebe thought maths was a cold and reactionary form of élitist thought. Phoebe thought that science in general was a crude product of masculist thinking, designed to separate knowledge and experience. Phoebe thought that her mother's life was a waste of time, and the dignities brought so painfully from it were merely a social conditioning that glorified maleness. Phoebe thought that the Labour party were a bunch of sell-outs, that women in professional life were a tool of the establishment. Phoebe had no time for her mother, did not want to know about her work, about her life, or about her friends. Phoebe was living in a community squat in South London. Phoebe was very clear, very fierce, and very self-righteous.

Halfway through the evening Rachel wanted to beg for mercy. She wanted to cry out, 'But I've always believed in women's rights and I've never shaved my legs.' But her wool skirt, her lambswool jersey and her own mother's string of pearls gave mysterious but conclusive evidence against her.

Then she felt furious, and fought back with all the skills of her well-trained and excellent mind. Whatever arguments Phoebe tried to articulate, Rachel demolished by exactly the methods Phoebe was most objecting to – meanings of words, logical skippetty-hops, dry irony and sarcasm, and the piling on and on and on of facts. Phoebe shouted and Rachel sneered and the two of them brewed up an evil storm in the calm sitting room of the north Oxford house that had been their shared home for so many years. Even as they sat on the antique chairs which had been Rachel's mother's, drinking the excellent wine that Martin had laid down, the two women exploded into space and went whirling across the timeless places where witch-women fly at night.

Even as they fought, Rachel felt that her principles were betrayed by the act of fighting, while Phoebe's were affirmed. And in a lull, in the eye of the storm, Rachel looked at herself aghast and thought that despite all her discipline, she had arrived somewhere that she never wanted to be. She had not kept control; above all she was not looking straight at the situation, she was not perceiving it, piercing it, looking before deciding, and that finally, therefore, Phoebe had won this round.

So that when Phoebe informed her that she was sharing her squat with a man called Jim who was her lover, instead of responding either with dire maternal warnings of the wages of sin, which might have gratified Phoebe, or with that impulse of tenderness and compassion and maternal solicitude which might have dignified herself, she said, snidely, disguised as earnestly,

'Well, that's something to be grateful for,' And even as she said it she remembered, appalled, that that had been how she had read her mother's expression when she had told her that Martin wanted to marry her.

But Phoebe heard it differently. Phoebe heard it with outraged virtue; Phoebe fell into a rant so complicated and emotional and senseless, such a mish-mash of ill-thought-out philosophies and ideas, that it gave Rachel time to back away from the fight.

Rachel, quite suddenly and clearly, knew better than to roar with laughter. That little moment of distance left her a space to recognise her fear. If she were not careful Phoebe would go away and she would never see her again and that was not what she wanted. She remembered that she had missed Phoebe and was glad to see her again. She realised that Phoebe, whatever she was now saying, had come home freely, and must be freely welcomed.

Suddenly Rachel was looking at Phoebe; she was, for a brief minute at least, paying attention. She saw all the stubborn passion that she herself had felt when she had wanted to go to Africa with Martin. She saw all the impossibility of apologising for vanishing as a child and coming back as a grown woman. She saw that they would fight again, because Phoebe needed to define herself as the the negative image of her mother, as she herself had done, as they all did. And finally she saw that although she was entitled to her anger, and even to her fear, there were things that once she said then could never be unsaid; and that she was a woman who never said those things, never, and would not say them now.

So she backed away, gracefully. Rachel's colleagues could have told Phoebe that no one was more skilled than Rachel in defusing an argument, in altering the course of a conversation. Her sense of good manners was so deeply embedded and personal that it flowed over into personal grace. So a little later Rachel went and changed and took Phoebe out to dinner and they talked together of foreign travel and places they had seen and been in, and of Rachel selling the house and moving to London and even of Phoebe's non-existent plans for the future. She seemed to have no ambition, no desire beyond the next month, no structure for her life. Rachel was bemused, but patient; Phoebe had come home.

That had been the limits of their relationship for the next year. Rachel was greedy, but patient. Phoebe was uncontrolled but passive. Some evenings in London Rachel would take Phoebe out to supper. Occasionally Phoebe would drift into north Oxford, secretive but there. Rachel once invited herself to Phoebe's squat. She had a dark conviction that they had cleaned it up because she was coming. It was strange – at one level it was appalling, squalid, freezing cold; at another it was oddly energetic and beautiful. She found to her surprise that she liked the girls better than the boys, who seemed rude and contemptuous. Whereas the women, filthy and undisciplined though they were, were friendly, civil. Phoebe's friend Lisa was even able to simulate some interest in Rachel's work and ask her quite elaborate and informed questions about women in scientific employment and what the difficult bits were.

The next time she saw her, when Lisa and Phoebe stopped overnight in her house in Oxford, Lisa revealed that she had been to Rachel's museum and looked at her dinosaur. She asked Rachel to lend her a copy of her book. Rachel was quite touched. Phoebe seemed irritated, and never brought Lisa with her again. Rachel tried not to mind, tried to smile benignly. But the fear of old age which had loosened its grip when Phoebe had first returned, tightened again.

The fear returned, despite the fact that her life began to improve in other ways. She was not so tired or so sad, and she began to enjoy herself once more. Paul had moved to London, and his youthful presence had started her working again. He did not let her off. His lovely face appearing around her door, his lovely hands; his faintly satirical, self-mocking enthusiasm; his sheaves of loose papers, each one always with only a single phrase or sentence in tiny writing right in the middle of the page; his constant questioning; all made her want to have things to tell him, things he did not know, thoughts he had not had. She saw more of him at this time than she saw of Phoebe, and he was a comfort and a delight to her, a relaxation compared with the careful restraint that she felt she had to exercise all the time with Phoebe. But she needed Phoebe, she needed her and did not know how to make a claim, and so she was frightened.

She was lucky in the end, as luck will always come to the people who want it enough, need it and dare to go and hunt for it. She had found her dinosaur, she could and would find someone to love and care for her in her old age.

Phoebe got pregnant.

Secretly she was surprised that Phoebe did not have an abortion; though she was pleased that Phoebe didn't. Secretly she was appalled at the thought of having Jim as a son-in-law. In the first place she did not like him, finding him a rude and aggressive youth, someone she was sure would never offer her comfort and probably discourage Phoebe from doing so. In the second place, more tenderly, she feared for Phoebe should she fall into his husbandly hands. In her fear she recognised that Martin had had good manners; he might not have been able in the end to allow her or himself the kind of marriage she Rachel had wanted, but in Jim she sensed an egotistical brutality. She disciplined herself rigorously, acknowledging that it might be only her failure to understand him, acknowledging that it might be a product of his passion; for, like herself and unlike Phoebe, she knew that he cared for his work in a way that controlled his life. But she remained appalled and frightened.

As it turned out, however, she did not have to face Jim as a son-in-law. To her surprise and initial alarm Phoebe had no intention of marrying Jim, or anyone else. Somewhere, about at the mid-term of her pregnancy, Jim disappeared from Phoebe's life, along with the other men in the house. Phoebe did not call it a commune or squat any more; she called it a Women's House. Rachel called it The Convent when she spoke of it to Paul, and Saint Revolutionary's College for Young Ladies when she spoke of it to Bill. She did not speak of it much to anyone else.

Some evenings watching the gentle north Oxford student babies being wheeled out in their shabby prams covered in bright hand-sewn patchworks, pushed by their sweet and soft-looking fathers, she felt sorry for Phoebe; but at least no father would do to Phoebe what Phoebe's father had done to Rachel. Sometimes she appalled herself, noticing her own punitive and victorious feelings, as though some great blow had been struck for women, a banner carried proud though invisible over Phoebe's swelling stomach.

Sometimes, more simply but no more usefully, she felt a purely social embarrassment at having a 'bastard' as her father's first great-grand-child, as Martin's first grandchild.

Sometimes she was furious with Phoebe for her passivity. Phoebe seemed incapable of making plans. Phoebe refused, Rachel felt, to face the fact that a baby was bound to mean some change in her lifestyle, in her so newly won freedom.

But she spoke of none of these worries to Phoebe, because more importantly, deep beneath these social reflexes, inside herself, Rachel felt a new and evil crone growing, flexing her ancient muscles, and plotting. Rachel was biding her time, practising the virtue of patience which her mother had tried to drum into her fifty years before.

In all her scheming she overlooked one possibility. When she went to the hospital, after the baby had been delivered, she fell in love. She took one look into the cradle, with its transparent plastic sides like a goldfish bowl, and thought, 'That's my grandchild,' and with the thought came a surge of feeling so strong and sweet that she almost wept. She had not felt that way since she married Martin.

She had not anticipated it, she was overcome with surprise. Her plots to reduce her own guilt for inattention by forcing Phoebe to be grateful, her hazy plans for her own security in old age were sharpened and shaped by love, by the desire, the need, to take care in some way of Maggie's safety and happiness and well-being.

'Darling Phoebe,' she said, turning to her daughter to share the moment. But Phoebe rejected her sentimental moment with a gesture. She had brought gifts for Phoebe, books and fruit and flowers. She had brought a little woollen suit too, but that too had really been a present for Phoebe. She was suddenly ashamed that she had brought nothing for Maggie. She knew at once that she would have to be terribly careful, terribly tactful about what she gave her; not her own father's left-over shares in South African Gold Mines anyway. She had to be careful.

It took nearly a year. A year during which she disciplined herself rigorously. She needed to; the first time she went to visit Phoebe, one evening after work, she found Maggie, certainly not changed into night-clothes, asleep in an open basket on the table in the living-room while the record player blared and the household carried on around her. It was a new thing, and she bit sharply on her lip.

She kept biting: she passed no comments on demand feeding, the absence of toilet-training, no bedtimes, no being-put-out-to-sleep-in-the-pram, in fact no pram. She even subdued her desire to ask what was so feminist and progressive about the slavish devotion that Phoebe lavished on the child, so that six months after the birth Maggie was still the only focus of Phoebe's attention. Phoebe was not working, or even reading and thinking, but was simply locked in on the baby. Sometimes it even seemed to her that Phoebe wanted her to complain, to protest, to object – that she was trying to provoke a row, a self-justifying self-righteous fight with her mother, that she was flaunting her version of maternity as a criticism of Rachel's. But still she held her peace. And she had her reward.

It became clear that Phoebe was finding life a struggle. Her friends talked a great deal about sharing childcare and being supportive. They were certainly touchingly affectionate, and delighted by Maggie. But inevitably there was a gap between their rhetoric and the daily reality. Rachel knew her presence, and her presents, were received with increasing gratitude. The charm of the house sank nearer towards the edge of squalor; it was too cold and none of them had any money. The winter was long and damp and dreary. Maggie did not flourish.

In February for the first time Phoebe asked Rachel if she would have Maggie to stay for a few days while she went to Amsterdam, for a conference. In April she asked again, this time simply so that she could have a break. Rachel, sniffing victory, delicate and careful as a night cat, moved in for the kill.

In late May she told Phoebe casually that she had finally decided to get rid of the Oxford house and move to London. She even went through the motions of looking at small and convenient flats near the museum. In July she proposed to Phoebe that she bought a larger house, and they divided it between them.

Phoebe by then was exhausted and defeated. She wavered. Then Rachel found an ally. To her surprise, Lisa supported the scheme. By this time Lisa, who teasingly called her 'The Dinosaur', had become a friend. Now they became co-conspirators. Lisa came one day to visit Rachel in her museum.

'Mrs Petherington . . . ,'

'Rachel,' said Rachel, it was the first time she had ever wanted to say it to any of Phoebe's friends.

Lisa smiled. 'Thank you.' Rachel realised that Lisa was desperate, was trying hard and was nervous.

'Rachel, you will never tell Bea about this will you? She'd kill me.'

Lisa got up from the chair by Rachel's desk and wandered about the room. Over by the window she stood looking out and fiddling with a plastic model of a *Tyrannosaurus Rex* that happened to be lying there.

With her back to the window she said, 'We can't cope.'

Rachel got up too. She planned to offer Lisa a glass of sherry but saw that this would not help. Sherry was too respectable, too close to what the poor girls were most fearing. She had not understood this in Phoebe's sulkiness, but she saw it quite clearly in Lisa's fiddling.

'Do you want some coffee?' she asked.

'Yes, please.'

Rachel did not ring the secretary for it. She needed Lisa's approval. Better to leave the room and get it herself.

Coffee cup in her hand, Lisa returned to the chair, and relaxed.

'You see we all thought we could. We all thought we ought to, I mean share the baby and nobody needs a husband and that stuff. At the moment I feel that *I'm* the husband.'

Later she said plaintively, 'I do love Bea, and we all adore Maggie, you know that. But she's depressed and the baby isn't well, and now I feel as though I'm betraying Bea even being here. And she won't take money from you directly.' She put down the coffee cup and looked fretful, 'I've got a job,' she said, 'not just a job, something I want to do. You understand about that don't you?'

'Yes,' said Rachel simply.

'Bea doesn't. Look I believe in it, I believe in the language of it, but it isn't who I am. I'm not twenty-three yet, I want to work and that means travel and . . . I don't know why I'm telling you all this, but you must understand that Bea is getting desperate herself, and I think that part of her would really like, really wants . . . I want to go to the States this autumn and I can't go away and leave her like this, and somehow that makes me angry, angry with her, and I hate that.'

'Yes,' said Rachel, 'I do understand. What should we do? What could I do?'

'I think,' said Lisa, 'You should just go ahead. Just buy a house, make it into two flats, just do it, somewhere that you would really like to live, as though it had nothing to do with her. Don't make her say she will agree, just do it. Somewhere nice and safe, with a pretty garden.'

And suddenly the two of them burst into laughter.

'Perhaps I should become an estate agent,' said Lisa.

'Lots of money in it,' said Rachel, 'but it's always better to do your own work. And I absolutely will not tell Phoebe that you came.'

Lisa stood up.

'Now you're here,' said Rachel, 'would you like to see what we do?'

'Please.'

For a brief moment they were completely equal, in love and respect and intent. It was a comfortable feeling for Rachel.

So she took Lisa's advice and bought the big house in Bayswater without discussing it any further with Phoebe. When she needed help and advice she sought it professionally, never from Phoebe; when she needed support or endorsements of her ideas she talked to Paul, not to Phoebe. She had the house divided into two flats, and although she installed the door that linked them internally, if asked she always said it was a fire precaution. When they were all together she never exchanged so much as a wink or smile of complicity with Lisa, but the two of them were united and intimate in discreet silent plotting. A person would have had to be stronger than Phoebe then was, to resist so much love and will-power.

Just before Christmas, just after Maggie's first birthday, the three of them, Maggie, Phoebe and Rachel, moved into the house. For Phoebe it may have felt like a defeat, but to Maggie and Rachel it was a moment of delight, a moment of victory.

And amazingly, it worked.

For the next ten years Rachel lived with a glowing certainty that it had been a brilliant idea, the second best idea of her life. Her fears receded. Her love for Maggie grew. Her tolerance of Phoebe became an ingrained habit. She went on working smoothly and usefully, past her proper retirement date. She enjoyed the new micro-paleontological work, and the biologists' contribution; the idea of being able to place her dinosaurs within an ecological environment was pleasing, satisfactory and engaging. She felt fit and well. She was useful to the two women upstairs and she loved her friends. It seemed to her a golden time and she never treated her good fortune with contempt. She went on being careful.

On her seventieth birthday she was interviewed for the *Life in a day of* column in the Sunday colour supplement. She chose to have the photograph taken in her office; it showed her looking authoritative and eminent behind her desk, with Maggie – ten years old, and wearing a pair of striped dungarees, playing with some model dinosaurs. The desk was covered with papers, but the room looked dignified, even beautiful, with photographs of both her father and Martin hanging prominently on the walls alongside a rather lovely watercolour of the Great Wall of China. The photographer had insisted on including a copy of her book, now with its new, rather garish paperback cover.

Rachel had liked the article: it presented her both as she liked to be seen and as now she thought she was. Perhaps slightly eccentric in terms of usual scientific life-styles, but competent, eminent, and justifying her years of labour.

And then . . . Ah, it was so hard to put her mind to it.

She was old and cold suddenly, why couldn't this cold old lady be left in peace and be allowed to get her sleep? Rachel heaved herself out of bed and put on her dressing-gown; it was a lovely dark red woollen one that Maggie, presumably financially assisted by Phoebe, had given her for Christmas. She was comforted by it, and so comforted she brought all seventy-four years of stubborn clarity to bear on her own life.

Recently she had become convinced that the facts could not be made to accord with her original conclusions.

Several things had made her change her mind, and none of them were pleasant.

First and foremost, there was the increasing weight of the scientific data. To that, try as she might, she could not and would not, close her eyes. Eyes she had rigorously trained for over fifty years. Where the eyes led, the intelligence and the passion had to follow.

Paul had fallen in love, and not with her, although she had never thought that he would.

She had learned a new truth about her mother.

And finally, primarily, absolutely, there was Maggie and Fenna.

She knew when the trouble had started. So innocently. Maggie had come home from school, waving a history book and calling out, even before she took her coat off, 'Rachel, why did you never tell me your mother was a suffragette?' Maggie had a picture, in her school text-book, of a group of women being released from hunger strike outside Holloway Prison. Their names were clearly printed underneath – although she did not need the names to know. Mrs Margaret Hunter-Pearce, Mrs Margaret Hunter-Pearce, Mrs Margaret Hunter-Pearce. A grotesquely dishevelled, gaunt-eyed, exhausted caricature of her elegant lovely mother. Her parents had been married in 1912. She had gone to prison as a new bride. A courageous young woman who had endured hunger striking and been released on license.

Why had her mother never told her, she asked herself? But she knew it was not a fair question. She had not wanted to know. She had not seen the evidence. She had stood there in Phoebe's kitchen, staring at Maggie's picture and a shower of memories scattering around her.

Her mother waltzing in the hall with a woman friend in 1919; laughing and catching up a tiny Rachel in an extravagant whirl; telling her solemnly, though still laughing, that women had won the vote, that they were free from a thousand years of inferiority. And the friend, also laughing, had said, 'Only because they are afraid of your lot, my dear, scared stiff of the young major's wife.'

In Java, in 1928, her father coming into their hotel with a month-old copy of *The Times* and a bunch of flowers. Kissing his wife and saying, 'Look here. You've done it. Universal and equal suffrage. Makes it all worth it, eh? Now behave yourself and pour me some tea or I'll have you back in prison. No women's rights out here, you know.' And her mother smiling and saying, 'It wasn't for women's rights, just for adventure, and now I've got you. Worse than a week in Holloway.'

Her arrogant nineteen-year-old self in a pair of rather dashing trousers leaning against her father's desk and complaining about her mother, so old-fashioned and prissy and not wanting her to go to university. Her father had said, 'You're way out there, old girl.'

'You always defend her. It's not fair.'

'It's you that's not fair, Rachel. You ought to know that your mother is in favour of women's progress. She just doesn't see why you can't brush your hair while you're doing it.'

'Oh, Daddy.'

'The pair of you are just as bad. You won't pay proper attention to each other. It's a shame.'

But she hadn't wanted to hear, she had refused to listen to him then, or to her memories ever since.

Rachel, who had prided herself so profoundly on her capacity to look and see had never looked at her mother with an honest desire to see. Had she ever looked at anything else? That had been the first problem.

Next she remembered Bill's most recent visit. She remembered sitting in the lounge of a delightful gentle hotel in Bloomsbury sharing their pre-prandial whiskies with pleasure; the pleasure reached out and embraced her own substance, the whisky itself, the fat chintz chairs not too brashly new and the sight of Bill, in the next armchair. They did not meet often, the Atlantic being wide, but their friendship was over thirty years old, and was itself a pleasure.

Rachel had come straight from her museum, and her leather satchel sat solid and workmanlike on the low table in front of the two friends. They would drink and chat and later they would go to a restaurant in which they had both eaten many such meals over the years where they would be joined by a retired professor of ancient history whose wife would let him out for the evening with relief. They would eat well and talk well and go home in taxis. Rachel felt her tiredness ease away, contemplating the soft beloved features of her old friend and the assurance of joy ahead.

As she enjoyed her whisky Rachel forgot a thousand things that were still and terribly true. That she was old and tired. And fat. She knew that Phoebe kept the ancient and magnificent photograph of her; she knew because some evenings, unbearably and degradingly, she walked through her daughter's home, peering, seeking without knowing what for. She was glad but not deceived.

'How's Phoebe?' Bill asked; they usually got the domestic details over as early as possible in their evenings together.

'Oh Phoebe,' Rachel grinned wryly, 'she's an opinionated cranky young woman if you want my opinion.' But she muted the statement into a joke with her smile.

'Like her mother,' said Bill affectionately.

'Like both her parents, come to that. Well, she's stuck at the job, which amazes me, and she seems to like it, and she seems so well and busy.'

'What a waste,' she wants to cry, 'what a waste. I don't understand. What did I do wrong. It wasn't my fault.' And all sorts of things unbecoming to an overweight old lady in her seventies, an eminent figure in her own field, drinking decent whisky in a discreetly expensive hotel. 'If I cannot love her,' she wanted to blubber out, 'can she love me? And if she cannot love me what will become of me? And I do love her, desperately and angrily and lovingly. I always wanted to be a good mother.' But she said none of these things.

Instead she said, 'She has delightful friends, I have to confess. She has a boyfriend and sometimes I think she may be getting what used to be called getting serious about him, a nice-mannered, clever boy – boy indeed, nearer forty.' Rachel paused, she did not want her daughter's boyfriends to be nearer forty, 'but, but, well, Bill you know, she's an adult, I don't ask.'

At this moment though she did not even want to think about her distress over Phoebe. Often she felt anger, frustration, guilt, irritation, but not tonight, not with Bill here and looking so smart and clever and being such a joy and delight. So she smiled instead, and the smile was as real as the hidden distress,

'I'll tell you one thing though, it is just not true that brains like muscles soften with under-use. She's so bright, she's so quick, and that goes on still. When she's in the mood, no one gives me more pleasure, the way she can take an idea . . . and juggle it, toss it around, always bouncing it about. Granted there's never much depth, because she won't follow through, but speed. I get envious, then I get cross because it is wasted on cranky notions and . . .' What she wanted to say is that she finds something venal in her daughter, a lack of discipline in every direction, a search after sensation, after emotion for its own sake that she cannot understand and that repels her profoundly, and she is ashamed and nervous of the feeling.

'And Maggie?' Bill asks after a pause.

'Maggie,' says Rachel, and her smile relaxes.

Maggie. Maggie. 'Maggie is a bell of clarity.'

Both Bill and Rachel looked startled at the passion in her voice. Rachel wanted to explain, wanted to express the deep and abiding tenderness. But she just said, 'Maggie has cut her hair into jaggedy spikes and paints them pink at weekends; it looks very striking. I have to tell you, Bill, that I am still besotted by Maggie, just as I have been since her birth and that being a grandmother is one relationship I am convinced I was born for. I don't seem to be able to produce the fears and disapprovals appropriate from my generation to hers. Adolescents, seen through her, appear the most glorious and delightful sub-species of *homo sapiens*.'

They talked too, of course, about Bill's wife Talia and his two sons and assorted grandchildren; they talked about mutual friends spread world-wide and about books and fame and Chinese porcelain.

'And work?'

Rachel smiled because Bill maintained his old duty to investigate fully. But her smile faded as she thought about how to answer the question.

For a moment she thought that she could and would tell Bill. That there was something wrong at the heart of the work, something fundamentally awry. That this, this is the one thing she has pure skill for – 'an intuition amounting to a genius of its own' – as perhaps the most eminent paleontologist in the world had written of her reconstruction. Something was wrong, and now the wrongness was fundamental, and could no longer be hidden. Indeed would be made public and then who would she be? She was frightened. From this sense of being wrong everything bad flowed; her clinging need, her clamorous fear, which bound her to Phoebe and made her hate Phoebe, the fear of old age and decrepitude and lingering unloved death. The fear that the dragon was going to tear her apart. The fears tangled themselves around all the words that she wanted to read, or the scholarship she wanted to consider, and there was no peace for her at all.

She wanted, so much, for a moment, to tell Bill all this. It surprised her and would certainly have surprised him. But he knew about this sort of thing, it was his stock-in-trade. Then she remembered that Bill's own work was enhanced, was formed around the same scientific base as hers and Bill might not want to let go and it was not fair to ask him to let go until she, Rachel, had done what she had to do. She was suddenly murderously jealous of the long quiet mutterings from Phoebe's flat; jealous of a different generation for whom friendship meant you not only could, but actually should, talk about Everything. But she, Rachel, did not know how to begin to do those things. She smiled at Bill and said,

'Work, work. I haven't done any real work in ten years; they let me keep an office and play about in it. It's time we both retired.'

Bill was relieved, though sad at his relief. He knew she was not telling the whole truth, but he did not want to hear it. He was old. The flight had been a long one and he was tired. He wanted to go out to supper and have Henry tell them both about what the bright young men were up to in his field. He wanted to watch Rachel gently and sweetly turn Henry inside out and back to front, bouncing like a puppy on ideas she did not understand and worrying at them, but with charm. Rachel was his friend. An exceptional, extraordinary woman; the sort of woman whose friendship glowed reflectively on his own sense of himself. He loved Rachel. He loved food and good company. Boston and work were far away. He asked the hall porter to call them a cab. They went out to supper.

That evening had been the beginning of knowing there was something wrong. And she had hated and resisted that knowledge with all the steady strength she had cultivated over so many years.

The available facts could not be made to accord with her own original conclusions.

She had been wrong, and the scientific wrong was standing before her still. She was a fraud. She had been wrong.

There were the scientific data. Of course over the years her theory had been modified; with more sophisticated dating and better understanding of genetic transference, no one, certainly not she, would use 'race memory' in the crude away she had used in the late forties and early fifties before Watson and Crick had cracked DNA. Paleontologists had been wrong before; Gideon Mantell had placed the iguanadont's spiked thumb on its nose as a horn. Being wrong about detail did not necessarily matter. What it had been, that part of her idea was a powerful metaphor for the underlying Darwinian understanding that everything developed slowly and steadily, carried along by the species' determination to survive. Gradualists, they were called, people who believed like she did; and they stood firm claiming for the life sciences at least that Neils Bohr was wrong, Einstein right, the Old Man did not throw dice, things were not random and haywire, order and progress was possible, scientific mechanism would eventually explain it all.

Suddenly there was a whole new wave of madmen. Great extinctions. The Cretaceous Catastrophe. The dinosaurs had gone not with a Darwinian whimper, but with a bang. The Alvarez iridium layer got everyone going, with extraterrestial interventions and long cycles. Rachel resisted it all. Stood with the Darwinians, the gradualists. Stood by her own reconstruction and the theories on which it was based.

She did not stand alone, but Paul changed sides. And then Paul would not let her off, waving the evidence under her nose and insisting that she pay attention to it, until sometimes she thought she hated him, felt haunted and harassed by him, bullied.

'Rachel,' he would say, 'OK, Rachel, what are you going to do with this?' waving some new article, some professional curio, some clever young man's clever little fact under her nose. Once he was living safely in his vicarage, assured of Simon's love, and apparently of God's too, he became almost magically her equal instead of her disciple. She knew that ought to make her glad, because he was, as she had known from the beginning, extremely good at his work, but she found herself wanting to cry out, 'Paul, please need me. Nobody needs me. If you're right my whole life is so wrong that I cannot bear it. Please need me and let me be right.' She did not say those things because she could not risk his friendship. Instead she was harsh with his ideas, almost cruel sometimes. But if it had not been for him she would never have confronted the problems.

A very bright young woman in Philadelphia had written an important critique of her dinosaur, and although she had dismissed it in print, without malice, and to everyone else's apparent satisfaction . . . well, it gave her pause. There was a problem with age of the sediment; and worse, the possibility – overlooked, she now knew, in her enthusiasm – that the dinosaur had not been fossilized where she had found it, that it was older than she wanted it to be, and that her reconstruction was shaky, was wrong. Smit and van der Kaars, from Amsterdam, produced a major paper arguing that the fossil record in Montana had been badly misread, that Cretaceous and Paleocene deposits had been all mixed up on the flood plain. If it was true at Hell Creek and Bug Creek, it could easily be true at Lone Point. They were arguing the other way: no mass mammalian development prior to the Cretaceous catastrophe, but should it work the other way too. Their article was a blow with a blunt instrument:

> Considering the large amount of Cretaceous sediments eroded by this meandering river, the occurrence of out-washed dinosaur fragments and other Cretaceous fossils is not surprising. In our interpretation a gradual faunal change is not justified. On the contrary, the evidence appears to underscore a catastrophic scenario.

She wrote a long letter to Tim Wong. She desperately wanted reassurance. Surely they had got it right? she asked him. His letter shocked her to the core. He simply did not care.

> My darling Rachel, he wrote. It was twenty years ago. It made our reputation and the educational sector of the museum world will go on loving it for years. Keep your head down and your expense account up. Now is not the moment to ask footling little questions about individual reconstructions. Van Valen is producing a major attack on Smit and co. We're not likely to be discredited yet awhile, so long as we don't ask too publicly too many awkward questions.

Her anger had been simple and pure. She had not felt so strong a rage in years. She had taken the letter along with the rest of her post to her bedroom to read it, and now she shredded the letter and carried the pieces almost disdainfully to her wastepaper basket. Looking up she saw the photograph of Tim, with Maggie and Phoebe, taken one summer when he had visited them here in London. In a single unpremeditated explosion she took the picture from under its glass and cut off Tim's picture with her nail-scissors. She shoved it to the back of her dressing-table drawer and returned Maggie and Phoebe to their position.

Anger did not help; nor did avoiding reading the threatening literature. Nothing helped. She dug her heels in and held out.

Then one day she read, almost casually, a humorous exchange between Stephen Jay Gould and Richard Muller in a back number of *Natural History*. Muller was proposing a sister star for the Sun, a weak star whose long orbit brought it crashing through the Oort cloud every twenty-six million years, shaking loose a devastating shower of comets, falling as Lucifer and the wicked angels had, and bringing devastation, mass extinctions to the earth. He called his star Nemesis, the death star, the bearer of disaster and judgement. Gould objected to the name.

> Nemesis, he wrote, represents everything that our new view of mass extinctions is struggling to replace – predictable deterministic causes afflicting those who deserve it.

It would also mean placing one more Western figure in the sky. It should be named for Siva, the Hindu God of destruction, who forms an indissoluble triad with Brahma the Creator and Vishnu the preserver, and would reflect the knowledge that extinctions not only destroy life but are a source of creation as well. The dinosaurs arose after one extinction, and mammals came into their own after another one killed the dinosaurs.

Rachel did not usually like to read this sort of debate, hating the idea of extraterrestial forces smashing up her predictable deterministic causes, but the mythology drew her and she looked up Muller's reply.

Muller had responded that Gould was unfair; he had no commitment to the name Nemesis. In his original report he had proposed four names. Only two of them were western, but his editors had deleted his other suggestions: to name the star after Kali, the Hindu Goddess who is the destroyer of men and animals and yet is infinitely generous and kind; or Indra, the verdic God of storms and war who uses a thunderbolt (comet) to slay a serpent (dinosaur); or finally George, the Christian saint who slew the dragon.

And then she could no longer escape, for Rachel's belief in her own theories was also under assault from Maggie and Fenna.

Fenna was Maggie's imaginary dragon.

Maggie was the most purely joyful thing in Rachel's life, the absolutely wanted child, the golden speck at the bottom of the Pandora's box of her life. Maggie was sweetness and light when she had finally ceased to expect it. Maggie had reconciled her to Phoebe's morals and politics, since without those Maggie would not have existed. Maggie was Maggie and was also the means that made possible her steady disciplined relationship with Phoebe, and therefore her home and her happiness.

Fenna was the purely joyful thing in Maggie's life. And Maggie was more generous than her mother or grandmother; she was determined to share her joy.

Fenna had appeared when Maggie was about five years old. At first she had been flattered that Maggie had turned not to an imaginary brother or sister or friend, but to her grandmother's work. But after ten more years she was forced to recognise that Fenna was no compliment. Fenna was her enemy. She was Fenna's enemy.

Fenna was an assault, an attack, on all that she had stood for. Fenna was the wilful instrument of her own professional disintegration.

Fenna was flame and fire, and moved on the wings of the night that were dragon wings to dance with taloned claws and mock scientific theory.

Fenna was the dark force of the imagination as well as its golden dancing; Fenna was chaos as well as order, and brought, on fiery dragon breath, the full danger of the chasm.

Maggie could play safely with Fenna and explore the land of dark flames and reversed colours that lies in the pit of disorder; Maggie could ride the rough neck, clinging to the glittering scales and interpret the wreaths of smoke that drifted from Fenna's nostrils when the great beast played at being tame. Maggie was safe because she never thought to deny Fenna's powers and floated with them, but the older women suffered under the assaults of this strange visitor from within the dreaming self.

Rachel could not consent. Maggie was as gentle as she could be, as gentle as any child who has grown up loved, loving and thoughtful; but Maggie delighted in Fenna and could not understand why her grandmother was afraid of the long scorching breaths, the flailing tail that swept the stars across the sky on windy nights and hurled them down beyond the horizon in exploding fireworks, the vast wings that shaped the storms of the universe. And Fenna had taught her a toughness, a scaled cladding against delusion, so that she knew quite well that unless and until her grandmother truly recognised and respected the powers of which Fenna was the prophet, then she could not really hope to be safe.

So Fenna unknotted the scientific shapes of Rachel's mind and each knot severed or untwined hurt her head. And the ones that she would not let Fenna melt with steaming breath hurt even more; they swelled into ugly lumps in her brain and kept her awake at night; they tangled themselves around all the words that she wanted to read, or the scholarship she wanted to consider, and there was no peace for her at all.

Fenna and Maggie persuaded her that she could no longer claim for science the priority over life and death and dreams that she had demanded for it. Fenna and Maggie persuaded her, very simply, that dragons were entirely real, were real products of the mind and eye and hopes and desires and loves and hates of life. Their reality, the reality of the imagination, was as central as her scientific causal reality.

So being committed – more lovingly and more clearly than at any time since she was twenty – to the disciplines of scientific truth, she had written the paper that denounced her whole life's work; and tomorrow morning she was planning to present it, pre-publication, to her board.

But she could not.

The Thursday before, after she had read the typescript and hidden it so abruptly in the drawer, she had come home and retrieved the photograph of Tim Wong and sellotaped the two halves together again with great care. She had to forgive him because she was tempted with the same temptation. Gradualism was, as Tim had said, not likely to be discredited just yet. She could stay on with dignity. Her dinosaur could stand its ground, its head held high, admired and feared by schoolchildren. No one would take it down in her life time unless she told them to. They would not dare.

Yet what was her life worth if she did not hold to the end to the careful and gradual evolution of scientific knowledge? There was nothing else. She had not made anything else.

But she could not. She simply could not get to her feet and say,

'Gentlemen, I, who have spent half a century telling people to look, to look at the facts, at the evidence and at the record have to stand here and tell you that I have entirely failed to do this myself. I have bent the evidence for my own emotional and professional ambitions. I am a sham. I am an amateur.'

And what would they say? They would say, in twenty different voices, 'Just like a Woman'.

She sat on the side of her bed and heard their mocking voices. And immediately she knew that it was not at sometime in the future, it was not in her old age and decrepitude that she needed Phoebe, it was now. Now. Phoebe could help her and if she could bring herself to ask, Phoebe would help her.

She wobbled with a doubt when she looked at her bedside clock and saw that it was nearly four in the morning. But she needed, she needed Phoebe. She got up and groped for her slippers, tied her dressing-gown cord firmly and opened the door of her room, a huge dinosaur pulling itself up from the depths. Slowly she started to climb the stairs towards Phoebe's room, seeking in her mind for what she could say, how she could awaken Phoebe and explain. Then suddenly from high above her she heard an enormous crash like breaking glass and wild terrified screaming.

Two

Phoebe had fled from Maggie in a panic, but when she had climbed the stairs and arrived in her room, she felt soothed. It was her own place, her sanctuary.

For years Phoebe had slept in baggy T-shirts. She slept naked only when she had a lover. She had learned over the years that when her bedtime hands reached for the T-shirt then the affair was over, and sometimes this happened well before she had even half-conscious stirrings that the fun time was passed and that the long slow tide had turned. Tonight's T-shirt had once been a vivid sunny yellow, but long-ago encounters with blue socks and red blouses in the washing machine had faded it to a slightly sickly beige. It made Phoebe feel sad. She indulged herself with a sentimental moment of missing Tom.

She was orderly. She undressed, pulled the T-shirt over her head and padded, barefoot, to the bathroom. Brushing her teeth she watched her face in the mirror and tried not to see in her own eyes the expression of worried concern that only a few minutes before she had seen in Maggie's. The toothpaste dribbled down her chin and irritated her. Then, remembering suddenly her momentary irritation in the wine bar, she ran the hot tap and began to scrub her hands, taking both soap and a nail-brush to the job. She liked her hands, strong with long fingers; she contemplated them carefully as she scrubbed, taking a quite superfluous amount of care. She grinned wryly at her reflection.

Her own self-knowledge annoyed her; she would like a little moment of perfect unselfconsciousness, although she recognised the problem: to enjoy a moment of unselfconsciousness you have to be selfconscious. She was not concerned with mystical ecstacy; only with silencing the mean and niggling woman who cast her cynicism on her every action. As though her whole life was an act lived out for the amusement or interest of an invisible audience.

Even in her park she watched herself at work, watched quite admiringly her own tall strong body labouring over the mowing machine, her long fingers planting, her wide shoulders digging. She would catch herself thinking, 'How interesting – there is a woman who could have got a first-class degree in mathematics, digging in a public park and enjoying it.'

Her hands were finally clean. She went back to her room and methodically took the bottle of whisky from the cupboard, poured herself a drink, and settled down on her bed to write her diary.

Disagreeable day. Finished the foul paths. Hateful job. Made a start on the pruning, probably a bit late. Got a delivery of shrubs etc. in the morning. No potentilla. Infuriating. Checked they had been ordered. These are the new ones I asked for specially, the 'Day Dawn', that I saw at Sissinghurst last . . .

She paused and ran back through the diary to see when she had been at Sissinghurst last summer . . .

June 1st.

A morning both damp and sweaty. Not nice. Sort of drizzly rain, but close. Lots of dogs; the middle-aged woman's puppy looks so funny still when he runs away from larger dogs, ears a-flap like Biggles. The daisies mostly scrunched up against the rain and the lilac mainly gone rusty at the edges and dingy-looking – also bridal veil etc. Finally mowed the leftover bulb ends; the grass looks oddly pale and plucked – like shaved underarms. In compensation the first of the roses – extremely pink; the herbaceous thingies looking good and the foxgloves just showing colour – yellow and pinkish probably. Best of all though the poppies – not devoured this year, in a strong fat clump quite suddenly in flower – an unbelievable red, and so big and dense and purple-hearted that they do not make me think 'Flanders field' but 'Hills of Nepal' instead. I watch every day and yet am always taken by surprise. The pansies continue extraordinary – most people seem to like the thick velvet blue ones but we also have a lovely delicate peachy colour – like the liquid aspirin, Calpon, that Maggie used to have – and the colour goes deep. Deeper than the poppies. The grass needs doing badly, also weeding. A young man with the most beautifully trained Dobermann was friendly. Two lovely Asian girls giggling all over the place and hiding, apparently from no one. It's still hard work but important to catch the first moments of things – not to generalise. This flower flowers at this moment. I should sit and watch a poppy break out – like butterfly from chrysalis – as delicate-winged and furry-centred. Still the image/metaphor again. How shall I learn to look-feel-tell without the gap. Poppy petals like paper, but not at all like paper, like poppy petals only.

3rd June.
Went yesterday with Sue (nice) to Sissinghurst. It was raining a bit and not the best time of year; and did not enjoy it so much – for the first time it seemed to me precious, both in concept and execution. Their aquelegia seemed over the top – looked like plastic flowers and the colours improbable, show-offy – though technically impressive. The orange/flame/red azaleas definitely too much. But white poppies with black centres, so black and white that I craved them, and some lovely viola in beautiful delicate shades. Also an espaliered Fremont-adendron – the yellowest yellow I have ever seen, and stiff open flowers, waxy – ugh – but for the colour, I must look it up. Evil herbs – witch garden (a bronze fennel like nothing I have ever seen) and some fabulous fernery which we must pursue. Didn't find the hydrangea that we need – Hever had a stand at Chelsea (???), or at Threave. But a very pretty Potentilla – Day Dawn – was flowering well. Easily the prettiest colour on offer: will definitely order some if possible, though a rather messy bush which will need watching. When the weather improves I must sit down and try and look at one square foot of grass (the lawns at S. were impeccable and shamemaking and wonderful – and for this purpose probably boring!) or something like that with the total precision of contemplation that Dillard brings to such a task. Aspiration. I must dead-head and weed this week. *Must* mow.

She skimmed on a little.

June 10th.
The weather has been appalling – just my luck, I pruned the

Bridal Veil back pretty hard after flowering and the wind was strong and it really took a beating. I did the Jew's Mallow too, but less hard because I overdid that last year and anyway both lots are against the wall so that it did much better. The wind was impressive actually, along with floods of rain, and brought down the tall lupins. In fact the whole place looks a bit of a mess – we're all both lazy and thwarted by the weather and the grass is way out of control, and too many weeds and a number of things – the lilies, the gypsophilia etc. in urgent need of staking. However the alum is doing extremely well and pushing up buds – looking slightly tropical and weird; the fuchsia have set their first buds, funny tight insect-looking things – though they are getting eaten to death – ordered the spray, but not yet arrived. The new climbers need to have their nets put in. However the 'new' bed at the west end looks great: the foxgloves were the perfect thing for it, quite a lot of them for a first year, and the weigelia is in flower. We need some forget-me-not in there next year, I think. Best of all are the calendulae, all white and spectacular even in the rain, but it all suddenly needs more time than it is getting – little things, weeds etc. and staking but also bigger things: paths, and the whole playground needs work and rethinking. Something has taken over the troughs: can't remember what this thing is called, it has yellow flowers and is supposed to provide quick ground cover – and it does!

Took my coffee break under the weeping ash over by Elmer St.; the branches were beautiful grey and black and the leaves a summer green full of dreams and that despite the fact there was no sun. There were also tiny toadstools here and there in the grass under the lilac trees on that side; the wind and rain have essentially polished off the azaleas, which now have a few battered petals drooping around and the stamens prodding up aggressively, twig-like. But the roses too are coming into glory.

Phoebe stopped reading, took another swig of whisky, flicked back to the present tense of the volume and went on writing:

. . . last June. It drives me bloody crazy. The weather is having a weird effect on everything. Last year I did no spring pruning before mid-March, and yet now if I don't get to the roses pretty soon we are going to have a disaster. But the daffodils are bright, and courageous (pathetic fallacy) and the garden peaceful, now that half-term is over. Tried to show off the herb frames to Lisa, who visited, but there wasn't enough showing for her to get interested.

But Lisa had been interested, actually. Phoebe noticed with dispassionate curiosity that she was deliberately recording how she wanted things to be rather than how they had been. She had knelt pruning the *cornus* with pleasure, and then Lisa had come and she had been pleased and smiling. When she had shown Lisa the herb frames, Lisa had been at the very least amused and intrigued by her, Phoebe's, excitement. Why did she then want to record the whole day so negatively?

She disciplined herself. There had been that lovely moment when the sun had warmed the nape of her neck and she had planned lilies-of-the-valley, in the deep shade under the shrubs and she had been contented. She ordered herself to write this down, to add it and the deep cups of the croci to counterbalance the nauseating paths and the undelivered *Potentillae*.

But it was even more of an effort now, after reading those happy, concentrated working notes from last summer. Her most recent entries in the diary read more as a moan about vandalism, lazy staff and the rotten weather. Though the croci were lovely, especially the gold ones, she had scarcely noted their flowering, only their collapse into raggedness. She acknowledged sadly her own decline, her own loss of concentration.

She shut the diary and picked up her book on Paracelsus, but the whisky, on top of the wine she had shared with Lisa, was beginning to do its job and she thought that perhaps, for once, she might sleep. She turned off her bedside light, snuggled under her duvet and curled up on her right-hand side like a child.

She was not afraid of the dark because, when she was very little, Phoebe had had the bright certainties of her father's mind to protect her. If she had been frightened at night she would climb out of bed and go to find him, in his study working, or stretched out beside her mother in their bedroom. He would wake simply and dispel her shadowy fears with the sharp-edged light of his knowledge. He would assure her of the complete non-existence of ghosties and ghoulies and 'lang-leggetty beasties'. He would set her simple chess problems to brood on instead, assure her that at night a person was always allowed to play white against black, and come with her to tuck her safely away again. His pyjamas were always neatly striped in firm colours and she was comforted to her core by the fact that he always left his slippers beside his bed, precisely where his feet would slide into them as he got up.

So she was never afraid of the dark. But she did not sleep.

Almost immediately, even while she still thought that she might be able to sleep, she felt quietly and insistently the call of her night-dark lover and she runkled up her T-shirt and felt up her own warm soft skin for her left breast. So near to her heart that she could feel its steady strong pulsing against her little finger, even while her other fingers caressed the breast itself, Phoebe had a lump.

She hated the word lump, an undignified name for something so strange and vital, so entirely her own and so secret.

When she had been pregnant with Maggie she had seen a young doctor who had referred to the foetus as 'Mr Lump.'

'How's Mr Lump today?' he had asked, with a facetious smile.

She had closed her eyes and not bothered to reply, but she had frequently used the incident as a joke since.

She could not bear the word 'lump'. Sometimes she almost took the risk of finding the word *carcinoma* beautiful. At dinner recently she and her friends had been laughing about names for children: how to revive the old custom of finding socially significant ones, like the seventeenth century puritans – 'Penitence' and 'Praise God' and 'Obadiah-bind-their-kings-in-chains-and-their-nobles-with-links-of-iron.' Someone had said that the first Victorian baby to be born with its mother under anaesthetic had been called Anaesthesia, and Phoebe laughing had said,

'Well I think Influenza is a pretty name. I shall have a son and call him Colitis, or what about Carcinoma?'

They had all laughed, and she with them. It had been a bold experiment, but she found it brought her too near to naming the truth, and so It remained unnamed. Unnamed and in the dark It grew. As powerful as all growing things.

Inside a bulb, a little ordinary bulb, that she had planted in thousands, the most extraordinary and bizarre things happen. A little dead-looking bulb, buried in the darkness, through the winter, had so much power stored in it. She had a hyacinth bulb in the kitchen, that she had grown in water, watching the lunatic thrust downwards and upwards, resisting the temptation to try and stuff all that force back into its oniony skin. A process that she did not understand, which forced her simply to marvel.

Growth had to be secret. At college they had sliced up bulbs weekly to see what was going on, but the process of knowing killed the process of growing. She could only see the force of life by killing, opening up and looking; and then it can never be put back together. It cannot even be X-rayed, X-rays kill and damage a bulb, it has to be left alone to do its growing secretly. Interference will kill it dead.

With a stab of fear she recognised fully for the first time that she might never see another bulb flower after this year, and that it was her own fault, she had done this to herself. It made her, briefly, furious.

Her fingers fumbled now, but there was no longer the strange mixture of panic and relief that six months ago she had felt when she could not find it. Now there was no possibility of that. If she stood naked in front of the mirror she could even see the way her breasts no longer matched. She had watched for that moment just as, even more reluctantly, she had stood in front of the mirror fifteen years ago and watched the pit of her belly for the first swelling signs that would make her pregnancy undeniable. It had now grown almost to the size of a small egg; a finch's egg, she liked to think, speckled and pretty, nestled there under her breast, above her heart, brooded over, kept warm and safe.

She cupped her hand lovingly over the breast and rolled onto her back. Her eyes opened and stared at the ceiling. She pushed her T-shirt up further and placed her other hand on her right breast feeling the pleasing smoothness of skin and the noticeable difference between the two of them. She could almost feel the inner power of the growth.

I lie here and It grows, It grows sweetly like a bulb in the soft earth, moistened by the fresh strong red blood so near my heart. Have I planted It myself? she wondered. Did I plant it like Blake's poem, have I watered It with my fears, night and morning with my tears? I told It not. That was the truth, she told It not and It would grow.

On bright mornings, on her bicycle riding to work against the flow of the traffic and feeling with great pleasure the solid muscle of her legs and back, she found the whole thing almost unbelievable. She, a perfectly sane modern woman, who for ten years had sensibly practised self-examination and had a dutiful smear test every third year; who preferred her cap to the unnatural and dangerous interference of the pill and who could insert it one-handed and without shame in front of new lovers, what on earth was she playing at? Indeed nearly six months before, when her competent fingers had first found the irregularity, and after a month she had felt obliged to recognise that It was not some freak of her hormonal cycle, she had assumed that she would take It to the doctor, like all sensible women did. She was not particularly afraid of hospitals. Despite a certain natural grief, she was reasonably sure she could live with only one breast if she had to. And anyway she knew damn well that the odds were against it being anything serious. She was thirty-seven years old and had breastfed a baby: she was very low risk. Of course if she were to be unlucky, then the sooner it was dealt with the better.

Six weeks later she realised that she had not yet been to the doctor, though of course it was a very busy time of year for her. Two months after first discovering the lump she had been with a group of women friends, one of whom was anxious about her own lump and Phoebe heard herself urging her friend to get it seen to, offering to accompany her if she were scared. And in her own duplicity she had felt the first thrill of excitement, of wickedness, of secret joy.

She had fallen in love. She had thought that was impossible for her, that she was a woman deficient in feeling, in power of feeling. And now she was at last the victim of a consuming passion, that was taking over her life, her destiny, her sense of identity. It was her closely guarded secret, the life she must defend with her own for everyone else would want to destroy it. The great pulsing power had got under her skin and into her body the way no lover in the past ever had, the way that even Maggie growing inside her had never done.

Once more she was furious with herself. She jerked her hands away from her chest and sat up sharply. Then she climbed out of her bed. She poured herself another whisky and carried it across the room to the window. She pulled back the curtain and looked out over sleeping London.

'Just what is the matter with you?' she asked herself fiercely. 'Have you gone crazy?'

It was not the first night she had demanded answers. The houses on the opposite side of the street again returned her no replies. They stood bland and respectable under the street lights, the safe steady homes of the bourgeoisie to which she had committed herself by mistake, through negligence, cowardice and the demands of the two women who were now sleeping silently, sandwiching her between them, squashing her flat, pinning her down like a butterfly on a board.

Once she had roamed the world, once she had travelled free and light in the beautiful sunny valleys of Kashmir and laid herself down to sleep untroubled. Once she had sat with her friends in an assortment of countries and rooms, getting high and planning the metamorphosis of the world.

Now she was trapped in this respectable house which looked like a hundred, a hundred-thousand others, and she could feel the great weight of Rachel and Maggie pressing on her, insisting she be strong, be good, be well. She, who had never chosen motherhood, was now mother to two women. She wanted to be held, she wanted to be cuddled, taken care of, loved, cherished, kissed, kissed sweetly and softly, tucked up in cool sheets and adored. She wanted to be mothered.

But there was no one to mother her. Self-pity swelled up delightfully. Even her friends wanted her to be witty, lighthearted, debonair. Even Lisa, who ought to have known her best of all, nagged at her constantly, expected too much of her, refused to see.

'Come on, Bea,' she had said rousingly only a few weeks ago, when she was trying to get Phoebe to help her, 'of course you can do it. You're a big tough lady.'

Phoebe had said, 'Lisa don't you know that inside every big strong woman there's a mimsy, little wet one trying to get out?'

Lisa had laughed, charmed as usual, and Phoebe had ended up spending the weekend helping Lisa to organise some other poor feeble woman's life for her. But for Lisa acts of maternal solicitude were chosen, self-enhancing little moments. For Phoebe they were daily, unchosen realities. Behind her in the dark were a long list of chores that never ended, that seemed to grow like weeds. Fetch Rachel's dry cleaning/write a cheque for Maggie's school trip/call plumber/get TV fixed/shop/supper/wash/clean/redecorate downstairs hallway . . . which she did not find scruffy yet, but which Rachel did. Rachel simply did not have the capacity to allow for that sort of difference. She was flexible and intelligent about ideas, and still thought there was no range of opinion on how often landings needed repainting. But nor did it ever seem to occur to Rachel that decorators did not arrive by magic. Ancient habits of class privilege and being cared for were ingrained in Rachel, deep in her unconscious; she did not seem even able to book herself a ticket to go on holiday without help. But Phoebe could not, on principle, accept the privileges, so she suffered the weight of Rachel's demands.

And Maggie made demands so innocently, so endlessly, so frivolously. 'You could make Maggie do more,' her friends urged her, but none of them had teenage daughters, none of them understood. None of them lived daily with the guilty, cross-making feeling that Maggie had never asked to be born, that she had never loved Maggie as a mother should, and that it would be an additional unfairness to lumber her with demands and expectations, that only her, Phoebe's, own moral passivity made necessary.

'I can cope,' she would say to her friends, and it was true, she could cope. But somewhere the weight of the two women squashed something in her, something called joy.

Leaning against the window pane with her glass in her hand, Phoebe felt tears welling in her eyes. 'I don't want a lot,' she thought.

About a year before, she had got a splinter in her heel: a deep fine splinter on the outer side of her right heel, a splinter that hurt a great deal. She could not get it out. It was deeply embedded in that precise square inch which she could not, not with any twistings and turnings, either see properly or bring pressure to bear against. And no one would help her.

Maggie had said, 'Oh yuck, Mummy, I *can't*; it makes me feel sick.'

Rachel had said, 'Oh darling, I haven't got my reading glasses up here just now.'

With a passionate resentment at their callous collusion, she had burst into tears, which they resolutely appeared not to notice. She had fled to her room. Couldn't they allow her even a thin splinter of weakness? Worse, she had let the splinter fester, hobbling and hopping, nobly not complaining, until the whole of the bottom of her foot was red and swollen, thinking, mean and childlike, they'll be sorry, they'll be sorry, waiting almost greedily for gangrene to set in and amputation to follow.

Phoebe leaned more heavily against the windowsill, folding her arms across her body. She tried to laugh at herself, but could not quite succeed. The London night was fresh and sweet, from far away she could feel rather than hear the sounds of a dreaming city. Against the tender skin on the inside of her elbow she could feel the weight of her breast through the soft material. She could feel It, alive and inviting, she could feel the presence of her lover; she reached out in imagination and embraced her dream.

Phoebe's new lover will tuck her between smooth sheets.

Phoebe's new lover will soothe and caress her, his hands will take her body and play with it, will pour power and tenderness and pain and health into it.

Phoebe's new lover will take her away to his own house, high and white, where she will be waited on by servants, all immaculately uniformed and universally charming, who will cater to her every whim and bring her breakfast in bed.

Phoebe's lover will encourage her not to sleep in a faded T-shirt but to splash out on a silk negligée, afroth with Belgian lace and pink ribbons, such as she has never dared to buy. But when it comes to bedtime he will, with his gentle hands, undo the tiny mother-of-pearl buttons, hang the confection carefully on a coat-hanger and carry her soft naked body to the bed.

Phoebe's new lover will not laugh at her for her weakness will not demand endless strength from her but will delight in her weakness, will treat her like the frail and sweet thing that she is.

Phoebe's new lover will carry her away to his own charmed land and all her friends, and especially Rachel and Maggie, will be sad to see her go, will be guilty and repentant and very unhappy.

Phoebe's new lover will decide about the plumber and let Phoebe, like a little child, like a beautiful woman, roam in his garden which will be as wide and sweet as the hills of Kashmir, and will never complain if she oversleeps in the morning.

Phoebe's new lover will indulge her every whim. Will know that she, despite hard hands and the bicycle, is in fact the lovable woman, the worthy woman, the woman to be cherished and cared for. Phoebe's lover will pay perfect attention to Phoebe; he will explore her whole body and open her mind with tenderness and she will be known as she is known.

Phoebe's lover will accompany her, on the last great adventure to the land beyond the rising sun, to the country she had once hoped to go to on her own: a land where numbers and patterns will be alive with emotion and meaning and where the inaudible note of the ninth planet will complete the perfect tune, will break and remake the octave and she will play it on a cello, her legs spread around it.

Phoebe's lover will love her body. Wildly. His passion will overwhelm her fear and shame, and she will no longer resist, no longer be forced to resist, to cut off. Phoebe's lover will bite, bite into her breast which is his until it bleeds and she will be smeared with blood, with deeper pain. Her lover will rip into her body with claws and teeth and in the pain she will be at last able to have an orgasm. Death will be what sex was always meant to be and which had eluded her too long while she dug in her garden and slaved in her house.

Phoebe was disgusted. Phoebe pushed herself physically away from the window and abruptly turned the light on. Phoebe did not believe in any of this stuff. She looked for the whisky bottle and then sternly refused that too, another lover that she would have to learn to do without. She must have something, she told herself, something to balance against this evil love, something solid and real and her own.

Intelligence, she told herself, intelligence and will-power. She had enough of the former and at least some of the latter. She placed herself – with considerable maternal firmness, as though she was, to herself too, a small child who had to be cared for with both affection and discipline – back in her bed. She handed herself her book and told herself to read until she was ready to sleep. The whisky bottle was discarded, as in the end the faithful teddy-bear was discarded. She was a big girl now.

Later, resolutely, she turned the light off once more and settled down again to sleep. Lying furled there in bed, she tried to conjure up the moments of her life when she had been happy. Happy consciously and knowingly.

She decided firmly to discount all the times before her father had died, before she had left university. Not her father's pride in her and the long Oxford afternoons when he had said, 'Come on, poppet, I want you to meet someone' and had presented her to his friends as a future colleague, a special treasure. Not the delightful summer she had gone to Wyoming with her mother and lived in a caravan on the prairie and been free to play all day among people who worked seriously and enthusiastically. Not, above all, the later times when she had been working well and smoothly without any consciousness except the consciousness of being wonderfully, richly tired when she finished. Not the whole period when she had still lived inside the charmed world of a loved childhood and happiness had been habit not incident.

She traced her life since then with careful attention, seeking and clinging to the good bits.

She could not bring herself even to think about her first year at Cambridge.

The two years she had spent on the hippy trail were mostly a blur. When she tried to tell other people about her travels she found she could not fix a coherent chronology nor recall with any reliability in what order she had visited those foreign countries whose beauty still stirred her dreams. Perhaps the dreaded They had been right and dope did indeed rot the brains, as alcohol most certainly did, damaging both short- and long-term memory. But it was not just that, it was also the violence of her uprooting, the suddenness of her flight. Fleeing her father's dead body in his bedroom and the realisation that her mother needed her. Fleeing the agonising knowledge that her first love had deserted her because she had been unfaithful.

But from out of that chaos she could extract moments of unassailable perfection, had stored moments of such heart-wrenching loveliness, that she could take them out now in the darkness of night-time London and contemplate them.

She had drifted through Turkey and Afghanistan in a transit bus belonging to some people she had met in Greece. There had been a strange beach outside Karachi, where a hot wet wind had blown in from the sea; the air had stunk with rotting fruit, piles of melons dumped by roadsides and sweating stickily under her naked feet. She had somehow gone on through India to Goa, soft and dreamy in the back of old cars and her skin had tanned across her shoulders and she had worn long swirling skirts made of local cloth in garish colours.

Now when she talked about it she would joke that they had thought, talked, planned around nothing but 'shit': how to get more dope and how to cope with the chronic dysentery. It was impossible to fix days from that first six or seven months. At some point she had coupled up with a fey, gentle Scotsman, who somewhere a little later had started using heroin, and had lost himself entirely.

Later, when the spring came, they met up with an American couple – a draft evader, and his girlfriend, both supported by reluctant and concerned parents back home. And together the four of them had gone north, to the more astringent highlands in the foothills of the Himalayas, up in the wild northern borders of Pakistan. The air had been clean and hard, the water milky white and unbelievably cold, and the colours of landscape savagely pure: the sky at night a darker blue than imagination could propose, with stars so crystalled that she had believed when high that she could touch them and freeze her fingers to diamonds. They had been offered a little house by the proud self-respecting mountain villagers and they had stayed there living on apricots and rice throughout the summer.

One morning she had woken before dawn, nestled in primal comfort with her companion. In the dark she had wriggled out and wandered a little way away from the hut.

She had sat in the dark on a stone watching the fading of the stars and then miraculously the sun on the distant mountains which were bright, burning with gold, while still down where she was sitting it was dark. She had felt she was the centre of the world, as though the sun was seeking for her alone. Clearing a shoulder of mountain the sun, with a wild suddenness, found her, pinpointed her and held her in its radiant arms. When the sun smote the valley everything responded to it. From a still bush not five yards away from her, a dust storm arose, a dust storm which was suddenly a cloud of butterflies, of white and yellow butterflies, more butterflies than she had ever seen at one time, moving in a single drift, but each one separate, entire and perfect, a dawn dance for the sun. And for all the thousands that rose up as many more remained, until she realised that the bush was itself covered with yellow and white flowers, and she was snatched up into that moment of glory of butterflies and flowers and sun: a moment which evaporated as soon as she was conscious of it.

For her, neither drugs nor sex had worked. She had tried them both and finally decided to come home; but that morning – those butterflies, that sudden chilling of the skin when she had left the sleeping bag, while inside her body was still warm with sleep, that sunrise, that bush which flowered white and yellow into the air but still remained white and yellow, those butterflies in whose honour she studied lepidoptery and planted likely flowers in her garden, that morning remained, and sometimes when a little drunk, when half smashed and half asleep she could have the shadow of it back.

One evening years later, at a travelling fair with Maggie, then about six years old, she had encountered the same feeling, but then it had belonged to someone else. They had been waiting for the Dodgems, a skill at which every eleven-year-old boy is a past master – knowing in advance just where and when the little cars will stop and rushing with the precision of ballet dancers to be the first by the car. However it was not a skill which Phoebe had perfected; her frustration and annoyance rose. She thought that they ought to have a queue, like every other ride in the fairground, but Dodgems were different and had their own rules, and the rules militated against the weak, the infirm, or even the well-mannered.

And in the midst of this irritation she had seen the face of ecstasy. Not hers. A young black man. Thin-faced, rather beautiful; expression so fixed, eyes so bright, that she read the needle lines on his forearms without needing to turn back the cuffs of his denim jacket. But he sat there, graceful, and when the tinny music and tinny cars stopped he did not move, simply reached in his pocket for the next payment and returned to the business of driving his car with intensity and extraordinary skill. Not for him the cruder pleasures of ramming into other people and squealing, but a beautiful elusive dance that protected his own magical space. She knew that he was actually both fully inside his joy and fully conscious of it. It was, she knew, the mystical experience which she was always seeking; it was commitment and delight. She felt a huge, unstoppable rush of envy and meanness. The next time the music stopped she took Maggie's hand and dragged her over to his car and in a voice that even she could hear was bossy Oxonian, the voice of dreadful women outside little boys' prep schools, the voice of her own mother at her most irritating, she said,

'Since you seem to be going on all night, perhaps you would be kind enough to take my little girl in with you. I'll pay for this go.'

She wanted to force him back into the world in which she had to live.

But he was a high priest, a guardian of the gateways.

'Sure Lady,' he said insolently enough to put her in her place.

He reached out one of those abused skinny arms, the denim as soft as chamois leather, and scooped Maggie out of her cross and jealous world and into his magic one. His car was battered blue and silver, its fat black rubber skirting apparently floating him above the tide of time and Maggie, with a delighted grin, entered with him into the music and the skill and the dance which suddenly became as graceful and fluid as hippopotami swimming under water. And Phoebe, backing away as though hit, found there were tears in her eyes.

That was what she wanted. What she had been looking for, for twenty years, what she had been looking for since the knock on her door which heralded her father's death. But she could never again risk the guilt that had followed the irritation at being interrupted.

She had drifted back to England, after her travelling years, almost without volition. After they left their hill village she could not cope with Sammy's addiction. She had parted from him in Kabul, hardening her heart against the hippy woman's duty to stand by her man, and turned westward, accepting yet another ride.

Somewhere between Iran and Turkey she had contracted dysentery again: no worse than many people's, but dragging. She had spent the first part of the summer on the beach of a Greek island. It had been hot, the sun pounding away for hours. She had felt sick, constantly sick, and the wringing of her bowels, hard enough to bear anywhere had become a nightmare. The dysentery had stripped her down, stripped her of both flesh and illusion. In a thin and painful place, sweating it out in disgusting public toilets or among scratchy bushes at night, she had realised that she was profoundly bored. The beach children here seemed sybaritic and impure compared to the brave ones who had gone all the way east. Weekend hippies with enough money to drag it out all summer. But too tired to turn east again, or travel down into Africa as some people were suggesting, she drifted north in the autumn.

England had seemed cold and blurred at first. She had no friends. She walked the London streets feeling absent from everything, weak and pointless. She was broke and could not bring herself to care very much. She occasionally thought of appealing to her mother, but something hardened in her; she would not go in defeat, she would not go begging, she would not offer herself up to her mother's 'I told you so.' A couple of times she found herself walking past the museum, almost hoping she would meet Rachel as though by accident, but she never went in. She did not want to see those sharp bones, making clear patterns in the dark rooms and see the widening eyes of her mother's colleagues as she introduced her shaken and shabby self.

For a few months she stayed in the flat of an acquaintance, knowing he did not really want her there, paying for his inconvenience by acting the part of his lover, although there was little passion in it for either of them, and no love. He went out to work during the day and she lay until late morning in the sweaty bed and could not bring herself to care.

And then as the weather turned cold and her health got better she became, almost by osmosis – as though from the dampness in the air around her – she became aware that something was happening, there was something in the atmosphere, something that had to do with her. She was waking up, waking from a poppy sleep, and the sharpness came to her nose along with all those other smells of a city in autumn. In pubs, at suppers with friends, and – as she grew more curious – in newspapers, magazines, in some turn of her flatmate's expression when, too idle to bother, she failed to cook or clean. Suddenly, almost unchosen, there were groups of women together, exchanges of secret glances and sudden spurts of surprising flame-like anger.

In November, when her boredom and her poverty were fully apparent to her, she met one evening a man whom for the first time in a long while she suddenly and clearly fancied. He looked like they all looked, but he wasn't. She could tell looking at him that he was somehow awake. He was as thin as everyone else, but it was the taut thinness of action, rather than the thinness of malnutrition brought on not by poverty but by laziness. He had a big and bony nose. His hands were too large. His name was Jim and he worked on a left-wing paper. His driving energy, his commitment, the clarity of his intentions, his – and she found the word with a sense of shock – his passion moved her. Not his body or his looks or his obvious interest in her, but simply the blood light in his eyes. She never understood why he fancied her – perhaps he had seen in her from the start the possibility of a convert, of a disciple: that would certainly explain why he got so angry later. Then they had just talked a little over their drinks, over the booming noise of the pub, and she had gone home less willing than ever to turn over on her back for the sake of a warm bed.

When they met again a couple of weeks later she went home with him without a moment of hesitation: she had known she would from the minute she saw him in the room – that if he asked her, she would go. They walked from the bus stop through the dark streets of Peckham, his arm not round her shoulder but gripping her arm above the elbow as though to prevent her if she might try to escape. They talked, or rather he talked and she listened; she did not tell him, fearing his disapproval, that she had been wandering in the Orient while he had been hurling paving stones in Paris. It was simple and exciting to walk with him thus, and she anticipated with some eagerness their arrival in his bedroom. But they did not make love that night.

He lived in a shabby house with no curtains. Later she learned that this was a point of principle. The light streamed out of the windows onto the two of them as they approached: it was welcoming and affectionate, the house reaching out like that towards them. Inside he led her into a large kitchen: the lino was torn and there were at least eight people there. He stood with his hand still round her arm, so that for a brief moment she felt like the prey, the dinner brought in by the great hunter, and then that faded into chatter and faces that gradually assumed names and shapes as he introduced her rapidly.

'Hi, everyone. This is Bea. How's things?' And, without more ado he released her in the direction of the women and fell into a heated discussion with one of the men. She sat down beside one of the women, someone made her coffee, someone passed a joint and the woman next to her gave a look of purely mischievous conspiracy. It was not for some months that she learned that the woman had grinned thus in what she had then supposed to be shared amusement at Jim's casual proprietorial grasp. It had not occurred to her then to be either amused or angry. The woman said that she was Lisa and this was Sue, and Jo over there didn't actually live here but next door, and various other informative snippets, but it was the wicked sardonic grin, the embracing collusion of the smile that had won Phoebe's heart. She knew she liked it here.

Later of course, when he was not quite so busy, they did indeed sleep together. Jim was the first man she had ever slept with whom she loved. Jim was the first man who expected her to have orgasms. Jim was therefore the person who introduced her to the fact that she didn't. He had an almost missionary zeal about it, just as he had about the IMG – the particular faction of the faction-ridden Trotskyite Left to which he had given his devotion – the miners' strike, the Troops Out movement and a hundred other causes.

'Tell me what you want; you do trust me, don't you?'

He was energetic, tireless and determined. He turned her on and she loved him, but she also got exhausted long before he did. Longing both for his pleasure and her sleep she would pretend. By that time she was so certain that she wanted to stay in the house, be with him, that she lied to him, with her body and her words.

But that was such a minor little detail. Jim held out for her far more important things. He introduced her to that crazy household of passion and affection, the one place that she could call home with her whole heart, a brief dream of paradise. The place where she had grown up. He had, like the Prince in Sleeping Beauty, brought her back to life.

His eagerness made her, suddenly, want to be intelligent again. Under his dynamic tutelage she started reading – not the literature of her childhood, but hard politics, sociology, philosophy, ideas, and experimental fiction. To please him she learned to talk about what she read and what she thought. He was, and she forced herself to remember this with gratitude, one of the best talkers she had ever met; funny and fast. Passionate, and unashamed. A man who could and would talk the hind legs back on to an injured donkey, provided it had decent proletarian credentials. They had all learned from him; she and Lisa still spoke, stylistically, as he had taught them to. He had set his mark on them.

Where was he now? Phoebe lying on her bed in her mother's house in north London, asked herself with a sudden rush of nostalgia. In what corner of what foreign field did he still keep the faith, further the revolution, wake up his current lover at three in the morning to discuss the delicate interweavings of class and race. She could not bear to think that he had taken all that pure wrathful zeal into marketing or insurance broking. Occasionally she half hoped to see him again, she would find herself watching faces rising towards her on the escalator of the Tube and wonder what she would feel if one of those faces were suddenly to be his. Where had they all gone, those extraordinary skinny left-wing men, who had bullied their girl-friends into the Women's Movement and been surprised when the hand with which they had so kindly offered freedom had been bitten so damn hard? Nearly twenty years later Phoebe still found it hard to suppress a little vindictive chuckle at the looks of growing shock on Jim's face – Jim and Lisa's Jonathan and Sue's Alan – when they discovered that their righteousness was not enough. Their women, far from being grateful, turned on them, snarling, in late night conversations telling them to shut up; far from setting them free to work for the Revolution, their women demanded that they take emotional responsibility and also clean the loos. And finally, only a year or so later, turned them out of house and home – put them on the street, as women who failed to be properly grateful to the fathers had been put for centuries.

But even as she chuckled, Phoebe knew now that this was not fair. There had been a time, a brief time, a glorious dawn, when despite her growing awareness of her own sexual failure, despite her anger and frustration, despite her own laziness and lack of commitment, there had been a time when she had been happy and hopeful and joyous.

It had not, as it turned out, been Jim that had made the happiness for her, but the house itself. However he, with his determined hands and determined nose, had been her way in. She did not know where he was now and she did not really care, but he had probably been the most influential person in her life: her handsome prince and Maggie's father. He had given her that household, a little society, warming itself in its own glow of virtue, insulating itself from the big bad world; but within its own limits it had been open and supportive. She had, during that year, woken some mornings giddy with courage and boldness, excited and certain. Motivated.

It had been, however briefly, a time when her body and her mind had fitted together so tidily and wholely that, waking up one morning and deciding that it was time to go back to Oxford and visit her mother, was neither traumatic nor casual, but straightforward. She had discussed it with her family; hugged Lisa and Sue, kissed Jim, left home, and taken the tube to Acton where she stuck out her thumb on the edge of the A40 on a smiling spring day and gone home.

Had that, she wondered now, been a mistake? A kindly lorry driver on his way to North Wales, chatting of his own daughter and his home, had dropped her at the roundabout at the top of the Banbury Road at about lunch-time. She had walked down through suburban Summertown, taking her time but without reluctance; watching the tidiness of the shoppers and the smartness of the shops with something akin to smugness – how little energy and vitality they had, compared to her own shopping street, with its untidy market atmosphere permeating even the Safeways and Boots which had tried to raise their modern, never-had-it-so-good façades in challenge to the poverty and squalor, and had failed.

Two blocks away from the house of her childhood it suddenly occurred to her that her mother might have left, that there might be strangers in the hallway, a different set of curtains hanging at the windows; her father's study might have been turned into a playroom for a new generation of North Oxford children, so different from herself in her prim Clark's T-bar sandals that she would not be able to recognise her own infancy in theirs. It would be too humiliating to have to contact her mother through her publishers or her employers. How could one ring a bell on a house door in respectable places like this and say,

'Excuse me does my mother live here?'

That was the stuff of melodrama, and now she was back in Oxford she knew she was somewhere, somehow, still too middle-class, too much her father's daughter, to want that. This was leafy north Oxford, this was the place of security. This was the corner to which she had tottered, her mother holding her on white leather reins, her legs encased in knitted leggings whose scratchiness she could still remember. This was the street along which she had run, a skinny and excited ten-year-old, to boast to her father that she was the only girl who had made it to the next round of the chess competition. This was the pavement along which, awkward and gawky, she had struggled to find a graceful, even a comfortable, way of carrying her cello to and from her chamber music group.

She hesitated at the corner, reluctant almost to discover that she was now, as of this moment, completely lost in the world, and for the first time she asked herself clearly why she had decided to come here. This was not home. Home was in Peckham, in the shabby house whose light spilled each evening out onto the street. Family was Jim and the others; family was her women's group and squabbling at two-thirty in the morning about whether women could be said to constitute a separate class because they had a separate relation to the mode of production, while still making each other coffee and giving each other hugs. And love was standing outside the local supermarket collecting signatures for the campaign to keep Family Allowance as a separate benefit. She had forsaken her people and her father's house, and had, like every other well-brought-up girl, established her own household and she should cleave only unto it, forsaking all others so long as she should live. She did not know why she had come. Not certainly to reassure her mother, but . . . to boast of her new self? To show off?

And then the moment had passed, and tall and tanned and fit in the sunshine she had walked down the green street with the gardens either side of her, and had known by an instinctive glance that her mother still lived there, that nothing had changed.

She rang the doorbell, listened to the silence within and felt a moment of panic. Then she laughed at herself, with an edge of self-mocking irony. All her self-righteousness had failed to inform her that her mother, a hardy professional, was certainly still at work in the city that she had left behind her. They had probably passed each other on the road. She went back to the corner and across to the nearby pub, where she sat sipping beer, munching a cheese sandwich, and waiting.

She had waited all afternoon – later sitting in the garden and reading. When the sun moved round she too had moved to the doorstep, her sleeves rolled up and concentrating half on the book and half on the remembered scene until her mother had arrived, walking up the street where they had both walked so many times before.

That had been the moment of her undoing. Her mother had got older, fatter and sadder. Phoebe felt an enormous, and unwelcome, surge of pity, of compassion and caring; and with it guilt. In one swoop the feeling swallowed her up and she had never got rid of it since. She saw in Rachel's face three years of loss and loneliness; she saw too the simpler anger that Rachel would never dare to express. And to cover up the dreadfulness of the moment, the pain of the knowledge that Rachel had become old, alone, and friendless, she had giggled and said something about having lost her key. She felt the deep need in Rachel's hug, and responded to it, but it was Rachel's need not her own.

She was furious. Her fury made her aggressive and she attacked. She was mean and horrible to her mother, snide, self-righteous and unkind. Only in her anger could she drown out the dark shadow that pity and guilt had cast over her. She hated herself for it, and went on and on, convinced that her only defence was to make Rachel throw her out again, and Rachel refused to be provoked. Finally Rachel responded and Phoebe had forgotten in her wanderings just how bloody clever Rachel was. How well she could keep control and use words and manipulate their meanings and score points. It was this ruthless clarity and brightness that she had run away from. She, Phoebe told herself, did not play those stupid games any more, she was direct and straightforward.

But her mouth motored on and what came out was simply, and childishly, rude. Phoebe felt foolish. Rachel seemed able to absorb everything that Phoebe tried. She was calm and sweet and later insisted on taking Phoebe out to dinner at some fancy little pseudo-Bohemian bistro. Then to her final and total humiliation Phoebe found that she was actually having a good time; she was enjoying her mother and her mother's easy authority and charm. *Her* mother, she thought with a most annoying pride, who was one of the few genuinely creative women scientists around and in whose success, were it anyone except her mother's, she would be rejoicing.

She went to bed in her own room, still full of pictures and possessions that had belonged to a previous and vanished Phoebe. She curled up in the position she had slept in as a child; and realised with a sinking heart that it was not only the most comfortable way of being in bed, but it was also one that you could not adopt in company. She thought that she never wanted to sleep with Jim again, that the bonds of love were snares and that she must at all costs leave as early as possible the next morning and never come back. She had a clear and frightening premonition that she would not be able to manage it.

Perhaps if she had not got pregnant . . . perhaps they could have pulled it off. Perhaps not. Now she no longer knew. She found it hard to remember with any precision exactly what had happened next. She remembered a little of the acrimony, of the mounting bitterness within the house, of their winter of discontent, which was so much part of and not part of the winter outside, and the miners' strike. But the light no longer poured out of their house and onto the street; the power cuts, although they supported them passionately, cut off their power somewhere. Jim and Jonathan especially were never there, and the arguments about washing up versus serving the revolution lost their gaiety and became mean-mouthed. Alan and Sue moved out, went north to do something else.

Phoebe had not seen Alan since, though Sue had moved back again briefly later that winter, saddened and distressed by Alan's disaffection. She had been part of a long stream of women who had come and gone swiftly, lives collapsing in one area as they gained power and certainty in another. Suddenly there were too many women realising that their happiness had to be taken at the expense of their men's – men who had promised so much and could not now deliver the goods; just like her father five years before. Lisa and Phoebe shared the painful knowledge that they had been connng themselves as well as their men.

How had a Conservative Government happened? Where were the golden days which Paris and Chicago and Grosvenor Square had promised them? In the meantime, the miners represented hope for all of them, but within the giddy cycle of excitements they were all edgy with new fears and old illusions.

After Sue and Alan left, Lisa and Phoebe had invited their neighbour Jo and her lover Sophie to come and share the house with them. Jim and Jonathan had been away, picketing and pamphleteering in Reading, had simply been not available, and Jo's squat had been suddenly repossessed and it did not occur to any of the women that the boys would mind. Sophie moreover actually had a job, had an income, which was beginning to be something of a pressing issue, inflation and the changing climate began to bite into their indifferent superiority to the outside world and they had given no thought as to how to fight that. Then the boys, as it turned out, minded bitterly having Jo and Sophie. Since, on principle, they could not say that lesbianism made them nervous and that the complex new demands made on them scared them, they found more underhand and aggressive ways of expressing their resentments. The women outnumbered them and plotted together. Having the other two women in the house taught Lisa something new about herself; she and Jonathan stopped sleeping together, which left them all short of space. Phoebe felt betrayed by Lisa's desertion. She and Jim talked together secretly about leaving the house and going off to somewhere 'more committed', but Phoebe could not bring herself to give up the only home she knew of, could not bring herself to choose absolutely Jim's commitments over the women's commitments. Jim did not seem to be there enough for them to talk it through and neither of them had any money. The women were there, there talking, struggling, excited, engaged and angry.

Jim got fed-up coming home, weary and sensing that things were going increasingly wrong, to find the women talking late into the night, ignoring him, even asking him to go away, to go to his own room, to mind his own business.

They fought. Jim was better at that than Phoebe was, and inside herself she sulked. He was actually far more articulate, better informed. She had no clarity to toss in his face as he tossed 'bourgeois deviation' and Engels in hers. At first, after their early fights, Phoebe would work on making peace, leave the women to be with him, offer herself in ever more elaborate rituals, but after a while repetition made this boring. Phoebe ceased even to bother to calm him down, to open herself to him. After months of weeping and shouting and apologising, she did not care enough. Sometimes they fought and sometimes they fucked and there seemed little difference between the two.

The house was escalatingly filthy and anarchic. It was not fun any more. The miners were defeated and so were they. And somehow in that cold and confused spring, somewhere in some loveless and last sexual act, Phoebe got pregnant.

By the time she realised what had happened, Jim had departed. Packed his bags and gone. It had in the end been a spectacular departure; Phoebe's final fling with overpowering emotion. He had told her that he had started sleeping with someone else, a 'real woman', he had said rashly. And although, now, twenty years later, she could understand his hurt and confusion and desire for revenge, then it had hit her squarely in all the areas she was most vulnerable. She had quite literally thrown herself at him, she had bitten him in the neck so hard that he had bled, she had scratched his face and torn his clothes. A new ferocious Phoebe, a Phoebe for one brief glorious moment allied to all those mad bad women, Jael and Charlotte Cordet and Boadicea; to Lilith and the Greek Furies and the terrifying armies of the Amazons.

But he would not fight back.

'For heaven's sake, Bea,' he said, 'grow up.'

She knew that if he wanted to he could have killed her; without apparent effort he held off her attack once the first shock had past. His reasoned calm defeated her. She looked only stupid. A stupid child in a tantrum. A child whose father had never allowed the tantrums, who had held rational behaviour out as the price of his love. There was no space anywhere, even here, even in this free world, she thought, which they had so boldly created, for wildness. All that got you was humiliation.

Jim had stomped downstairs wiping the blood off his face with a handkerchief and later it had been Jo and Lisa who had packed his bags and told him never to come back to the house.

When she realised that she was pregnant, her one clear emotion was that he should not know. She would never allow him a reason to pity her again, to hold her in contempt. It was one of the more simple reasons why she denied the pregnancy, even to herself, for so long.

Now her memory refused the whole thing; simply refused to countenance the next few months. Phoebe could remember no details, could recall only with an effort that was profitless, the numbing passivity that had fallen on her.

She had never convinced herself of the reality of her pregnancy, she had never done anything about it. She kept the pregnancy to herself – or rather kept it from herself, and from everyone else, for too long.

Now, quite suddenly, Phoebe was wide awake again. She sat bolt upright in her bed and said aloud,

'Damn,' and then, 'damn, damn, damn.' She was meant to be thinking about happy things. She was meant to be persuading herself that life was worth living. Why was she so damn slow? Why had she not made connections between the secrecy, the silent, passively gloomy, growing of Maggie inside herself and this new, equally secret, growth? Why had she not made the connection and what, in any case, was the connection?

She lay down on her back again, almost smelling the sharp odour of the whisky; just awake enough to resist it, just sleepy enough not to make the climb out into the cold worth it, and felt numb with fear. Lying there she was aware for the first time that night of Maggie above her and Rachel below her; both, she imagined, sleeping sweetly, and again the grinding weight of compassion and guilt swept over her. She cannot mother her child and she cannot mother her mother; everything she did inclined towards death. What would happen to these two women who had done nothing to deserve her evil body and heart between them, what would happen to them when she was dead? Had she simply had Maggie so that someone, somewhere, would have to love her and take care of her?

At one level, of course, it had worked, because throughout her pregnancy Rachel had been carefully and systematically nice to her. Rachel would appear, warm and generous, with smiles and a determination to be friendly and tolerant. Rachel had been, apparently, more relieved that Phoebe should be an unmarried mother than that she should have to have Jim as a son-in-law. Lisa, who had first noticed this oddity in Rachel, had found it hilarious, had even teased Rachel about it directly. But Phoebe had felt a harsh jealousy that she did not like in herself when she realised how well Lisa and Rachel got on: she did not want that. She wanted somehow to have her mother for herself, but only so that she could reject her herself. She did not want Lisa to have any part of Rachel, and she did not want Rachel to have any part of Phoebe.

Almost in tears, Phoebe took her breast in her hand and squeezed and banged at it until it hurt. In the pain there was both forgetfulness and satisfaction, just as there had been when Maggie was born.

Her labour, at least, stood out sharp and clear.

The pregnancy itself was lost in a fog. There had been the long drift through cold spring into hot summer; the long sinking into the mercies and bossiness of her friends and thence into the arms of the medical profession; the final humiliation of accepting, because she was too inert to refuse, money from Rachel. She remembered indistinctly the sense of her body being gradually taken over and pumped full of something that was not Phoebe. She had experienced mounting terror at the thought of a new role in which she would certainly prove a failure – a woman who could not do her work, could not save her father, could not love her mother, could not satisfy her man, was most unlikely to make any sort of mother.

Then rising like dawn from the mist, the pain was utterly and entirely real. So, with it, was the focused love of her friends. They had not approved of the baby; they had thought Phoebe negligent at best for getting pregnant and not taking appropriate action; they had chivvied her through the later months of her pregnancy with a mixture of indulgence and irritation, cross both that she was pregnant and that she wasn't taking it seriously. Lisa and Jo had taken her to clinics, booked her in with midwives, read up on birth technology, warned her about smoking; and all with an air of adult exasperation towards a wayward child.

But when the pain came they were there. A little scared, since they were then all very young and had believed the stuff about painless childbirth, and a little over-excited by their own courage and naughtiness, but completely present for her – not as grown-ups to a child, but as women. It was in the pain that she found their love and tested it and found it so true that the bond would never break.

A night, a nightmare of pain. A night, a nightdream of love. Inseparable. A period of almost literally climbing the walls, turning away from the world and kneeling up, holding the end of the iron hospital bed, and Lisa's hand firmly on the pain, firmly on the small of her back pressing, pressing, pressing away the pain and the fear, keeping her in contact. A long plateau in which the never-ending surrealism of pain muted down into boredom and there was Jo laughing bravely, veiling her fear and doing great lines from *Gone with the Wind* in a deplorably bad imitation of a southern black accent.

Staying was the point; they stayed there with her and that enabled her to stay there with them. And even then her flesh would not give up its alien growth without a struggle. She went down too far, too far into the riding waves of pain, deep under water and drowning. The midwife muttered her spells, and from far away Phoebe could hear voices calling her, siren voices that called her back to the pain and the reality. Not angry but loving calls, which the midwife tried to hush because she had never encountered young women who could yell abuse so lovingly;

'Bea, you goddam asshole, just try. Lazy bitch.'

Phoebe, knowing the strength and command of Lisa, was comforted and, in some other place, almost amused to hear the midwife shocked, ordering Lisa to be more gentle. There was no gentleness like Lisa's fierce love; and she tried to respond to that while another darker voice called her to unconsciousness and silence. In the end she saw the giant fish-hooks come down down into her and she thought they would haul her out of the depths, but they did not. They had not come to rescue her, but the child whom Phoebe would not let be born. Forceps hurt.

Then suddenly everyone was no longer concerned for her as she lay there, but for another woman; a tiny fierce woman whose fault it had all not been and Lisa's gigantic, striding power melted into softness, soppy for the baby.

'Ah, Bea, look – just look.'

But she had turned her face to the wall.

Guilt and exhaustion is what she had felt for the next year. Everyone adored Maggie. She had seen that instantly the next afternoon; in

Rachel's eyes she recognised the same melting joy as she had seen in Lisa's. And she loved Maggie, too: how could one not? How could one fail to love a small person so infinitely resolute to follow her own path? How could one not admire a woman so clear as to her needs that she did not care whose flesh she carved her way through, who did not care whose sleep she shattered in the small hours of the dawn? How could one refuse tenderness to someone so frail and tiny, to someone whose bones one could break with the flick of wrist, to someone who greeted one with smiles and later whoops of purest delight, who wept if one left them, and would die if one neglected them? But she, who had run fifteen thousand miles to find her freedom, she who had driven Jim out of the house rather than wash his dirty teacups, was now a slave to someone who never washed their cups, who was never interested in her ideas, who never wanted to talk, hear, understand, sympathise, who hurt one's body as no one had ever hurt it before and who chained one forever to mountains, not just of washing-up, but of washing itself.

The launderette was two and a half blocks from the house; probably less than three hundred yards. Six nappies, even wet ones, did not weigh that much, and there were others who were willing to help. In the launderette it was warm and cosy; here Maggie made friends and fans and she had inconsequential conversations which mysteriously made her a member of the local community in a way she had never been when she had been fighting for the area's well-being.

None the less, throughout the autumn and the cold winter that followed, those three hundred yards became three hundred years each and every time, the sign of her defeat, the sign of her capture – she felt herself a wild animal tamed and she devoted herself to Maggie with what appeared to be maternal passion mainly because she felt guilty at her lack of joy in it.

Maggie, it quickly emerged, induced a turning of mood in the rest of them. Rachel was kinder and gentler towards her than she had ever been before; but she also required Phoebe to take responsibility for the baby, to be a good mother, to take heed for the morrow. Phoebe could accept that, it was how grandmothers were meant to be, but when she turned to her friends, looking for guidance and inspiration, she did not find it. When it came to childraising, although they were libertarian towards the baby, they seemed conservative towards Phoebe's needs: demand feeding and endless devotion seemed to be required of her.

'You're behaving like a goddam husband,' she said sulkily one night.

Lisa looked startled, but was stern. 'I'm beginning to feel like one,' she said.

Lisa had got a proper job at last, as though tired of waiting for the Revolution.

'Look, Bea, I feel like a shit as a matter of fact, but I can't live like this – this little ghetto, where feelings are the most important thing in the world. I want to get out there. I want a decent job, I want to do something useful, and something interesting. I'm not and I never have been a hippy, I can't just "hang out" any more. That bit is over now.'

Phoebe felt accused, felt useless. She also felt worn out, oppressed by the cold scruffiness of the house, and the energy of her friends. She tried making friends with other women who had children, exploring ways of shared childcare; but faith was not enough, they were bogged down by impossible travel arrangements, endless irresponsibility and hopeless public transport. She had no money.

Rachel proposed an alternative. Rachel wanted to move to London, and thought that perhaps they could share a house.

'Not share it, Phoebe, split it. You'd be independent and I could babysit for Maggie. You could get out more, it would be good for you, darling.'

Phoebe said to Lisa, 'If I go and live with her it will be the end. I'm a sucker for middle-class comforts. I'm not tough enough to toe the line.'

'Oh Bea,' said Lisa affectionately, 'Don't be such a puritan.' Lisa adored Rachel, which frequently made Phoebe cross.

Lisa however was full of her own schemes. She had gone to work first for a radical magazine, perched in a cramped office behind Kings Cross. When she had acquired a range of basic editing skills she started looking round for what to do with them. Soon she aligned herself with a small group of women who wanted to break into publishing.

'We need to control it Bea; why should those fat cats get rich off our books?'

'What books? Shiny hardbacks for middle-class feminists. Masses of American theory and no socialism.'

'We could do better, then. What books do we need?'

Phoebe was seduced suddenly. 'Well, some decent history for one thing, I suppose. And some fiction; women must be writing better books than they seem to be publishing.'

'There you are, you see. You, the Women's Movement, on the street and in the home, need me!'

They forgot briefly that they were having a fight; instead they had a happy half-hour of fantasy about what books they could write and read and live with.

Phoebe said finally, 'OK, OK. But we'll all be so busy reading all this wonderful stuff, and learning from the big bad world about how to market it, that we won't have time to do anything else.'

'Look,' said Lisa, 'I never thought that the Women's Liberation Movement would be spread by word, rather than action, but that is how it is.'

'Only if we let it be.'

'No there are skills; we need those skills.'

'You'll have to wear a skirt to the office.'

'Don't be silly.'

Lisa had a good degree from some northern university and had little trouble finding herself a job in a proper publishing house – 'Biding my time,' she said laughing. 'You wait.'

What Phoebe had realised quickly was that Lisa liked working. Lisa had a passion for working. And at first it was nice because there was more money coming into the house, and they could feed the gas monster and have hot water and fires. But Lisa had less time for her, and was meeting new people, refining a way of living that even a year ago she would have claimed to despise. Phoebe could not, try as she might, despise it for her, because it was so obviously making Lisa happy; while she, clinging to a nostalgic and increasingly sentimental vision of the household, was patently not happy, not useful, and not passionate. She felt envious, but unable to change. She could not find in herself any source of passion. Jo and Sophie were working too. Phoebe began to feel like a housewife. There she was, ably supported by active and intelligent people while she sat at home feeling cold and tired and guilty.

That winter Maggie did not flourish. She seemed little and mingy, pale and tight. She coughed, and when her nose was plugged up it was difficult for her to suck properly; she cried to be fed all through the night and Phoebe got more and more tired, more and more passive and despairing and guilty.

In the spring, almost without knowing how it happened, she accepted Rachel's invitation to go and live with her in the new house she was buying in London.

The day she moved in she knew she had been defeated, that love, love for her mother and for her daughter, had defeated her. The passion she had tried to feel for feminism was not enough, it did not give her enough strength to stand up for herself against the demands of these two women who wanted her, needed her and demanded her.Even Lisa thought the move was a good idea.

Phoebe was now wide awake again and irritated with herself. She did not feel she was doing very well in her attempt to persuade herself that her life was full of joys and worth living. Without turning on the light she sat up and reached for her bottle and glass, faintly alarmed to discover she could find them both by feel alone. Her friends did not think of her as a drunk and Rachel would be truly shocked if she knew about the long nights of insomnia and secret alcohol. She was shocked herself, but that shock was muted by the greater shock of realising that even now she was not certain that she would keep the appointment she had made for the morning. Shocked and ashamed.

Of course, the fourteen years since she had moved into the Bayswater house had not been years of unremitting misery and depression. Soon after they had moved in Maggie and she, too, had begun to thrive. Rachel was undeniably wonderful with the baby; and took such joy from having Maggie with her that it was impossible for even Phoebe to feel much guilt about the times when she was free. As Maggie became more settled, and ate and slept better, Phoebe's own health and energy returned, and with it a determination to get some sort of job and pay for her own keep. Oddly she never felt the least guilt in accepting money from Rachel to help her bring up Maggie.

She had scrambled through the middle years of the decade. At first she had scraped a more or less adequate living as a free-lance journalist. She did not require a lot of money, would indeed have despised it. She was only half aware that Rachel was heavily subsidising her rent, because she was living in a part of London and a sort of house so different from her friends that she had no easy comparisons. Feminism was, briefly, news, and women feature writers were welcome. Phoebe was good at looking into things, she discovered; never brilliant, but perfectly competent.

Then for a couple of years she helped set up a women's bookshop and café run on high but unmanageable collective principles. Initially it seemed quite exciting to her, but she quickly realised that she was unable to care with the intensity felt by the other members of the group. She did not believe that it was going to change the world or that every minute detail was worth the drama and emotionalism that the others seemed to want to pour into it. Maggie became an excuse to leave the endless collective meetings early. Afterwards she knew that she had tried, but had not tried very hard. She had not tried hard enough because she did not care enough. She resigned finally from the co-operative over a minor political skirmish about which rooms in the shop would be open to men. She felt a superficial moral righteousness and a profound fear about her own boredom.

Both her mother and Lisa had been cross with her; they both had felt she ought to settle down. She felt infantilised by them, but also felt bitterly that they were not fair, and she was bored and frightened at the thought of remaining bored all her life. She went vaguely back to occasional journalism and found it increasingly difficult to sleep in the evenings and get up in the mornings.

One evening Rachel invited her to dinner, to meet some old family friends who had recently retired from academia and moved to London. Rachel and Phoebe did not often invite each other to formal meals, although they often ate together with Maggie. Rachel's friends had, as usual, been charming. They remembered Phoebe from Oxford days, and she could not fail to notice their thinly veiled compassion for Rachel that her brilliant daughter should have turned out so odd, so unsatisfactory. Somehow, somewhere, she got the impression that they were congratulating themselves on Martin and Rachel's failure; on their very irresponsible approach to Phoebe's education. They were obviously delighted to be able to use Phoebe to prove their conviction that child stars burn out if they are not raised to be as dull as anyone else's children. Had they been jealous, thirty years ago in Oxford, of the young Phoebe's special status? Phoebe now wondered, with an inner smile, remembering the evening when, aged about twelve, the master of her father's college had rearranged the high table to make her his senior guest. Certainly they now boasted insistently of the marital bliss of their daughter and the solid Civil Service progress of their son. She felt more at her ease realising that long ago had they had probably minded bitterly that the Petheringtons' little daughter had been so much more extraordinary than their own. She felt furious on her father's behalf and oddly compassionate on her mother's. In inviting her Rachel had proclaimed the absolute acceptability to her of her daughter even though she knew that Rachel did not feel this.

Because feeling grateful towards Rachel made her uncomfortable, she turned her attention to the other guests, a couple of solid neighbours whose grandchildren played in Kensington Gardens with Maggie during the holiday visits. The mixture of gratitude and discomfort made Phoebe unusually charming and civil. The husband, a gentle and kindly man, had recently had a minor stroke. His doctor had told him to ease up. He confided to Phoebe that what made him sad was his garden.

'Planned it for years to give me pleasure in my retirement and now it's just getting into a mess. Amy won't do it and I can't find anyone even to come in and keep it tidy.'

'Can't, Graham, not won't,' said his wife.

'I know, dear,' said Graham and they exchanged a pair of smiles so sweet and affectionate that Phoebe, despite herself, suddenly liked them.

But the Oxford guest said, 'You'd think with all this unemployment . . . there seem to be an extraordinary number of people around who don't want to work.' He gave Phoebe a sly look.

She really only said it to annoy these old friends of her mother's. She said, 'I'm free-lance; any job is a job. I'm reasonably fit. If you'll teach me I'll come and work for you a few hours a week.'

Amy smiled and said, 'It's hardly the job for a socialist-feminist revolutionary, Phoebe. Tidying up rich people's gardens.'

At any other time Phoebe would have thought she was being mocked and taken offence. Now, dazzled, she realised that Amy was in fact praising Phoebe's commitments, on her side rather than on the side of the pompous arrogant ex-professor. She grinned back.

'I don't know. We could call it community work, couldn't we.'

'Yes, indeed. Or rehabilitation for old age pensioners.'

Graham joined in, 'I'll find out what the union rates are tomorrow. TGWU?'

Even Rachel was willing to share the subterranean joke. She broke off her conversation and said,

'Better make it NUPE, Phoebe, much more radical.'

'But worse paid.'

'Anyway,' said Graham, 'I do draw the line at being described as "public". Perhaps I shall ask the farm workers' union. They're bound to have the lowest rates.'

'And no London weighting,' added Amy.

'True,' said Phoebe, 'but I'd probably get to be a Union Official immediately, owing to the lack of competition in the Bayswater Chapel, and then Graham would have to give me endless paid hours off to attend to Union Business.'

Rachel said courteously to her other guests, 'Any suggestions then? What do the rest of us pay our servants these days? Twelve pounds a year and a free uniform?'

The professor's wife said something about how difficult and expensive it was to get a good cleaning woman, and the professor responded uneasily, insensitively, aware that he was not getting the respect he was used to in his Senior Common Room. He started blustering about the general election and an end to the inflationary spiral. But when Graham left later, with something of the earlier benignity still binding him and Phoebe together, he had asked,

'Were you serious?'

'Why not?'

'I can't tell you how grateful I'd be.'

'No need. Shall I come about eleven next Wednesday?'

So by a collusive accident Phoebe had become a gardener.

Not all at once of course. At first she had just worked a couple of hours a week for Graham. What had surprised her was how much she enjoyed it. Graham was not just a kind elderly man, he was a passionate and knowledgeable gardener. He wanted her to do more than dig and weed. He wanted her to be interested. Soon she realised that he was singing her praises to his friends, because other similar garden owners rang her up and asked her if she could do a few hours for them too.

In her bedroom now, sipping her whisky, she acknowledged for the first time in her life that if she had to make a list of the happy times, it would properly have to include the hours she had spent with Graham in his garden. When he died six years later he left her all his gardening books: not just the technical instruction manuals, but coffee-table picture books, historical studies and a collection of exquisite, hand-tinted Victorian flower drawings, and a Beatrix Potter original which, she now knew, would keep Maggie in shoes for the rest of her childhood if Phoebe could have brought herself to sell it. It was the first personal bequest she had ever received, and the first time in years that she had cried.

About six months after the dinner party she realised that, for the first time in her life, she had turned down a decent journalistic commission in order to start work for a crazy old lady off Ladbroke Grove, whose garden specialised in old roses, and who was insistent about sterilising soil before new plantings.

A few months after that she had said to Rachel,

'Mummy, I'm thinking of going back to college.'

She shut her heart firmly against the look of incredulous joy that lit Rachel's face.

'Really, Phoebe? Where are you going?'

'Capel Hill, I should think.'

'Capel Hill?' And, then after a pause, in which she saw Rachel's joy cancelled out by fear, 'Is that in America?'

She had almost laughed. That was a plot against Rachel she had never thought of, to take up maths again but to do it in the USA. That would show the old bag. It was too late now though.

'No, it's in Enfield. I want to be a gardener. You do City and Guilds and those things there, and then the Council will employ you. GLC or DoE, or the Royal Parks people.'

Rachel had been nonplussed. Even now a ten-year-older Phoebe could not suppress her amusement. Rachel had wanted her to settle down to something, Rachel had wanted her to get some proper qualifications and chose a career. She had done so; Rachel had not known how to handle it then, and still did not know ten years later.

The memory of her own amusement encouraged Phoebe suddenly. There, she had been happy in Pakistan; she had been happy in the Peckham house at least for the first year; she had been happy working for Graham; she'd been enthusiastically interested at college and during the first two years after she had qualified; she had been completely delighted when she had got the job she now had: a tenants' association garden in a dreadful estate in Hackney, but where she, with a community group, had planned the garden from scratch and had made a small desert blossom like a rose.

All right then, she thought, her courage high, she had also been extremely happy while she was having her affair with Tom. It had simply been fun, the sort of fun she had with her women friends, except that she had also desired him, and he her. It had been splendidly undemanding; because of his family, she did not see him more than than a few times a month, always meetings snatched at short notice and with absolutely no expectation from him that she would be available. Apart from the holiday in Italy, they had not spent a whole night together more than half a dozen times in two years, and never at her home; always when they could find excuses for them both to be in other cities. Before she knew him she had never stayed in real hotels with private bathrooms taken for granted, and coloured TVs and room service for all guests.

She had met him at one of those dinner parties which had now become the nexus of her social life, replacing conferences and meetings, although few of the individuals had changed. One of those dinner parties which she loved and mocked almost equally, where people envy each other their success while feeling faintly guilty about their own. Friendship networks so old and intimate that the differences and difficulties could collapse into wild mirth at any instant, or could flare into fights which, however vicious at the time, would not actually change anything nor prevent her and all her friends coming together again soon after, at identical but different pine kitchen tables, scattered in a loose lop-sided circle around central London.

The detached, amused part of Phoebe sometimes thought that her main feeling at these parties was a wish that she, and everyone else too, would dare to improve the quality of the wine, but they were all too self-consciously afraid of being mistaken for Yuppies, despite the fact they were mostly a little too old and slightly too poor. Property prices and psychoanalysis were mentioned shyly, rather as Rachel might mention sex, but once in the air everyone turned out to be immensely knowledge-able about both, as well as about the contemporary cinema, the wickedness of Thatcher's government and the perils of current educational reforms. Those that had children struggled desperately to keep them within the state school system and also to see the frequent failures of others to succeed in this as being somehow a rather nasty disease, with compassion and sorrow the appropriate response, rather than the fierce bell-like anger they would all have produced reflexively only ten years before.

Another part of Phoebe hated herself for this cynical internal grin, because these were her friends and she was indubitably one of them, and could not imagine being otherwise.

She and Tom had met because they had had a playful debate about whether and in what sense you could say that coal pre-dated miners.

'Of course,' said Phoebe, showing off a little, 'miners come before coal. That's what Engels is trying to say, all that stuff about there not being mines and machinery in Siberia, where the natural circumstances ought to favour it, but only in England.'

Tom grinned an enormous grin across the table and said, 'You're cheating, because a) what are your natural circumstances if it's not the very existence of coal, b) I don't believe Engels said it at all and, c) even if he did, that doesn't make it true because he was working with an outmoded scientific model. New physics and astronomy have done for all that. In the beginning there was carbon, and after several generations of Super Novae there was the solar system and then there were a whole lot of trees and they all fell down plonk into bogs and got turned into coal, and that led to the dinosaurs and that led to the mammals and that led to humans and that led to the miners.'

Phoebe was impressed; she laughed with pleasure and said, 'And it's all in God's purpose and plan, eh? Then he got peevish and decided on a rain storm and the dinosaurs were so overgrown that they wouldn't fit into the ark so the flood destroyed them all. Seriously, coal doesn't exist outside of a market condition, OK? and you can't have a market condition without someone to extract the damn stuff. Hence, miners first, coal second. QED.'

They looked at each other quizzically, trying to decide how much emotion the other was prepared to invest in this. Did they really want to argue? Clearly they each believed there was a real issue, and that the other was intelligent enough to pursue it. Phoebe decided to give it a go. She gave him a tentative smile, suggesting, she hoped, her pleasure in the game and drew a breath, when he said.

'Oh my God, I know who you are. It's that let's-get-on-with-it expression. Hell.'

She was totally baffled. Please, not Goa in 1969, she thought. Please, let it not be some man she had slept with and now could not even remember ever having seen before in her life.

He had attracted the attention of the rest of the table. He was suffused with laughter.

'This woman is the first woman who ever beat me at chess. In Cambridge, twenty years ago. You cannot imagine how furious I was. She made the first breach in my armourplating of male superiority. Where the hell have you been ever since? I have a debt to pay off and I still want to beat you.'

'You would now. I haven't played for years.'

'Good. You have changed though, that sweet little fringe and those neat pearl earrings.' He smiled, 'It's OK, you don't have to pretend you remember me; this instant recall is but an outward symbol of the soul-scarring effect you had on me. I was just one of those Tweedledum and Tweedledee corduroy-jacket-wearing chess buffs who hung around the club. Women were rather more conspicuous. Why did you stop playing?'

'A long story,' she said, 'I'll tell you sometime.'

She heard the invitation, the promise of a future, in her voice and was surprised. However when the party broke up and he offered her a lift home, she was quick to negotiate secretly with her hostess for her bike to remain unmentioned in the stairwell until she came back the next day to collect it.

He drove well and efficiently. She watched his profile in the dark car and it pleased her, soft floppy hair and a decent nose. He seemed relaxed and simple. They chatted impersonally about the dinner and how they each came to know their hosts. When he stopped outside her house he said,

'We must meet again. We've got unfinished business, you and I.'

'Chess or miners?'

'Both.'

'You could come in now and have some coffee.'

'Unfortunately I have to get home. But I'll come another time, please.'

'Come on Saturday afternoon? We can play chess and I could probably correct your anti-materialist views on the coal industry in a matter of moments.'

He laughed, 'Mine anti-materialist? Mine are materialist; yours are mystical-Marxism, the opiate of the middle classes. Actually I can't come on Saturday, I have family commitments. What about one evening next week?'

'Are you married?' she asked him abruptly.

'Yes,' he said, 'do you mind?'

'Funnily enough, I think I do. I suppose your wife doesn't understand you.'

'On the contrary, she understands me very well and I'm still free to play chess.'

'Thank God for that,' she laughed. 'Come next Wednesday if you can. You can meet my daughter.'

'Are you divorced?'

'No,' she said, and watched a tiny nervous flicker on his face. 'I'm only not divorced because I was never married. I have a delightful little bastard who can chaperone a long-delayed revenge match.'

'You're on.'

She opened the door of the car and climbed out. She knew perfectly well she was going to make love to him sometime, so there did not seem to be any hurry. She waved happily as he drove off.

He beat her easily at chess the following week, but when he came again she had been thinking and remembering. After a long game in the kitchen which ended in a draw, they went upstairs and made love. He was undemanding, unemotional, light-hearted and pleasing to her. Once Phoebe had started playing chess regularly again she realised she could probably have become considerably better than him quite quickly, but she did not want that enough to work on it. They played together a couple of evenings every month, but after that first time by mutual consent they never made love in her house, any more than they did in his. He and Maggie got on well and he was calmly nice to Rachel.

Phoebe tried to build up a little guilt about his wife but failed to do so. Because she never had to be his lover in front of Maggie or Rachel she had no need to worry about that either. Occasionally she could see a gleam in

Rachel's eye, as though she might suddenly ask him if his intentions were honourable, but for the first time in her life she learned to be grateful for her mother's good manners.

He was fun. He would turn up at her garden with a picnic in the late afternoons, laying out a white cloth, champagne and strawberries under the shadow of the tower block and the bemused scrutiny of the local youth. He would stay for just an hour or so and then gather up the equipment and disappear.

When he was working out of London she would join him. She saw more of England driving with him in his car, or walking through cities while he attended to business, then she ever had before. He planned carefully so that there was always time and no panic. And she loved his body, the astringent unsweaty cleverness of it, that gave with delight and asked for so little back.

Their Italian holiday had been different, a tiny golden time, snatched out of nowhere and more than either of them deserved. Last spring he had said,

'I have to be in Rome for six weeks. It'll be so hot I thought I might rent a place in the country, but it might be a waste of money. Julia and the kids are going to her parents in Cumbria. What do you think?'

Phoebe went skiing early every spring. She had learned as a girl and given herself a week's holiday for a thirtieth birthday present. The extreme delight of it had almost shocked her; it was her one personal extravagance. Now she thought that she could give it up for three weeks in the Italian sun.

'I don't see why not.'

'Bring Maggie,' he said, 'she'll love it. I'll find you somewhere with a pool.'

'Tom, can I afford that?'

'I shouldn't think so,' he said, 'not all of it, but I need it too and can write if off as expenses.'

'Cor,' she mocked in her best cockney accent, 'kept woman now, Phoebe Petherington, you ought to be ashamed of yourself.'

He seemed to find that adequate gratitude.

So he found them a tiny cottage just south of Orvieto, in the grounds of the villa of some Italian friends of his who had departed for the northern mountains, a villa with a pool and a shady veranda along one side and an unspeakably romantic view down the steep hillside towards the floating cathedral. She had taken Maggie off to the sunshine.

She had not travelled for pleasure since she had come home from her long sojourn and she had wiped out of her memory the simple delights of hot sun and cheap wine. She had risen at dawn each day, when the sky was still apricot-coloured and swum naked and alone as the sun rose. She had lain with Maggie beside the swimming pool and had let her whole body soak up the sun. Tom spent the weekends with them and drove up many afternoons from Rome to dine with them and stay overnight. He took them for drives, showing her the extraordinary beauties of Umbria. It was hot and gentle; Maggie was playful and contented.

One day she would remember forever. It had been another perfect morning. She had woken earlier even than usual, with Tom beside her, sleeping contentedly and openly on his back. Knowing it impossible to sleep again, she had lain there for a while and listened to the silence of sleep throughout the house. Then she got up, half cross to be awake when other people were still sleeping and half pleased with the intensity of quiet and peace. Downstairs she made herself a cup of coffee and carried it out onto the patio and drank it at the table, smoked a loose-rolled sweet Italian cigarette, and watched the coming of the dawn. She had swum, very conscious of the water, cooler after the night, swallowing her into itself and the darkness retreating before the splashes of her arms and legs. The sky would begin to change from grey to silver gilt, then peach, but still the sun did not rise.

After swimming she had felt completely alive and glad to be awake and have this time of her own, which had been a gift to her from Tom and Maggie. She had gone for a walk up the road, beside a field of sunflowers, and although the sun had not yet risen she could sense the whole field turning away from her and each flower raising its face towards the eastern hills over which the sun would shortly leap. She had felt the whole silent movement of that field, each straining golden head, instinctively, blindly, passionately turning towards the light. And equally instinctively, she had turned with them, leaving the road and taking a cart track along the upper side of the field. Above her the fields rose steeply, rough grass and scattered olive trees, which in that light looked immovably ancient and grotesque. Below her the muttering sunflowers continued their ghostly and invisible movement. Suddenly, the track fell away sharply, in front of her feet, and she felt before she saw the expanded horizon. She had looked up; and like the sunflowers she was facing right into the heart of the brightness which preceded the sun. The eastern mountains looked black and shapely, silhouetted against that great apricot-coloured fire. She had been on the very edge of the steep hills which surround the basin in which Orvieto sits; and the basin itself was alive and moving, swirling with smoke, with smoky white mists which filled it almost to the brim. Then and there the sun rose abruptly and she could see the city, bright and sunlit, floating on the mists, a magic city of mediaeval romance.

That sleeping peaceful beauty had been almost too much for her. Only a couple of days before Maggie had pointed out how the great cathedral dominated the city, like the spines along a dragon's back, while the other buildings lay in a rough sprawl. She had laughed then at the vivid imagination of the child, but now for a brief moment she saw the city as Maggie saw it, basking in the first rays of the sun and oblivious to the dangerous mist below that might suck it in before it could wake up and take wing against the now blue blue sky.

Then far away, only emphasising the silence, a cock had crowed, shrill and certain. With both laughter and irritation Phoebe had returned to consciousness ironically amused at how nature could behave with such excessive romanticism.

But the day had insisted on playing itself out in the idyllic pastoral mode. Tom, when he woke later had insisted that they should absorb some culture, had chivvied them both into his car and driven them first to the Villa Lante.

'You'll love the garden, Bea,' he insisted when she had looked longingly, lazily, at the swimming pool. 'It's one of my favourites. It was built by a series of cardinals as a hunting lodge.'

'I don't like those high Renaissance gardens much,' she said, though unaggressively. 'There are never enough flowers, only designs. And I'm meant to be on holiday. Gardens are work for me, not leisure.'

'You'll like this one,' he said firmly, 'partly because of the water; it all flows downwards, the whole garden works its way downwards. And also you'll like it because the house had to be split into two separate halves – the garden takes priority over domestic comfort. And also you'll like it because the cardinal who designed it was a practical joker and built in all sorts of extremely infantile jokes so that he could spray water onto his innocent friends while they were eating their dinner or trying to watch little masques. You will like it very much.'

'Is that an order?' she teased him, but indicated her consent by beginning to search for her shoes.

'No,' he said, hugging her, 'It's a present.'

She laughed and accepted his gift. And he had been right. She did like the garden, its delicate wit and gentle scale. They had walked up the worn stone staircase, arm in arm, with their beautiful girl child dancing around them. And Phoebe was so relaxed that it actually amused her to realise

151

that everyone who saw them would assume they were a boring married couple, English middle-class tourists.

Afterwards they had eaten lunch and then despite the heat had started home. Then on the way back he had suddenly turned to Maggie and said,

'That was a garden for your mother, now I have one for you.'

He wouldn't tell them anything more, but drove by tiny back roads, through impossibly steep villages to the grotesque gardens of Bomarzo. He had scarcely known Maggie, could not have known that he could not have chosen a better treat than this mysterious park, with its vast statues carved out of the living rock: the huge-mouthed cave with its mighty teeth, the vast stone giant, his shoulders visible through bushes a hundred yards away, half hidden in greenery; and above all, the great carved stone dragon with its broken wings, and wild Chinese eyes. The three of them entered a place outside time, on a day of such stillness and heat.

Later that evening they had been sitting in a restaurant and Maggie had looked at Tom and said, her delicate face and long neck almost visibly aquiver with pleasure,

'Thank you.'

'What for?' he had looked almost startled by her vehemence.

'For the nicest day in my whole life.'

Phoebe, her body content and her mind rested, had heard her daughter without a flicker of guilt, or envy, simply with affection.

Would she have enjoyed him so much if she had thought the whole thing permanent? she asked herself sternly now, sitting up in bed and shaking off the poppy and mandragora effect that thinking about that summer had on her. Would she even have started the relationship if she had not been reasonably certain that in the end he would not leave his wife? Perhaps not, but she did not care. Who had been the loser? On paper, she had; and perhaps his wife. He had, in the classic language of such things, had his cake and eaten it too. But what was she supposed to have lost? Nothing that mattered to her.

That, of course, had been the rub. She had not cared enough. He told her so at the very end.

Just after Christmas she had travelled up to Birmingham after work one evening, to spend the night with him. The weather had been bitter, she had been tired and stiff. Sitting on the train she had suddenly thought that it was not worth it. She could have been at home, warm and snug. She could have been at Lisa's house, laughing. She could have been alone with the dark shadow in her breast, nourishing it quietly and secretly. But

Tom and she would go skiing at the end of the month. It would not be damp and she would not be so weary. She tried to jolly herself into enthusiasm.

Their moods did not meet that night. He was ebullient, excitable, verbal, and passionate.

'I'm tired, Tom.'

'My sweet love, you're tired a great deal too often. Are you well?'

The tide of her secret lapped around her; soon she would be too tired all of the time. Soon she would lie down in the arms of a stronger lover than Tom would ever be and fall asleep. The thought of being so discovered made her careful. She put her arms round his neck and said, 'Come to bed and hold me tight.'

Hopefully as well as affectionately, he did so; undressing her as she lay on the too-large hotel bed and stroking her shoulders and upper arms. He never ceased to be amazed by her physical strength.

'Why don't you look muscly?'

'I've told you. These are real muscles, not the detachable falsies you get in the gym.' She was rather proud of herself and could not suppress the smug tone of voice.

He smiled. 'Real breasts too. No detachable falsies these.'

If he had been less aroused he wouldn't have done it; if he had been more aroused he wouldn't have noticed. He ran his hand half playfully, half seductively round her left breast and then stopped. The whole room stopped. Her whole life stopped. His hand felt rigid, and then his thumb moved delicately.

'Don't,' she said sharply, and sat up.

'Darling,' he said. He reached out to her but she did not move into the offered harbour of his arms.

'Why didn't you tell me?'

'I suppose because I didn't want you to know.'

'What does your doctor say? What are you doing about it?'

She couldn't think of a lie quick enough. He just stared at her.

'Are you insane?'

After another long silence he said,

'Bea . . . I'll leave Julia. I'll come and live with you. Please.'

'No.'

'Is that why you didn't tell me, because you were thinking of me, of her . . .'

'No. I didn't tell you because I knew we'd have a scene like this and I don't like it.

'Of course we're having a scene like this. I love you, Bea, you know that.' He tried to lighten his mood, grinning at her like a schoolboy, 'Apart from anything else we could make love at breakfast-time, lunch-time and tea-time.'

He had found out her secret and she hated him. She said, 'Apart from anything else I can't imagine any sex worth giving up tea-time for.' As soon as she had said it she knew that it was true and that made her sadder and crosser. But he looked so hurt that she tried to make a joke of it,

'You know me. I adore crumpets; and I loathe romanticism and that "all for love and the world well lost" stuff. I've loved you because I like relationships to be comfortable and not too much hard work, and sex to be civilised. I prefer doing the crossword puzzle anyway. You've never made scenes and I don't want them.'

But although they both tried to smile still, neither of them failed to notice the past tense she had used for the word 'love'.

'You'll never want anything of me, will you?'

'Well, not dramas, and miserable marriage breakups and guilt and scenes and deathbed proclamations certainly,' she had replied. 'Nor have you wanted them from me. You'd never have stayed around so long if I'd pushed you about.'

He had not quite known what he wanted to say. He had not wanted a drama, demands, excitement, but he had somewhere wanted her at least to complain that he did not.

He said almost sulkily, 'I've been behaving badly for two years, and you know it, and you don't even mind.'

She knew what he meant, but she would not help him out. She was not going to have a fight with him. She would see him occasionally for the rest of her life, and she wanted to be able to chat to him, invite him for more games of chess, more visits to historic gardens. She would never make love to him again, though. She did not care enough. She kissed the balding patch on the back of his head as she clambered off the bed and went to the fridge to pour them both a drink.

'You don't care, do you?' he said with amazement. 'I don't mean just about me; I mean you really don't care whether you live or die. I can't cope with that. You just don't care enough.'

They did not say that it was over, neither of them. They did not need to. She went on the skiing holiday he had paid for and accepted his excuse about his daughter's measles without a moment's hesitation.

She had thought it would be a pity not to have him around any longer: Rachel and Maggie both liked him and she had not told either of them

154

about his wife. She preferred such a relationship to a more driving one. She had always known she was devoid of passion: she worked at her garden and talked to her friends. It was all she would ever have. She missed him, and missed the companionable secrecy of their relationship, but she was not miserable about it. She was more miserable about not being miserable. She felt her inability to demand anything from him, to need to demand anything from him, was a mark of failure. She would have liked to fall in love with him.

And instead she had fallen in love with her own tumour. 'You must be insane,' he had said, and she was. All love was folly; a grand passion was madness. This was a love worth dying for, at last. And all these pleasures, these frail joys that her most stringent discipline over the last couple of night-time hours had summoned up for her memory, they were simply not enough. They were not worth living for.

Her mother had once told her scornfully about a crazy book produced on the contemporary new wave of evolutionary theory: a book which abandoned Darwin and returned to his predecessor, Lamark. Or rather, as Rachel had been at pains to point out, a misunderstanding of Lamark's theory of learned characteristics being inherited. The author of the book had argued that evolution was a product of desire: a wingless animal, unconsciously, wants to fly – it wills a wing, a pair or wings, or a longer neck to reach the trees, or swifter legs to escape its predators. It is this will which is inherited. The book claimed that cancer and other deformities were mistaken wills, were new organs to meet new needs dreamed up in the deep unconscious, and that therefore they should be treated not with surgery but with interest and affection – humanity was limiting its potential by cutting out the tumours, blasting the cells. Phoebe, like her mother, did not believe a word of it, but part of her knew it was true.

She had wanted to fall in love, she had willed it, and her body had produced the lover, close to her heart, fed by her own blood, watered by own needy greedy wanting. Secret and adored.

She knew it was not sane. She knew it was insane and dangerous, what she was doing. She knew it so clearly that three weeks ago she had made an appointment to take her breast lump to a doctor. But she had done it in a very peculiar way: she had booked in to a private Well Woman Clinic under an assumed name. The appointment was now for tomorrow. She was amazed at herself, but she had done it, and now in the early hours of the morning she did not know if, even so, she would go.

Who was he, this dark and secret lover who had inflamed her with so great a passion? Was he Death astride his dark charger, was Death the moment of consummation, the moment of glory?

'Tell me,' she commanded herself, 'tell me what is going on. What is this certainty?'

She was in a new place where she had never been before. She had run off with her lover to a new country which was strange and beautiful and dangerous. In this new place there was an orgasmic sweetness in the thought of dying. She was pierced to the heart and made alive with the consciousness of passion, of love, of choice . . . She had found a sweet lover where there had been no love. The patterns were broken because she had broken them. This love was a new pattern, a new Catastrophe Theory and she was happy in its embrace. She wanted the world to go away and let her live with her lover in a secret palace, give herself over to his embrace, to be beyond responsibility and care and hard work and sanity.

Her hand was caressing her own breast now, probing with such delicacy, feeling the hard resistance, the anger of her lover. Soon, soon if she has the courage, it will not matter, it will be too late for anyone to protest, to come to her with sensible and sound advice. Soon, soon her lover will take over her whole body forcing his way deeper than any lover before – not just into her vagina, or, like Jim's sperm, further in to her womb. This lover will penetrate every corner of her body, her lymph nodes, her spine, her lungs, kidneys, liver, brain. This lover will be irresistible and she will be taken over entirely by him. She has only to consent, to be passive, to welcome him and he will take her home, will welcome her into his kingdom and his kingdom will be her flesh.

But she did not consent.

'No,' she said aloud. 'No.'

'Why not?' he asked sweetly.

She wanted to say, 'Because of Maggie and Rachel and Lisa and the garden and duty and sunshine,' but alone in the darkness she did not believe in any of that.

'No.'

Suddenly, overpoweringly, she needed her mother, she needed to be taken in her mother's arms, like a little child and to be held there.

'It's four o'clock in the morning,' she told herself. 'You cannot wake up an old lady just to listen to your insane and morbid fantasies.'

But she knew that this was more important.

She had never asked Rachel for anything. It was difficult. Rachel was not an easy person to go to with such a strange and garbled fear. Rachel would try to be rational and calm. Rachel would not want to hear. But it was not to Rachel that she would go, but to her mummy.

She turned the light on and got out of bed. She was shaking with fear. The moment she spoke to Rachel the die would be cast, and she would have to go along the road of sensible health planning and operations and anxieties and reality. She would have say goodbye to passion and secret joy. She put her knickers on, and almost smiled, because even now she would not go to Rachel without them. She walked over to her door, practising the sentences with which she would wake Rachel.

'Mummy, wake up and listen to me.'

When her hand was on her doorknob she paused; the call of the dark was so strong, it slowed her movements down. He was calling her. Promising her. She wavered. Her hand tightened on the handle and she pushed down on it. Then she heard an enormous crash, a bomb exploding somewhere very near, a great roar of shattering glass and, after a moment's stillness, screaming, ear-splitting, horrible screaming, from just over her head.

Three

Maggie's room, her own place, had been made for her the summer she was eight by Phoebe, Paul and Uncle Wong. Lisa had helped and Rachel had encouraged. Even now Maggie remembered the making of it as a time of rare delight: when all the people of her life came together and did something for her. The result of such a burst of love and energy from such an assortment of individuals was inevitably extraordinary.

It was a magical room, carved out of the attic and reached only by a wrought-iron spiral staircase which Paul had rescued from some abandoned church. High above the house the room floated lightly. The ceiling sloped down tightly to the floor, making dark shadowy edges which were well nigh impossible to clean, and three odd narrow passages ran to the three dormer windows, which cast odd blocks of light into the main spaces of the room. But there was also a huge skylight, facing both ways and divided across the middle only by the roof beam of the house itself. By day light flooded the room and by night darkness, because no one had ever worked out a satisfactory way of curtaining these great expanses. Phoebe continually meant to buy blinds, blinds that would be ingeniously fitted into little runnels either side of the glass slopes, but it was one of those domestic chores that she had never managed to complete.

Maggie now slept on a low bed draped with a Chinese spread covered in dancing dragons and spinning suns, exactly underneath the centre of these windows, and on clear nights the moon rode over her head, and the clouds, illuminated a sickly yellow by the vastness of the city, would race past. Because there had never truly been enough height and the angle of the ceiling was so acute, nothing was ever quite symmetrical and balanced, and cupboards and wall space were eccentric and fortuitous. Maggie clung to the privacy of her room, as small children do to their teddy bears; she never invited her friends there, preferring to contain them in the large sitting-room below. This was her place, her secret place; hers and Fenna's.

The first night she had slept there she had known. It had taken only a little practice to discover how to lie there, flat on her back, and slowly, with great care, peel away the roof beam and open back the two vast panes of glass. Even from the beginning she had lain naked and adoring under the moon and Fenna could come and go as easily as the clouds did.

Fenna is Maggie's dragon.

Fenna is the one purely joyful thing in Maggie's life.

Fenna is flame and fire. Fenna moves at night.

Fenna is flame and fire, and moves on the wings of the night that are dragon-wings, to dance with taloned claws and mock at hopes of safety.

Fenna is the dark force of the imagination as well as its golden dancing; Fenna is chaos as well as order, and brings, on fiery dragon breath, the full danger of the chasm.

Maggie and Fenna belong to each other.

For Maggie, this is the primal sentence. Not the first words spoken, but from before the surfacing of memory she has known this. It is her first self-conscious sentence. It is the sentence around which she has shaped her identity.

To deny it is therefore impossible. To break it down is extremely difficult. Dangerous. The words will remain, indubitably. 'Maggie', 'Fenna'. There is no question about them. And 'each' and 'other'. 'To' as well. Maggie feels no doubt about that: so small a word, so small and so necessary a word is bound to survive, to slip through the net of destruction that she and Fenna – no, that she herself, alone – will loose on the cold sky tonight. But 'belong' – she is fearful that for her at least the word may explode, may vanish in a puff of smoke as delicate as the smoke that trickles from Fenna's nostrils when he is asleep; as delicate as the fronds of smoke that drift mysteriously from the end of Phoebe's cigarette when she gestures impatiently in conversation. Maggie might no longer belong, to anything or anyone, if she did not belong to Fenna.

Fenna accompanied Maggie into consciousness. There must have been a time before Fenna, just as there must have been a time before words, but Maggie cannot not conceive of either. How could it have felt to be lonely and dumb?

But at the same time Maggie was still young enough to hold two or more things in her mind, clear and contradictory. Her mind, like the women in her house, was still laid down in strata, each virtually impermeable to the others. All this about Fenna was entirely true, but she would not have said it, would not have known how to shape such sentences. If she were asked where Fenna had come from she would have told a quite different story: the story of the arrival of Fenna.

Her Uncle Wong, her grandmother's friend, who was now under a shadow so deep that without being told, Maggie knew she must not mention his name, her beloved Uncle Wong had given her Fenna. When she had been about five he had come to stay, returning from Hong Kong and, like other wise men from the east, he came bearing gifts. He had given her an egg; an orange egg about four inches long and made, of all things, of soap. She had felt disappointment waiting to pounce, but swiftly he had assured her it was a magic egg, that if she washed with it carefully it would hatch. She had for nearly a month washed fanatically, with all the clarity and determination of which five-year-olds are capable.

After about two weeks, long cracks had developed in the egg, lines of longitude. Even so young Maggie was not a child to cheat; it did not occur to her to prise the egg open, only to stay longer in the bath and to forget to take the soap out of the water, when she climbed out herself, pink and skinny. At last, from the thin end of the egg, a rounded point appeared, and, three evenings later, in the bath, the egg had suddenly split in half. Encased in the soap was a tiny green dragon. In one hand she held half the soap with the embedded dragon in high relief, its tiny green wings minutely scaled, its long head thrusting forward and its tail descending to the soft nobble which had first appeared. And in the other hand was the orange soap holding the shadow of a dragon, the clear and perfect indentation of a three-inch-long green plastic dragon.

After the careful brooding, she had hatched a dream. That was Fenna. She had shown him with pride to both her mother and grandmother and had carried him to bed more deeply satisfied than at any time since she had been weaned from Phoebe's now forgotten breasts.

For the next few days she had carried the tiny dragon everywhere. And then she had, as children do, lost him.

To comfort her desolation and guilt Rachel had told her about the Mongolian desert, where she had been as a little girl, hardly older than Maggie was now, to look for dragons, which she called dinosaurs, and where years later Russian palaeontologists had found the great fossil eggs in which the sleeping baby dinosaurs could still be seen. She told Maggie about the palace of the Princess Tang Li, north of Beijing, which she had visited with her own beautiful mother, Maggie's great-grandmother. In that place there had been intricate gardens, where water wheels turned musically and water lilies bloomed moon-white, and giant goldfish floated under them. And there had been green and gold and scarlet dragons painted on every wall and woven into every silk hanging. There had been stone dragons, and jade dragons so delicate that they disintegrated at a puff of breath. There had been copper dragons and dragons painted on porcelain so fine that light filtered through them and their colours seemed to change as you looked. China, Rachel had told Maggie, was the place for dragons, where it was hot, and where in the villages great paper ones were paraded with veneration. And being as usual in the mood to get things right she told her a Chinese dragon story.

Rachel's Dragon Story

This is a Chinese story, Maggie, and in China they used to understand dragons better than here in Europe.

Once upon a time there was a man who thought he could be a dragon-master. He was a scholar and for many years studied to learn the ways of dragons; he was proud but not stupid, and he learned all that the books could teach him, and then he set off on a long journey and captured two baby dragons and brought them home as pets. He had learned everything that dragons need, but he had not understood any of it.

He built his dragons a garden, the most beautiful garden in the world, and although he surrounded it with an iron wall which he believed they would not cross, he made the wall beautiful for them, lavish with filigree work and sweet with hanging plants. He built them a pagoda of solid jade and embellished it with precious gems – not realising that to grow up a dragon must accumlate its own hoard, must steal it from Emperors and princes. He had a pond dug for them, so pretty and sweet, surrounded by bullrushes with a delicate arched bridge and floating with water lilies – not realising that a real dragon needs a whole ocean to sport in, needs the spume of the white capped waves, needs the great storms and clanging icebergs, needs the coral islands of the southern seas, needs the dark rains and winds and currents to make its blood flow green and its whiskers curl ferociously.

The scholar fed his pet dragons on the choicest tit-bits, bringing them rump steaks of the purest virgins and a daily supply of swallows' flesh – not realising that such things, for true dragons, are treats, are after-dinner delicacies and no more a fit diet than endless chocolates would be for you.

As you can imagine, his pet dragons did not grow very large, but they did grow lazy and fat and tame.

And then one night, one bright and starlit night, a true free dragon came by to pay a call. He looked down on the pretty garden and saw the two of them snoring there, their front claws tucked neatly under their chins which rested on silk cushions and their tails dipped tidily into the pond whose waters did not stir enough to move their dreams to wildness.

The great dragon was angry but courteous, and he woke them up in as mannerly a way as he knew how. Immediately they invited him to join them, singing in their slightly squeaky voices of the charms and luxury of their lifestyle.

'What?' cried the great dragon, his deep brass-gonged voice ringing out and causing several of the gems to tinkle off the jade pagoda. 'What! Come down and snooze in a garden when I am a dragon, an ocean-lurking, sky-flying free dragon; when the mother wind that keeps the world spinning caresses my scales as I fly across the moon and bring warnings and hopes to the fiery heart of the world; when I can dance aloft at dawn, so that the rising sun turns my every scale to a pure diamond and the tides and rhythms of the oceans slow down in delight. Have you gone insane?'

'Well,' they answered a little sheepishly, 'this is so much cosier.'

'Cosy! Do you call yourselves dragons? What of your great calling? Your dragonish duties; your dignity and pride?'

'But we cannot escape,' they whinged. 'See, he has imprisoned us inside an iron wall. You see we are real dragons; all dragons dread iron.'

'Dread, yes,' he replied, 'but fear can be defeated. Come on out, you miserable cowards.'

'Oh, no, thank you,' they both said hastily. 'It might hurt our Lord's feelings. And he does look after us so well; we are truly comfortable and urge you to try it.'

The great dragon snorted a cloud of fire, and gonged back at them, 'Stay then, you foolish worms. I came to help you escape and you have insulted me, me and all true free dragons with your petty invitation. I'll leave you to your fate, but I warn you, tame dragons never come to any good. Just wait and see.'

And he roared away into the night, the rough scales on his throat catching the breeze of his anger and making a hissing hum as he vanished.

But he was right. For soon enough their scholarly owner grew bored with his dragon studies – as well he might since his samples were such boring dragons – and decided to investigate the secrets of the turbine jet engine instead. Of course he needed to finance so improbable a research programme, so he sold his dragons to an Emperor, who had them minced up and served to him garnished with spit-roasted swallows' tongues, at one of his less important banquets.

And Maggie had giggled and had indeed been comforted.

To comfort Maggie's desolation and guilt at the loss of her little dragon, Phoebe had suggested that the dragon, having gained his strength from her love, had flown away. Being for once in the mood to get things right, Phoebe had brought home from the library a book about dragonflies. Not a children's book at all, but a modern illustrated coffee-table book with careful, delicate photographs.

As a child she had not had time for many fairy stories and did not now know them to tell to her daughter again, but instead she showed her the pictures. First the ugly lumpy larvae, the precision closeups showing its undershot jaw as it chomped its way through its subaqueous world. Then the tight cysts, not unlike Maggie's soap egg, glued onto the reed stalks, and swelling, swelling, splitting until finally the pictures captured the moment when the dragonfly broke from the chrysalis, crawled desperately up the reed stem and unfolded its glorious wings in the sunshine, spreading them out to harden, to firm up, to set, to grow strong. It was shimmering, incandescent, as the colours deepened and the long blue-black tail unfurled and stiffened until it gained the strength to fly.

'Perhaps you were the sun for your little dragon; and now she is strong enough, she wants to be free.'

'He,' said Maggie obstinately, and with unusual tenderness, Phoebe did not contradict her.

Thus Maggie was comforted.

And that night, from these gifts, Maggie had resurrected Fenna. Using the solid material of history and science she had recreated, restored, raised up Fenna in her imagination and he had never gone away. For ten years he had been her constant companion.

Now, arriving in the safety of her own room, Maggie undressed, folding her clothes and putting them away with an unusual neatness for a fifteen year-old. In her case this was a consequence of living with two women like Phoebe and Rachel. Phoebe loathed housekeeping so profoundly that she felt guilty about it and always did it with a disciplined and joyless rigour, expecting everyone else to do so too. Rachel, on the other hand, thought that tidiness was simply a moral necessity, along with generosity, thoughtfulness, good manners and clarity. Phoebe, who might have been a slut, had in fact become exactly the opposite – she had not time or patience or tolerance for anyone she considered to be exploiting the manual work of other women. Since Rachel had sneaked her Mrs Gordon into Phoebe's half of the house, misunderstanding and not caring about Phoebe's impotent fury, Phoebe had become even more rigorous about Maggie's tidiness. The mess in the kitchen was typical of neither of them, and should have announced to them both the distress of the other. The fact that they had not fought about it should have announced their despair.

Maggie had never bothered to resist their reasoning, and she folded her clothes partly from the natural instinct of obedience, and partly because she had never been entirely sure that these external appendages did indeed belong to her, Maggie Petherington, or if perhaps they were loans from the mysterious outer world; loans that would doubtless be called in some day.

She undressed without turning the light on.

She was not afraid of the dark, because when she was very little Maggie had had the last few scales of Fenna's tail to suck on while she fell asleep. The scales across Fenna's shoulders and haunches were as large as dinner plates, and thick, heavy and dry – they changed colour in different lights, from dull pewter through to a dark red, the colour of dried blood, or the murky green of the lower waters of the Amazon River. When they were wet from rain or swimming in the oceans, the light might catch on some deep oil in them and they would glimmer shadowy rainbows of colour, like oil spills on a road. The scales on Fenna's belly were as large, but softer – pastelled reflections of his back, glimmering in pearly tones: oyster, and creamy-grey like dawn, or pollen yellows and dusty pinks. But the scales down Fenna's tail grew gradually smaller and smaller, the darker shades of his back and the paler shades of his underside blending together, and at the very tip, small as a child's thumb, they were minute and a shade that, when she tried to match it to paint sample cards was usually called *eau de nil*. She had sucked comfort with the distant vibration of Fenna's breathing rumbling down to his tail tip, and he had spun stories for her and woven them into dreams.

Fenna's Bedtime Story

This is an old story, Maggie, even by the datings of dragon lore. Times have changed and now courageous young men on noble horses come out to kill us with their spears. In this bright new world there is no place for the dragon: no one wants the shadow, wants the dark magic which is as old as the caves in the hills where we dwell. It is not easy to kill a dragon, but it can be done, and there are many handy manuals to teach an aspiring hero the tricks of his trade. It is much much harder to tame a dragon, to embrace a dragon, and to love and accept the darkness and the fear. There are no manuals for this struggle, for it can only be done by those who have pure hearts and sharp wits and the wisdom to know themselves.

Once upon a time, long long ago and far far away, out in the dreamlands, there was another Margaret just like you. I do not know whether we dragons loved her or hated her; her will was like iron, as fast clad as our scaled hides, but her heart was like a songbird in the morning and she was as lovely as the lilies of the field.

They say she lived at Antioch in Pisidia during the reign of the Emperor Diocletian. Her father was a magician; he knew something of the old magic, but he turned it against the little people to whom it belonged, and demanded their money, their livestock and even their children to appease the gods with rivers of blood.

But Margaret laughed at him, and when she heard about a new God who sacrificed only himself, and gave bread and sweet wine to the people, she became a Christian. All magicians can be tested by laughter because corruption cannot stand mockery; and when his daughter laughed at him he drove her out into the wilderness, and she lived in the wilderness with the wild beasts and angels ministered to her.

Hunting one day, Olybrius, the grand governor of Antioch, saw her and seeing her innocence and her loveliness he was jealous and immediately wanted to destroy both. So he had her captured and brought to his palace. He wanted to marry her, but she laughed at him too, and said she had already made her choices and they did not include giving up her God and replacing him with a somewhat vulgar and certainly brutal man. Not surprisingly he was livid, and having failed to realise that those who laugh easily do not fear easily, he tried several means of torture to get her to consent. It says a great deal about the natural stupidity of tyrants that, having discovered that torture works extremely effectively in intellectual or political cases, they immediately assume that it will work as well in the inspiring of desire in young women. By and large it does not, and it certainly did not in Margaret's case: she merely laughed all the more, and sang the taunting hymns of her new faith, about how tyrants would be put down from their thrones and the humble and the meek raised up.

Then Olybrius' fury flared and even the ground shook in fear. Deep deep in a limestone cave where the stalagmites grow less than an inch a century, but still tower so high as to humble the cathedrals of the surface, the shaking fear of the ground woke a dreaming dragon. Called by

Olybrius' anger, the dragon rushed on crimson wings, down from its home in the cold north. The flame from its mouth passed over the western lands like a comet and woke millennial longings in the hearts of Roman legionaries, who eked out their twenty years of cold service dreaming of victories and of eating fresh figs under the olive trees of home.

The dragon homed in on Olybrius' wrath, which called him across the continent. Cross at being so abruptly awoken from his sleep, he spotted Margaret and licked his great lips with glee. Virgin flesh was not so easily come upon in those days; and a virgin garnished with terror was an unexpected breakfast treat after his long sleep. He swooped across the market square in Antioch, while the crowd fell back appalled, and opening his huge mouth, like a salmon to a fly, snapped Margaret up. Without missing a wing beat, he bore her high above the city and flew on. He was just shifting this succulent morsel in his mouth before grinding her bones, when he heard an extraordinary sound; he heard a gurgle of laughter. So shocked was he, and flying so fast, that he gulped and swallowed her whole.

And now both fear and joy fell upon the dragon. He flew on, his great red and gold wings beating the sun-filled Mediterranean air, his huge scarlet tongue hanging out of his mouth in a desparate effort to cool down and not blow out any smoke and flames. And when they were over the blue Aegean sea, many miles from Antioch, he circled widely, descended, and alighted on a small mountainous island, on soft green grass beside a grove of apple trees.

When the dragon had flighted across the market place of Antioch, and Margaret had found herself swept up between the huge teeth, she had laughed like a child at the brief glance she had had of the panic around her; she had laughed from the pure unexpectedness of her escape and at the terrified way the mighty Olybrius had nearly swallowed his moustaches. But now in the belly of the monster she learned what fear was. Inside the great dragon it was very hot and very uncomfortable; it was also very noisy, since the dragon's stomach rumbled like a volcano. The dragon's internal boiler was situated very near to its stomach, and since he was making tremendous efforts to cool down, there were also terrifying hissing and grinding sounds.

But more: Margaret had been brought up in a household where true magic had been corrupted for profit and was therefore rightly feared as dangerous. She knew, without any consolation, that she was at the mercy of everything which was most ancient and fearful. The terror of death was upon her and, sensing this, the dragon's appetite awoke again. The walls of the cavern where Margaret was sitting began to ooze with digestive juices, pungent with the smell of sulphur, and the quicklime of the morgue. The acid began to eat away at the edge of her tunic, the bottom strands of her curly hair. She longed for a weapon, for even a hairpin, and knowing that she did not have one, she knew too that she was totally defenceless, unarmed and alone. She could feel the great flight of the dragon and sensed that she was high in air and travelling fast towards the sunset; she could feel the great muscles of the dragon's wings send ripplings down the stomach walls and she gave herself over to death.

And in the moment that she laid herself open to dying she heard the whispery voices of the wild beasts in the wilderness:

'Yeah, though I take the wings of morning and fly to the uttermost ends of the sea, yet thou art with me.'

It was true, she knew, that dragons were huge and fierce and wild and mysterious; but it was also true, as she also knew, that not everything that was huge and fierce and wild and mysterious was necessarily evil, necessarily wanted to kill you. Her God had made the dark at the same moment as the light. He had made the shadow, the wildness and the passion. Nightingales sing only in the dark. In the dark there are new joys. The dragon was the same as her wild longings, her fierce and stubborn courage, her desire to fly.

Then she felt the great gliding swoop, the downward hover and the bump as the dragon landed. In a still moment of total blackness she could feel the sinewed strength, the velvet softness of the dragon's tripes.

'At least,' she thought, 'I will die touching something beautiful.'

Her heart soared as she realised that this was a new adventure, an adventure through darkness into the greater darkness which might, just might, be even more beautiful than the slow throbbing of living blood, richer in iron than the veins of any mine, passing through mighty arteries, driven by the rhythmic pounding of the great beast's heart.

So she waited eagerly. Suddenly far above her head she saw a little shaft of light. It grew until it was a window and out through the window she could see down a long tunnel; and beyond that the sun shining and the mountains rising over the fruit trees. Wider and wider, the dragon was opening its mouth. He wanted her to come out. It was a scary journey, scrabbling over that slippery great red tongue and passing through a great hall of teeth and palate, each pillar taller than she was and as sharp as a knife.

Stepping out on to grass she turned and knew that she was one of the few in all history and legend who could safely look a dragon in the eye. So she did. 'Thank you,' she said.

The dragon was ashamed. 'I wanted to kill you, but I could not.'

'Well,' said Margaret laughing, 'I wanted to kill you too, but I could not either.'

The dragon heaved a huge sigh of relief and politely turned his head to let out a huge smoky belch; then he settled down for a dragon-like snooze. Margaret kissed the side of his cheek and went to gather daisies in the grass and make a daisy chain to lead her new friend and spectacular pet through all the illuminated and flower strewn pages of Christian manuscripts.

Maggie had fallen asleep rejoicing.

So now Maggie was not afraid of the dark, even though the great windows exposed her to the full moon and turned her own skin white and pearly – a reflection of reflected light. That light came originally from the same source as Fenna's fire, from the heart of the golden star, from the sun itself – but it was light crashing around space at speeds which defy relativity, rolling like waves, bouncing like particles, rebounding off the dead desert of the cold moon and hurled thence, down through nearly a quarter of a million miles, forced through the steadily slowly moving liquid molecules of solid glass which made the windows.

Maggie lay there on her back, stiff, formal, upon the great silken swirls of her Chinese bedspread, her feet tidily together, her arms spread wide, cruciform, and her rib cage rendered elongated and tortured by the moon shadows. The moon was at her feet and she was clothed by the sun and so she waited.

By a strong act of will she kept the roof on her room. She would not allow it to open up and expose her directly to the moon, and to the distant but approaching dragon. Fenna, by all the ancient laws, could not come to her until she invited him; but he could, and did, will her to invite him, and the will of dragons is strong. Once upon a time Fenna had brooded on a hoard for so many years and with such desire that it had quickened and grown, diamonds breeding and bringing up their young under his weight. The unimaginable heat and weight of Fenna had pressed the ooze in the cave, pressed so hotly and heavily that the molecules of mud were squeezed apart, breaking up into carbon atoms and hydrogen atoms, and his weight had compressed the carbon atoms into diamond crystals, and more and more diamonds until his hoard was a lure to garish youths, who had toiled up to his cave and exchanged riddles and blows with him, but when he had fixed them with his ancient evil little eyes, they retreated abashed to sing his praises. The force, the weight and heat of Fenna's will was no small thing, and Maggie had never before tried to resist it.

Nor was resisting enough. It was only the beginning. But St Margaret of Antioch had been swallowed up by a dragon too, and she had climbed out again, fresh and free, to become the matron saint of women in childbirth. This gave her hope, for it was nothing less than a re-birth that Maggie was aiming for.

Maggie would not close her eyes, because that would be cheating, but she shortened her focus so that it rested precisely on the window-panes, and although they were not dirty and the moonbeams seemed to shine straight through them, they were there. If she fixed her focus with enough concentration she could envisage the invisible barrier. All she knew of self and love she knew through Fenna, and now she had to send him away. Suddenly, lost in misery, she could not even remember why.

Lying on the bed, naked and waiting, Maggie lost her nerve. She knew that she could not do it alone. But surely she owed her beloved that honour at least, the honour of single combat, which is a dragon's privilege.

You do not go out after a dragon with hounds and huntsmen; nor with gangs of labourers to dig pits and set fires and lay traps. No, you polish your armour till it gleams, you sharpen your lance and you mount your white charger, you raise your banner, you bid farewell to the grieving city, where the crowd stands in terror and hope at your preparations and your parting. Then you ride out alone, across the springing grass all beset with tiny jewel-like flowers; you ride up the rushy mountains and down the rushy glens and come to the mouth of the dragon's cave. Then you draw your sword, wave it over your head and call the dragon out. Some dragons banter words with you, more devious and less answerable than the Sphynx herself; they spin word games which you must not play, and then in the end they come out and fight like men, until you can plunge your spear into the soft white spot where their plated armour is thin.

Maggie was tempted to that particular plot, for the story had been told that way so many times, and it is very hard, at moments of crisis, to re-cast the language and the shape of old stories. But she had lived with a dragon for over ten years, and she had lived in a house filled with strong women, so she knew that there was something very wrong with that scenario.

In the first place, she did not plan to kill Fenna, although she recognised that he might die of grief or loneliness. In the second place she was naked not armed, she was lying not riding, and she was the heroine not the hero. This was a new battle.

Moreover the young hero was never alone; he always had a pure princess, waiting for him, holding the thread of life which would protect him from the flames and the teeth and the dark belly of the monster. It is women who have to go alone; whose lovers do not have the patience to wait at home and pray for them. Maggie however had no intention of doing this alone. Her courage returned. This time she was not going to permit Fenna a re-run of the old plot; this time she was indeed going to make a brand new story; her own story. She knew her own limitations. She had been brought up by clear-thinking women.

The effort of thinking up a new way to tackle a dragon, a beloved dragon, daunted her for a minute. Her doubts came back. She allowed her steady gaze to flicker from the glass which she had been holding firm. Immediately and frighteningly she could feel Fenna's will power. She honestly could not hold him off alone.

Then her eyes fell briefly on the painting her grandmother had given her. In the picture, St Margaret held her power over her dragon steadily and calmly. She had not killed him, she was leading him away from the open mouth of the cave and towards the distant city. Her holy obstinacy, her sulky refusal to bend her stubborn head to emperors, fathers, lovers, or dragons had proved strong enough to conquer even the need to kill.

Inspired, Maggie called on St Margaret for aid.

St Margaret had passed several dreary centuries in heaven; people very seldom sought her intercession nowadays, and then it tended to be superstitious old women with sentimental requests. Since the Second Vatican Council she had even been removed from the Universal Canon, by ignorant prelates who – full of their scientific and rationalist approach to the institutions of sanctity – insisted she had never existed. Since the beginning of the modernist theological era, she had not even had the once-yearly chore of taking her urn and collecting up the incence and imprecations put up, however formalistically, for her own feast day.

In the middle ages Margaret had had a wonderful time; women had understood then that it was not to other mothers that you turn in childbirth, it is to those women who have lived it, who have been down between the dragon's teeth, have travelled the dragons' pathways and have lurked in the dark and boiling belly of pain, have been chewed and digested and emerged. It is free virgins whom women need in childbirth. She had been busy and useful day and night. But nowadays they call on new and brasher saints, whom St Margaret had not even met – Saints Epidura and Psychoprophilaxia.

So St Margaret had sat in her empty court feeling neglected for decades. Now she heard Maggie's intercession with delight. Another tangled virgin called on her for help against a dragon, called on her though she had thought that her time was past and the dragons had all departed.

With a smile so radiant that the light in heaven itself sparkled, she leapt into action. And, down below, laid out there on her bed, Maggie felt the full strength and joy of a bored woman given something useful to do flowing through to her.

St Margaret held the dragon's will by the power of her own legend. Fenna knew both fear and respect. The old passionate story had come between him and Maggie, and he trembled and retreated. Poised between Maggie and Fenna, St Margaret took her stand. She plucked a great hank of silk thread from the girdle of her spinsterhood; tied one end of it to the wedding ring of her virginity and, looping the two ends of the hank over either wrist, spread her hands and invited Maggie to take the other end and wind a neat ball. Maggie, who had never learned such useful arts from either of the women who had brought her up, had to be shown what was required, but soon the smooth rhythm of one woman winding and the other co-operating by swinging her hands in and out as the thread unwound, pleased and comforted her.

Soon Maggie held a golden ball of thread and St Margaret had one end of it firmly attached to her finger.

Freed, thus, from the weight of the dragon's will, and safely assured of being able to get home again Maggie turned her mind to her own task and went travelling down into the labyrinth of memory and desire.

Just as Maggie could not remember a time before there was Fenna, and a time before there was the big house and the three women living in it, so she could not remember a time when there was not the constant tug of tension between her grandmother and her mother. She could remember though the time when she realised that she must, for love of them both, never let them know that she was aware of it. It was that night that Fenna had taught her to fly.

She had been eight. She had already known, half consciously, that she liked her grandmother better than she liked her mother, and loved her mother more fiercely than she loved her grandmother. Rachel always had been safer, Rachel's adoration was guaranteed, secure and clear. When Maggie had hugged Rachel as a child, her small arms stretching wide to reach round her bum, Maggie had been able to feel the solidness of her, the deep-grounded certainty that Rachel exuded. When Rachel looked at someone, she saw what was there to see. No one else could look at things the straightforward way that Rachel looked at things. Maggie trusted that, trusted the clear steadiness, the certainty that Rachel would do what she said; and what she had said, and went on saying quietly, calmly, efficiently, was that she loved Maggie. She paid attention.

At eight Maggie had not known that her grandmother was famous, but she had seen that people had something in their manner when they looked at Rachel; later she learned that that something was respect. Rachel deserved respect. If there were games to be played or work to be done or stories to be read it was always to Rachel that she would turn; Rachel who went out and came in when she said she would and said 'yes' or 'no', not from whim or temper, but with authority. Rachel was as safe as a rock.

Phoebe was different. Maggie could not depend on Phoebe and knew that she would not. But it was Phoebe that she wanted. Phoebe was unreasonable and distant and dangerous. Phoebe had too short a fuse, and it was impossible to guess how she would be, each meeting had to be gauged with care, and it had always been so. She could not be certain that Phoebe wanted her and needed her. Maggie knew all about Phoebe's restless unhappiness, her discontent. She did not know if she herself were a part, a cause of it. She wanted Phoebe to concentrate on her. She wanted Phoebe's long bold stare, so different from Rachel's serene regard – more dangerous, more challenging. She wanted Phoebe to feel passionate about her. She needed Rachel to stay alive, but she needed Phoebe to be alive.

She knew the tension that existed between Rachel and Phoebe. She could sometimes experience it as a physical thing – a slender cord strung between the two of them, as though they each held one end, and she, she had to balance on that tight rope, poised and tricky. She had to perform for them with the spotlight on her and she knew that no trick would be good enough. If she danced without a safety net Rachel would find her foolish, and if she refused to attempt a wild and abandoned triple somersault with twirls and flourishes, Phoebe would not notice. It was easier really to learn to fly.

That day when she was eight she had disappeared, or as Rachel tried patiently to call it, 'wandered off'. They told her over and over again that she must not do it, but she couldn't help it. Usually she could not remember why she had wandered off. Neither of them seemed to realise that she never planned it. Just somehow, somewhere between the sweet shop and her house, between home and school, between tea-time and bath-time, she would lose concentration. Something would attract her – a cloud, a flower, a fat lady on the street – and she would drift away from the track unthinkingly. She knew that her grown-ups were frightened and she did not want them to be frightened, but she also knew that Fenna was a mightier protection than all their loving care could ever be. She could walk safely in the forest of city streets and that no harm could touch her.

She would just wander off; and then later she would come to, wondering where she was and remembering that they would be angry with her again. That day she had wandered off between leaving her mother's kitchen and arriving in her grandmother's sitting-room. She was supposed to do this, unless it was raining, by going out the front door and down the area steps, rather than through her grandmother's bedroom. There seemed hardly time for anyone to wander off, but wander she had, and she had come to swinging happily on a swing in the park playground.

As soon as she realised what had happened she had jumped down guiltily and run home. There was only one big road to cross, but it had a zebra crossing and she had been road-safe at Phoebe's insistence for years. But she was scared of their anger – not their anger with her, but with each other, so she ran. Arriving, she saw that the front door was still open: perhaps she had not been gone long, perhaps they had not yet missed her. She skipped up the steps and into the house. She could not have failed to hear them.

Rachel was saying, 'It's not naughtiness. I agree she has to learn, I agree she can't go on like this, but it isn't naughtiness. She's . . . I don't know, can't you see?'

'Oh, Mummy,' Phoebe sounded rough, cross. Maggie was too young to hear that as anxiety. 'For God's sake, you know that isn't the point. The point is that you muddle her, you muddle her up. I'm not surprised she has to get out sometimes. I'm not bloody surprised. I wish I could.'

There was a pause. The grown-ups were above her in the stairwell. They were in neither half of the house, but in a space that did not really exist for Maggie, who never asked herself which half the house was whose, since the whole house was, for her, theirs. She could sense that Rachel was being careful; after the pause Rachel said, very calmly and reasonably:

'Are you sure it's me that muddles her? I think it's partly you. You stand against everything I tell her, obstinately and in her hearing, you give me no support, but as soon as it's convenient to you, you pack her off back downstairs.'

'She's my child.'

'I never contest that.'

'Yes, you do.'

Maggie, down below, knew that Rachel had bitten her tongue before she had snapped out 'Oh no I don't'.

Rachel was horribly sensible if you tried to fight with her. She was so horribly sensible that it could drive you, as Maggie knew it was now driving Phoebe, into complete tantrums and screaming, because Rachel would not share that part of the argument. It was not fair. She could feel her mother's irritation rise to balance the calmness that her grandmother threw over the fight.

'I can't cope with all this any more,' said Phoebe, and there was a screech in her voice. 'If we have any more of this nonsense, we're going to have to move. I shall take her away; I shall take her abroad and that's final.' Maggie knew, even as she heard it, that Phoebe did not mean anything of the sort; it was the kind of thing that Rachel dragged you into saying.

Then Maggie heard what she did not want to hear; she heard Rachel, who was always so controlled, so strong, so clear, she heard Rachel whimpering, begging,

'No, Phoebe please. Please. Perhaps you're right, perhaps I do interfere. I'll try. I'll try.'

She heard her Phoebe sounding ugly and fierce. 'You'd bloody better.'

And Maggie whisked herself down the stairs, out of the house and fifty yards along the street. She approached her home again, and entered noisily and tearfully. She took the punishments meted out to her without a murmur. Then, curled up in bed that night, she told Fenna that she must not do it anymore, she must not wander off, he must not let her. She must never ever do anything that might make them fight. She had to be careful and clever.

So Fenna taught her how to fly.

She would never forget the first time, balanced high on the steep roof of the house, huddled from the wind against the chimney-stack, Fenna's great shadow hovering over her, although Fenna had surely not been so hugely vast then as he was now, his shadow had not obliterated the stars, threatening their very existence. She had been joyful and terrified and Fenna had urged her to trust him.

'Trust, leap, jump, trust,' he had commanded her.

And she had leapt.

Caught in an eddy of storm, she had feared herself falling; and then between her and the ground below there had been a stillness. She had found herself in the safe nook between Fenna's sail-like wing and the crenellated and fantastic fortress of his spine. But she was not resting in the hollow, she was floating in it. She was flying, just within the still pocket of air, but enough to know that she had the power. Fenna's mightier flying, inside which she had her little flight, lifted her up, higher and higher. Then poised above the shining city, among the burning stars, Fenna had paused, dropped one great wing, tilted over, tipped her away from his side and she had flown free.

They had danced on the night winds through the dark hours and before dawn she had flown safely home, filled with a new and fierce joy which was the warmth of Fenna's fiery breath and the width and grace of freedom from gravity.

It was also another burden of secrecy. When she had been a tiny child, and Fenna had still been a small, manageable and undemanding dragon she had often spoken of him, to her mother who had grinned, to her grandmother who had smiled, and to her schoolteachers and friends, who had laughed indulgently. But as she and he both grew, people smiled less often and Fenna himself began to insist on secrecy and darkness. A child who was not allowed to wander off to the park, would certainly not be allowed to fly off to the planets.

But by keeping him secret she had given him too much power. Now here, lying on her bed while St Margaret held his dragon power in check, Maggie knew she had indulged Fenna too long, that she had fed him and petted him into overweening size and pride. Now he even dared to challenge his maker.

His maker, she repeated to herself firmly; she was his maker, and he had no existence without her, without her consent and her will and her passion.

But although she said it she could not be certain that it was true. She could not be certain that she wanted it to be true. For he had given her gifts beyond dreaming. Fenna had given her freedom and power and joy; she would not call those things illusions, because without them there was nothing worth having in her life.

She did not know if she could live without him. What could be the point of life without that great sweeping tail that could scatter the stars across the sky, without the dark rumbling tenderness when they slept together after their soaring adventures. Could she live without magic and intimacy?

But she would have those things for ever; she would have them in her head, in her memories and her dreams, and no one could take that away from her. It was time to put away childish things. She must remember them, but not brood on them. She must move forward.

She must look at two other things, hard and solid, so that she would be strong for the battle ahead.

It was getting harder and harder to pretend to be ordinary. When she had been little it had been easy, and now it was not. When she had been little, temporary lapses and been easily passed over. Her early school reports were peppered with comments, complimentary or judgemental, depending on the teacher: 'Margaret has a very active imagination',

'Margaret must learn not to go off into day-dreams', 'Margaret does not yet seem to have learned the difference between fact and fiction'.

But while these were unfortunate, and inclined to make Rachel crumple up her forehead and lecture her on the scientific method and the importance of mental clarity, there was no real danger in such remarks. They were just little signs warning her that she had failed to keep Fenna the perfect secret that he had to be.

When she had been little, once Fenna had taught her how to fly so that she no longer went wandering off, there had been very little time when she had been left alone. The night-time, the time after she had been tucked up in bed, that was the proper time for Fenna, for flying and dreams.

When she had become a teenager however, she had more time alone, and when she was alone it was so much harder to remember. She flew more and more, like this last evening. It had not been fully dark when she had been flying. It had certainly been risky, landing in the tree round the corner. She had been lucky so far; she had not yet been caught, not yet been dragged off to some shrink and asked for explanations. She was even lucky in a way that her mother never paid any real attention. If they found out . . . if they found out, Phoebe and Rachel would tear each other apart, and her with them; it they found out, Fenna would be lethally furious. It was too dangerous. It had to stop.

The more she flew, the more irresistible it was; like a drug, an addiction. She knew she was doing it more and more, taking more and more risks. Sometimes it was as though the risk and the pleasure had grown together, nourishing each other. But . . . at school less than a month ago she had lost her temper with her maths teacher.

She hated her maths teacher anyway, and that dislike was fuelled by Phoebe's frequently repeated conviction that the woman was a moron and taught not mathematics but 'sums', a subject apparently lower on Phoebe's scale of values than home economics and office skills:

'You've got a bloody calculator,' Phoebe would yell, 'she ought to be teaching you to think.'

The maths teacher hated Maggie too, because one Parents' Evening Phoebe had turned up in overalls and working boots. She did not look like anyone else's mother. Everyone else's mother came in neat and respectful skirts, and were accompanied by neat and respectful fathers who sought wisdom and understanding from the teachers. Not Phoebe. Maggie thought Phoebe did it deliberately; Phoebe was normally rather well-dressed in a casual sort of way, and had the best fitting proper designer jeans and lovely hand-knitted posh jumpers; she had plenty of skirts and frequently wore them. But she had to turn up at Maggie's school in her working clothes.

When Maggie tried to tell Phoebe about her gruelling embarrassment Phoebe just laughed and told her she was turning into a bourgeois little creep and should perhaps be taking domestic science and dress-making.

'It's called Textiles nowadays,' muttered Maggie furiously, knowing that this was irrelevant.

Maggie knew that many of her school-friends admired Phoebe; they thought she was rather splendid, especially since they had all got into ecology, but this did not help Maggie. It was not enough that Phoebe should turn up looking like a manual worker – ('But, for God's sake, Maggie, I *am* a manual worker') – and wearing a button on her overalls which said 'This facility is under threat from rate-capping,' which made boys on buses make obscene jokes; she also had to take on the maths teacher.

The maths teacher had been, Maggie knew, contemptuous and rude and sexist, but Maggie felt that Phoebe should have put up with it for her sake. Phoebe was selfish. She certainly did not, in the vast school hall, in front of two hundred other parents, in a very loud voice, *need* to tell the maths teacher that she was a moron and incompetent to boot. She did not need, while wearing boots with the mud still on them, to give the teacher an advanced lesson in maths. At the top of her voice. Nor to tell her that it was women like her who prevented girls doing well in sciences. Nor that the reason she had sent Maggie to an all-girls' school was not to protect her from evil-minded youths, but to protect her from the sort of teaching that she seemed to be getting.

Maggie had wanted to die. At the same time she had fiercely wanted to be proud of Phoebe, to support Phoebe's admirable fight on her behalf. She had felt trapped by the old mesh of loyalty and shame.

Phoebe, in fairness, could not have known that the maths teacher, shamed in public, should take to hating Maggie with a spiteful glee, though she would probably not have cared if she had. Maggie had dealt with that as best she could, taking it quietly and never complaining about the minor injustices which a teacher can inflict – work returned because of untidiness, petty sarcasms, rigorous enforcement of minor school rules. Then, one day, she had lost her temper, completely, suddenly and, even to herself, shockingly.

Maggie had been amazed at her own fury, rocked by the power of Fenna within her, breaking through the cool disdain she tried always to preserve in front of this loathsome woman. Twenty minutes later she found herself inside the Head's office, white and trembling, so obviously terrified that the Head herself was taken aback. Maggie knew the source of her own fear: in her anger she had so nearly, so very nearly, launched herself into the air, growling a dragon's fury, sparks flying not from her eyes but from her mouth, raining blows from above, hovering over the teacher like St Michael over the devil. And if she had . . .

If she had, all hell would have broken loose. Fenna would never have forgiven her. Fenna would have killed her. She would have been locked up in a mental hospital, or alternatively taken off for parapsychological testing and Rachel would have been unforgiving. Rachel believed that mechanistic science could explain all phenomena, even those of the heart and soul; Rachel would never have forgiven her, the last place of safety and affection would have been taken away.

Fenna had become too powerful. Maggie did not want to be a crazy person. She wanted now, at any price, to be able to sit in the rooms of young women who could be her friends and not feel that she was travelling in territory stranger than the night caves that were Fenna's home. She wanted life to be like it had been earlier that evening. She wanted to be able to sit there and be like them, to sit there and sip Coke and not to have to worry about whether she would laugh at the right moments. She just wanted to be free of the burden of her own special powers. What was appropriate and necessary at eight, was inappropriate and dangerous at fifteen. She was stuck.

Stuck in too many ways.

As she lay there on her bed Maggie suddenly raised her arms, breaking the iconic cruciform of her pose, and ran her hands over her naked chest. She was fifteen. She knew that she should have breasts, that she should be menstruating; that, judging from the giggled conversations of her friends, she should have at least wanted to find out about love and sex. One more guilty secret that Maggie felt obliged to keep from everyone was the deep fear and disgust that she felt at the thought of sexuality.

That was Fenna. Fenna did not want her to menstruate, Fenna would not allow her to desire. She was not just Fenna's friend and child, his daughter of delight. She was also Fenna's hoard; and Fenna had kept from her until too late the awful, consuming greed and jealousy that, from before the dawn of time, all dragons have had about their hoards. Dragons can lie for dark centuries brooding over their treasures, bedding down on frozen flames that will never see the light of day. Dragons love virgins, but they hate the creamy smell of female desire that will bring the young men to their caves, to steal and kill. Princes on white chargers are like bloodhounds, over mountain ranges and mighty oceans they can scent the whiff of virginal longing and are drawn to it like wasps to jam jars. The wise dragon so captivates his maiden that she never even has a second for longing, that she turns not from him to stare out across the wide meadows and lakes of adolescence.

Now at last Maggie had realised that something had gone wrong. The power of flight, the companionship of joy and dream had been bought at too high a price.

Fenna did not want her to bleed, and because Fenna did not want it, she had not wanted it either. Taught by Fenna's crafty and ancient wisdom she had learned well the deft turns of deceit. It was easier for her than for many, for she had always lived in two kitchens, under the different and indifferent ministrations of two cooks. She knew she ought to be furious that her mother had apparently not noticed that she did not bleed, that she did not eat, but until recently she had always been grateful. Now she felt that she could have used Phoebe in her struggle with Fenna. Phoebe lived in a totally other world, a world she could not even begin to penetrate, a calm world of profound indifference, which is not the world that Maggie lived in, nor the one she wanted to live in. Often she was afraid that when she sent Fenna away she would become like her mother, that there would be nothing, nothing left. She had realised from when she was a tiny child that Phoebe did not love her as she loved Phoebe, and as other mothers loved their lovely daughters. Loved by Fenna and by Rachel it had never occurred to her to consider herself unlovable, but now she needed a counter-weight in the real world, and her mother would never be that for her.

Her mother would not come into the arena with her, strip naked for combat, risk her life and her neutrality for Maggie, and Maggie recognised that tonight with a new sadness. She knew that if Phoebe needed her, if she could even imagine that Phoebe might ever need her, she would have no problem, no problem at all, dealing with Fenna. That evening, as her mother had stood at the kitchen door with the shadow of future old age lurking behind her, she had felt for the first time what it was to be a grown-up, what it was that she was missing in the never-never land of Fenna's spell. But Phoebe had not wanted her there, had not wanted her love and concern and caring. She had to face the fact that Phoebe was not, not then and not at any time, going to pull Maggie out from the night-time and into the daylight of loving and needing. Phoebe was not going to devour her in love and thus keep her safe from the great fangs and wraths of Fenna.

Who, then? There was her grandmother, solid and real, who could offer her stories nearly as miraculous as those that Fenna told her and which would have the miraculous ponderousness of fact. If she took her problem to Rachel, Rachel would listen and she would be on Maggie's side. She would be willing to try, but Rachel was not able to understand about Fenna. Rachel hated Fenna. She walked too firmly in the world of the day, of science. No one, not even Fenna, could actually stand up against Rachel when she had once got the bit between her teeth: she was better at the game of controlling, containing, winning, than anyone else that Maggie knew. She was very strong.

But Rachel stood against the powers of myth and imagination. That, Maggie knew, was why Rachel was so unhappy now. Maggie had known, for months, that something was wrong with Rachel. When she looked at her grandmother with the sharp eyes that Fenna could lend her, she would see that solid outline waver, dissolve, crumble. At first she had thought with a shock of fear that it was old age, that old age was like silicon, water-soluble, it flowed into you and as you dried out, it hardened, recasting you in blurred shapes and muted tones. But now she thought that it was not that, but something worse; Rachel, who had always known things, did not know them properly any more. Rachel was in trouble deeper than her own; Rachel needed her help this time. She could not ask Rachel to help her.

There was only herself. This battle must be fought by herself alone, and if she lost, she would lose alone. Then, almost magically, as she realised this, something stirred inside her and that something was excitement and courage. The same glorious sensation as she had felt that instant when, poised on the highest diving-board, she had known that this time she really did dare, that moment of poise and thrill before the free-fall.

She clenched her fists, spread eagled her arms and legs and called, exultantly, to St Margaret that she was ready.

And St Margaret, her cheeks glowing with the realisation of her strength, the knowledge that she indeed held the great dragon at bay while this new young warrior prepared herself for combat, felt a moment of disappointment, anticipating a return to the bordom of heaven. She almost offered herself for the fight, the surrogate, the already-victorious. But she looked down through the glass skylight and recognised in Maggie's cropped hair and long white body the same contours that she had seen in that other virgin warrior whom she had inspired into battle. This was a new Joan: another of these modern women with their new language and new dreams who could follow where she had led, if she were generous enough to let them fight their own battles.

So she removed her right hand from the glass skylight and placed it instead over her left finger with the ring and the thread. Then she withdrew her will from Fenna, leaving the dragon free to go or come as he would.

Fenna came.

Maggie had braced herself against Fenna's wrath, but dragons are deeply wily, they are tempters used to souls far more subtle than any fifteen-year-old child can be. They have lent forms and skills even to the great serpent who beguiled Eve, who swallowed Jonah and who wrestled in the wilderness with the young man from Nazareth. Fenna did not come wrathful now, Fenna came sweet. Came again as the little dragon of her infancy. He slipped through the skylight and sat at her feet, small like a baby, sweet like a beloved puppy. He sat and looked at her, and licked her toes with such a gathered pure tenderness, such a chuckled tickliness, that it was heartbreaking. Fenna came offering now only love, huge steady love and joy and that seemed the hardest thing to resist.

And then there was a harder one. Fenna came sad. Fenna shows those great scaled flanks, untouched for centuries, uncaressed, unloved. Dragons dry out easily, their scales turning dusty and arid. The great Dust Bowl which Maggie has seen only from the air, was once the long flank, the turning of the armpit of a dragon greater than Fenna, the great dragon laid out across the world its tail cooled by the oceans of the Antarctic and its breath, no longer fire, turned to ice around its head in the most northerly places of the globe. Fenna cried out to Maggie, 'Need, need, want. They have told you lies. There is no evil, there is only dragon.'

Fenna said, 'I need you.'

Fenna came full of love and sorrow and joy. Maggie was too surprised, too taken aback to resist him. Like all the maidens, in all the stories, half seduced and half petrified, she consented to Fenna's plans and he swept her high on his great wings and bore her away over the roofs of London and higher and higher cavorting and caracolling through the star-spun night. Now, as from the times of childhood, she rode Fenna, seated in the deep hollow of the meeting place of scaled neck, veined wing and rising battlement of spine; a throne protected from the great gale of his flight, as safe as the rocky cradle secures the foetal child, leaning back towards the bumpy spine as she had leant before, she gave herself over to their journey.

Now the Thames was a thread of silver below them, and Fenna flew as he had never flown before. The Mediterranean was a bowl of dark green glittered with lights too tiny to count. They were sweeping over the ancient continent of Africa, the everlasting wastelands of the desert no more than a patch on a great patchwork quilt. Fenna dived low over southern Africa, where his shadow presence in the night would simply meet with old dreams and young magic, and he plunged into the dancing spume of *Mosi oa Tunya*, 'the smoke that thunders', now called the Victoria Falls. Their deafening boom tossed up lunar rainbows; and Fenna gave them to Maggie for playthings and they dissolved in dark brightness between her fingers. The huge clean moon stood at her right hand, lemon-yellow and patterned with shadow. Before her marvelled eyes the Southern Cross lifted itself off the horizon and hung glowing, silent and fierce.

Now they were too high to see the great waves of the southern Atlantic carry the whales on their singing pilgrimages. Two hundred miles from land the fierce Amazon river stained the dark water darker, red with the silt it carries down from the secret jungles and mountains of the New World. The Andes, serried like dragons' teeth, sparkled as the sun rose behind them, chasing them eastwards across a peach-coloured ocean dotted with green islands.

Now Fenna rose, higher and higher, and, holding all his power for one sharp second of perfect concentration, revealed to Maggie the crazy onrushing of the galaxy where everything spins through space so fast that the observer is locked in stillness. For one blinding moment she knew absolutely that Galileo should have died for his truth, and yet had also been right to retract because he had still not known one particle of the whole. For, as the speed of light rushed down upon her, she heard, in the untimeable pause between the upbeat of Fenna's wings and their down swoop, she heard the singing of the spheres, the harmony of the universe which turns, turns, turns in the atom and in the infinite and is unmoved in its own movement and is all one single force.

Now, in the dream influence of the moon, Fenna told Maggie to look down on all the kingdoms of the world, and across China she saw the snaking of the Great Wall. On the southern side she saw the mandarin silks of the beginnings of civilisation and the huge courage of the Long March; and on the other, to the north, the eternal silence of the greatest desolation. She looked on north, north, north, through desert and tundra, to the unbroken cruel peace of the polar seas. And Fenna awaited her thanks for a journey so beautiful and so unique, the gifts that only he could offer her.

Maggie was ready to give him the glory, to return to him and stay with him forever. Then she heard, barely a distant whisper, but clearly, her mother's voice telling her that the Great Wall of China is the only human-made object that can be identified from the surface of the moon. She heard her grandmother informing her that out there, in that Mongolian vastness, was 'The Dragon's Tomb' where her own great-grandfather had gone to find the dinosaur eggs.

Empowered by their voices, she drew a deep breath and, scarcely audible in that vast space where they were floating, she said, 'Fenna, it's over, go away.'

Fenna laughed, an ancient laugh, a sweet summer thunder laugh that echoed off the dancing planets. When he had done laughing, he told her,

'I do not believe you.'

He told her that she would not be able to let go of him, that his power was deep, deep in her bones and she was bound to him for ever.

'Fenna,' she told him, 'please. I know I cannot go unless you let me, please let me go. I love you. But it is too much. Let me go.'

'No,' roared Fenna. 'No. No. No.'

And now the anger Maggie had feared was loosed. The great flames poured from his mouth, rivers of fire across the cold darkness of space. The comets that streaked the skies and scared the ancients were powered by Fenna's breath. The meteors that burned out the dinosaurs two hundred million years ago were the gouts of flame and phlegm from Fenna's nostrils. His flailing tail swept down a third of the stars of heaven and cast them on the earth. The great City of Babylon was fallen, fallen before his fury. The lost island of Atlantis was swallowed up in his wrath. The roots of the World Tree were shaken by his writhings, and the old Gods stirred and marched out to Ragnarok.

In the epicentre of the maelstrom, with the moon at her feet and crowned with the stars was Maggie, surprisingly unmoved.

'Fenna,' she told him sternly, 'I can out-tantrum you. You may be a dragon, but I am a child. I am just a little girl, I haven't even started my periods yet and little girls can tantrum louder and then can sulk deeper than anything else in the universe. That is my power and you have strengthened it in me.'

In speaking, in making conscious the secret hidden power of little girls, Maggie became a woman.

Fenna wanted nothing from the woman. It was the child he had desired. Fenna loved Maggie, and knowing that all was lost and love had departed, that she had betrayed their long friendship, that she had asserted herself over his mastery, he howled and, dropping his shoulder, hurled her out of her safe nest and into the immensity of space.

She fell. She fell. She fell as Lucifer, the ancient dragon, had fallen first, long long ago before the creation of the world. The ancient race memory of that fall stirred in Fenna's marrow and he was appalled. He was broken with compassion as he watched her crashing like a falling star, pulled by gravity and centripetal forces towards the consummation of the sun and in a moment of weakness he relaxed his will. There was space then for her free-fall to be guided, even as Lucifer's had been guided, across the vast vacuity, down to a home prepared for him by his enemy.

Now Maggie learned that falling and flying were different and the difference was fear. In the naked fear of falling in a space so huge that she did not know whether she was falling up or down, inward or outward, she met a fear so great that it burned away forever all the other fears. The fears of sex, of adulthood, of life; the fears that Rachel and Phoebe would tear her apart, the fears that they would not; the fears of love and hatred. She would never be frightened of them ever again.

All her little fears were burned away in the great fear, the fear of ceasing to be, of falling falling falling and never landing. Knowing that fear, she abandoned all pride and she called into the darkness for someone to come and rescue her. She called on her mother to leave the little green park, leave neutrality and passivity, and come to her aid; she called on her grandmother to leave the grand study, to leave scientific fact and come out here and save her. She called to St Margaret and St Joan and to all the women who have fought the burning and conquered the dragon. She called to Hermione and Joanna and all the girls who had gone already along the paths she had rejected, called to them to wait for her and place their steady walking boots on solid earth to catch her. And still she fell and fell.

Because she has called, they can answer.

St Margaret tugged firmly on her thread. Maggie felt it in her hand, frail, attenuated, overstretched, but tautened by the love and knowledge of all the women. It would lead her safely home.

She, too, could afford compassion, even as she fell; compassion and wisdom. She cried out suddenly into the enormous silence. She cried,

'Fenna, go to Rachel, go to Rachel!'

Rachel is the crone, she knew as she spun downwards. Rachel is the one grown old and weary. Rachel needs, Fenna needs, they need each other. The moon is turning. Now is a new moment. Go to Rachel, the barren one, and fill her with the harvest of fire.

'Fenna, I command you. Go to Rachel.'

Then Maggie followed the thread back through the atmosphere barrier. She was blasted by the friction of re-entry, scorched by her wild rush through particles and atoms of welcoming air, hurled through the orbiting phase. She crashed through the glass of her own skylight. In a shower of diamonds, in a dust cloud of shattered stars, in a bee swarm of broken glass, battered and bleeding, she was hurled face downward onto her own mattress and she lay there and screamed with fear and relief.

BOOK THREE

How much energy and time we wasted in all our endless love tragedies and their complications! But it was also we who taught ourselves and those younger than we that love is not the most important thing in a woman's life. And that if she must choose between love and work, she should never hesitate: it is work, a woman's own creative work, that gives her the only real satisfaction and makes her life worth living.

Alexandra Kollontai

One

Because they were both already awake and on their feet it took neither Phoebe nor Rachel long to reach Maggie's room. Phoebe being younger, fitter, and a storey and a half nearer was first. Barefoot and in a panic, she missed the bottom step of the wrought-iron spiral staircase, stubbing her toe and grazing her right shin. Maggie was still screaming above her and she did not even notice until later that her own blood was added to the devastation of Maggie's attic. Picking herself up, she shouted,

'Coming, darling!'

But she did not pause to listen for an answer. Seconds later she shoulder-charged the door, and found herself in an eerie moonlit room where she could distingish nothing, except the deafening howls which seemed to reverberate off the walls. Disoriented, she could not for an instant even locate her daughter. She groped for the light switch, but could not find it. All those years ago they had thoughtfully placed it unusually low on the wall to make it easy for the child Maggie had then been to reach. It was about the height of Phoebe's thigh and, after a flustered second, she remembered that decision with an instant clarity. The electrician had been very irritated by their insistence. And even while she remembered, she was also scared by the mystery of the moonlight, by the disorientation and, above all by her daughter's screams. They seemed to her unearthly; a new combination of loss, pain and fear: they were howls she would have made herself only half-an-hour before, if she had known how.

Then the brighter light of electricity drove out the ghostly moonbeams and she saw only her daughter, her child, flat out on her bed, naked, apparently bedecked in diamonds and rubies, a fierce tattoo of glass and blood.

'Christ!' she said, and the next moment, forgetful of her own safety, she had Maggie in her arms, shushing and soothing as she had never in her life done before.

Outside Phoebe's open bedroom door Rachel paused, wondering if her daughter had heard the explosion and responded to it. Then she became aware of the noises of Phoebe's ascent. Despite her anxiety she registered both the relief that Phoebe should have acted so promptly and a tiny flicker of jealousy, which she quickly quashed. She was panting, she realised, and hung for a moment on the newel post of the spiral stairs and waited for her heartbeat to calm down. Maggie's screams died suddenly into moans, and she knew her darling was safe. She even considered a discreet retreat to her own lair, but recognised that she lacked such disinterested nobility. With her hand on the iron banister, she started to pull herself towards the rooftops.

The scene that greeted her at the top was already less frightening than it had been when Phoebe arrived. The light was on and Phoebe was sitting on the bed with Maggie's arms wrapped convulsively around her, her scarlet and sparkling body thus partly hidden from her grandmother. Rachel was, though, more able to take in the ruin of the room than Phoebe had been.

The great skylight had shattered. All the other windows on both sides of the room had imploded. The great metal roof-tree which held the house together had bent inwards as though from some giant's blow, and listening, Rachel could hear tiles still slithering down the slope and crashing into the street forty feet below. They would have the fire brigade round in a few moments if the external noise had been as loud as the internal one. Rachel even thought of going down to Phoebe's bed room and using her phone to reassure the outside world, and protect themselves from its invasion. But before she could move, Phoebe looked up, saw her and said,

'Mummy.'

The appeal was stronger than Phoebe had ever made before. The years reeled back, her old saggy breasts seemed to respond and she crossed the room without realising it, wrapping both her children in the Chinese spread and taking them into her arms like a mediaeval St Anne with Virgin and Child. For a silent moment the three of them sat there. Abruptly the full moon passed across the gaping wound in their roof and no longer shone directly into the room. The neon quality vanished and they were all together as one flesh with three faces.

Released from the spell, Rachel took a deep breath and knew her duty. She said, with a rigorous assumption of calm and maturity.

'Whatever is happening here?'

Phoebe looked up and smiled with simple gratitude before she said,

'I don't know. Maggie, darling, what happened?'

Maggie's sobs were becoming more natural, but she still had her arms tight round Phoebe's neck and her head pressed against Phoebe's breast and her voice was muffled.

'I fell. He dropped me and I fell.'

The two adults looked at each other. She was shocked? Still dreaming? Phoebe looked to Rachel for help, and Rachel was frightened. Panic, though, would not help, she told herself.

'It's too cold in here,' she said, 'Maggie, darling, do you think you can get up, because even your mother cannot carry you down those stairs, you're too big. And I don't think this room is safe for the moment. Is she badly hurt?' she asked Phoebe.

Together they gently uncovered the child and inspected her. There were still splinters of glass gleaming on Maggie's shoulders and high flat breasts. There was a longer gash on her right elbow and a bruise forming at the top of her arm. Both of them noticed with shock how alarmingly thin she was, frail to the point of vanishing. She was shaking all over but seemed miraculously free from serious injury. Rachel offered her her dressing-gown, but Maggie seemed to want to keep the Chinese silk around her. Phoebe lifted her to her feet and they started towards the door.

At that moment Rachel heard the electronic siren of a fire engine. 'Maggie,' she said firmly, 'I'm sorry to make you do this but you have to. You have to decide, right now, do you want to go to the hospital or stay here?'

'Stay, please,' said Maggie; now she was on her feet she was returning to them rapidly. 'Please.'

Then she added, 'I'm OK, honest.'

Rachel and Phoebe exchanged half-smiles. Rachel said,

'Phoebe, I'll go deal with the authorities. They'd probably better check that the whole place isn't falling down and I'm afraid they'll want to see Maggie, but I'll get rid of them. Take her to the kitchen and try and wash some of that glass out.'

Phoebe was suddenly grateful for her mother's calm and decision; if anyone could get rid of the London fire brigade it would be Rachel. Suddenly Rachel leant over and kissed Phoebe quite gently on the cheek, and then she turned and led the way downstairs.

Maggie did not want to take her arms away from Phoebe, she needed to be held. Phoebe was both gentle and firm. In the light of kitchen she sat Maggie down and started to brush gently at her shoulders, but after a minute or so she said,

'I think the shower would work better; let's go to the bathroom.'

She made Maggie kneel down and lean her head over the bathtub, just as she had when Maggie had to have her hair washed as a little child. Under the warm water and the delicate probing of Phoebe's fingers, Maggie relaxed. After a few moments she was saying very natural and quite irritable 'ouches' when Phoebe prodded too hard. They could hear Rachel's commanding voice out on the landing, showing the firemen up to Maggie's room. Quite suddenly Maggie giggled and, imitating Lisa's voice, said,

'Good old dinosaur.'

Her release from tension released Phoebe's fears. Suddenly it was she who was shaking and crying,

'Oh Christ, my darling, I thought you were dead. I've never been so frightened in my life.' She wanted to be as mature and sensible as Rachel was, she wanted to be reassuring and maternal and all she could do was cling to Maggie and sob and sob.

Now it was Maggie, soaking wet and still oozing blood who turned and took Phoebe in her arms.

'Mummy, Mummy, it's all right. I'm all right. I'm OK.'

Cuddling her mother, petting her, she felt almost exultant. The two of them clung together, soggily, hugging closer and closer until Rachel knocked on the door and asked them to come out. Phoebe wrapped Maggie in her towel and called Rachel to come and hold her while she found them both some clothes. The two women passed in the doorway and exchanged glances of pure gratitude. In her room Phoebe pulled on her jeans and a shirt, and snatched up a thick pullover and the bottom half of her track suit for Maggie. Then suddenly she changed her mind and reached into her wardrobe for a new pair of tight stretchy ski trousers that she had hardly worn. Maggie was a very young woman, she thought that if she had to face a gang of young firemen she would be more comfortable in something smart. She was amused at herself for thinking of it, but saw, back in the bathroom, that Maggie appreciated the thought.

Rachel, perfectly dignified in her dressing-gown, made the firemen cups of tea. Maggie sat huddled on a kitchen chair and Phoebe held her hand. Under Rachel's serene autocracy the firemen agreed that there was nothing much to be done now, that the house seemed safe enough but they should not use the attic until someone 'from the department' had been and inspected it the next day. And finally Rachel swept them from the kitchen and down the stairs, chatting amiably as she went. Phoebe offered Maggie a cup of hot chocolate, and ten minutes later Rachel returned smiling and quoting,

> 'They took peculiar pains to souse
> the pictures up and down the house;
> until Mathilda's aunt succeeded
> in showing them they were not needed.
> And even then she had to pay
> to get the men to go away.'

Both Phoebe and Maggie smiled warmly, remembering the frequent readings from Belloc with which Rachel had edified their childhood. Phoebe made all three of them hot chocolate.

Later, Phoebe tucked Maggie into her own bed. She kissed her tenderly, then grinned and said,

'I tell you what, you can take tomorrow off school.'

Maggie seemed safe, warm, relaxed, sleepy. Then she opened her eyes and said,

'Mummy, can I have my St Margaret picture?'

'Now?'

'Please.'

'Of course you can, sweetie.'

She climbed the stairs to get it, crunched her way across the glass-strewn room, feeling a strong rush of her earlier panic, and unhooked the painting from the wall. It was quite small and she could hold it easily between her hands. It had hung in Maggie's bedroom for as long as Phoebe could remember: she had not looked at it properly for years. Now, with it in her hands, she knew absolutely that it was not a worthless Victorian copy, as Rachel had once told her. It was very old. The virgin saint was leading the dragon on a slim gold chain across a field of flowers towards a distant and elaborate city; she had a thin white face and an expression of nonchalance, almost tedium. It was a strong talisman for a little girl, for a young woman. Phoebe smiled, and allowed herself an unusual and agreeable start of gratitude to Rachel, not just for her consistent kindness to Maggie, but also, freshly, for her generosity and understanding towards herself.

She found Rachel still in the kitchen, looking old and weary. She was sitting at the table with her chocolate cooling in the mug between her hands. She raised her head when Phoebe came in. She thought how strained and tired her daughter looked.

'Sit down, Phoebe, I'll warm some more milk for you.'

Phoebe let her. Outside the sky was turning pale. It was morning. Looking at each other with a new respect, they both wanted to say something to mark the importance of this dawn. They were both too tired.

Two

Maggie woke up. The pale April sunshine flooded the room, but it was different from usual. She felt the change unconsciously, and with it an unaccustomed warmth. Dozily she felt her arm ache. Then the whole night flooded back into her memory, and she realised her loneliness and desolation. Instinctively she sought through the whole cosmos for Fenna, and knew she would not find him. There was nothing there, except the comfortable warmth. She opened her eyes and was aware of being in her mother's bed, where she had not been for over ten years. Phoebe was still asleep beside her, curled up and with her back close to her daughter's: Maggie enjoyed the moment of comfort, adding it dreamily to the shadow that was also there.

She felt strange. She was still wearing Phoebe's trousers and jersey. Perhaps that was why . . . surely she had not wetted herself? She reached down with her finger and drew it out covered in blood. A simple adolescent embarrassment flamed her face: she had ruined her mother's new, and pale blue, trousers. She was frightened that Phoebe would respond to this news with excessive enthusiasm, congratulate her, want to celebrate in some humiliating way, even ring her friends and tell them. She sat bolt upright, and there to greet her was St Margaret serenely leading the tamed dragon towards the city. Encouraged, Maggie prodded Phoebe.

'Mummy, I'm bleeding.'

Phoebe woke up quickly, as though she had been waiting for Maggie's summons, but not quickly enough.

'More glass, darling?' she enquired without turning over.

'No,' cried Maggie, 'and Mummy, I've messed up your new trousers.'

'Oh,' said Phoebe, who now understood, 'it doesn't matter, they'll wash.' Then, hearing something more distressed in Maggie's voice, she became maternally reassuring. 'It's probably last night, Maggie; a shock can easily change your cycle.'

'I don't have a cycle,' said Maggie crossly, feeling that her mother ought to have known. 'This is my first time.'

'Christ!' Phoebe sat up immediately and then, overwhelmed with hangover, tiredness and surprise, flopped down again abruptly. It made them both giggle. For a while they lay there, recouping their dailiness, setting up this soft laughter against the horror of the night, close and easy together.

Then, businesslike, they faced the day. Phoebe dealt with Maggie's immediate needs and took her trousers off to soak in the bathroom.

'You'd better put on one of my tracksuits, we're not meant to go up to your room until they've sent someone to inspect it or something,' she called on her way to the kitchen.

She slung the milk saucepan casually on top of the other unwashed dishes in the sink, unbothered now by the mess, aware that Rachel had seen it all last night and had said nothing. She put on the kettle, craving her morning cup of coffee. Soon Maggie joined her, and made toast. Still floppy from giggling they were careful to avoid catching each other's eye, but there was warmth and repose enough there to set against the hardness of the day's demands.

Rachel woke in her own room, tired and uncomfortable. She was too old, she told herself, for all these midnight cavortings. She turned herself over in her bed, and snuggled down for an extra, self-indulgent and rare hour of sleep. But her eye caught her bedside alarm clock and she pulled herself properly into wakefulness. All her temptations had dissolved the moment she had heard Maggie say,

'I fell. He dropped me and I fell.'

The final quiet half-hour in the kitchen with Phoebe had only made her conscious of what she had then known was now necessary. She did not like what her life demanded of her, but she knew painfully and absolutely that the moment for truth had come. So this last time she wanted to be in her office, correct and professional at the right time. The board meeting was at four o'clock, but she had paperwork to do and she must at least speak to Clare before then. She lumbered out of bed, reached for the too recently removed dressing-gown and took herself off to her bathroom.

A little later, neatly dressed in tweed suit and cashmere jersey she climbed the stairs to Phoebe's flat. She had expected to find them both still in bed, and was surprised by the noises from the kitchen, but she poked her head round the door and saw Maggie sitting at the kitchen table eating Weetabix in a reassuringly healthy way. She could sense the goodwill between the two of them, and it encouraged her. She crossed the kitchen and kissed Maggie on the head,

'Are you all right, my darling?' and then, almost surprising herself, she passed on and kissed Phoebe too. 'And you?'

'Yes, thank you.'

'Well, if everyone is all right, I think I had better go into the office today. I have something very important that I ought to do.'

Phoebe was surprised; she had somehow thought that after Rachel's sterling conduct of the night before, she would now take charge, go on looking after them all, manage everything for them and leave her free to walk the road that she had to walk. But in her mother's kiss she had learned something of the importance of whatever it was that Rachel had to do. Her mother so seldom asked her for anything, she realised with a jolt. It was she, Phoebe, herself, who imposed all those expectations upon herself, not her mother. Now in some obscure way Rachel was asking for something, for help, for reassurance, for permission.

'Of course we can manage,' she said and grinning added, 'I'm a big girl now.'

Then suddenly that was not enough. She returned her mother's kiss and said, 'Good luck.'

Rachel was used to being the tallest woman in a room. She seldom remembered that Phoebe was actually taller than she was. Now she could feel the solid muscle of her daughter's arms and she wanted to lean against her and draw comfort and strength; but she pulled away and looked at Phoebe with that straight, clear, appraising look that was her hallmark. She did not ask any questions. She said goodbye to Maggie and then, just as she was leaving the kitchen, she looked directly at Phoebe and added,

'Good luck yourself.'

Then she went down the stairs, collected her satchel and left the house by Phoebe's front door.

Phoebe and Maggie had a trying and tiresome morning. The fire brigade reappeared, bringing them some council inspector, who obviously wanted to evacuate the house. They probed and measured and cross-questioned Phoebe in the most condescending manner, made worse by the fact that they clearly did not have a clue as to what might have happened. Phoebe wanted to scream with temper, or indulge in wicked and vicious sarcasm. At the same time she was certain that Maggie did not want to have to cope with that. She bit her lip and kept her peace, and even made them cups of tea with the same grace that her mother had demonstrated in the dark hours of the night. Maggie kept catching her eye with an expression of knowing amusement, but at the same time she obviously hated having these men stomping through her every possession and destroying any remaining magic in her secret chamber.

Finally the men gave up, grudgingly admitted that the room was safe, and left muttering about 'freak accidents' and 'acts of God'. They recommended a glazier, a brush and an insurance claim. Phoebe thanked them wearily.

She and Maggie brushed the room out as best they could and the glazier arrived with an enormous sheet of polythene for the roof. He set to work steadily on replacing the panes of the side windows. Phoebe went back to the kitchen, heated up some tinned soup and made tuna fish sandwiches. Then she called Maggie. Their shared tiredness was too great; they could not replace the goodwill of the morning. They sat limply messing with the food.

But Phoebe knew that she must act.

'Maggie darling, I don't have a clue what happened last night, but I think you do.'

Maggie looked unattractively sly, sulky and fearful all at once, but Phoebe doggedly pushed on.

'Darling, I'm not going to ask anything about it, but there is something I have to know. Is the house really safe now?'

'I think so.' Maggie looked away from her mother, 'Yes. The house is quite safe.'

Phoebe held her breath. She could feel Maggie's distress; Maggie needed more than to have her care about the house. More, but not too much more.

'And you, darling, are you safe?'

'Oh yes,' said Maggie with such bleak sincerity that Phoebe knew she must go on. She must keep her appointment at the clinic at all possible costs.

'In that case I want to go out this afternoon and do something. Something important.'

Maggie only repeated her question of the night before, 'Are you OK, Mummy?'

But now it was a time for truth and Phoebe said,

'No. No, I'm not OK. But I want to be. That's what I'm going out for. It's to do with getting better, getting OK.'

And Maggie came round the table and standing over Phoebe gave her a long silent hug.

Meanwhile Rachel had taken a taxi to the museum; she had entered by the back door and exchanged a smile with the doorkeeper. She crossed the dinosaur gallery, carefully averting her eyes from her own display, unlocked the solid door and arrived in the security and peace of her own office. Deliberately she sat herself down at her desk and examined her post. Carefully she opened the drawer where the two copies of her paper lay and took them out. She started to read and for a moment lost her rigid self-consciousness in admiring delight at her own writing, its clarity and generosity. After a while, though, she pulled herself together and, leaving one copy on her desk, took the other down to the secretarial room and asked if someone could run her off two more copies, ideally before the board meeting.

Rachel was popular among the staff, always courteous and concerned and never asking for the impossivble except with great charm and self-deprecation. She got an enthusiastic response, 'Of course, Mrs Petherington, I can stay in through my lunch-break if need be. I'll see to it.'

'Thank you so much, I would really appreciate it. I'm just sorry that I didn't give it to you sooner. It was very stupid of me.'

She went back to her own office and sat down at her desk again. She put her elbows on the desk and rested her head in her hands. She had seldom felt so old or so tired or so wretched. Then she picked up her internal telephone and, very civilly, asked Clare if she could spare her half an hour or so – yes, before the meeting; yes, as soon as possible.

For the ten minutes before Clare arrived she leaned back and looked around her with a sense almost of satisfaction. She had burned her boats.

The interview with Clare was very trying. Clare was at first protective and maternal, then weepy and emotional, and finally, when the implications of what Rachel was doing became clear to her, she was furious.

'You can't. You absolutely cannot do this to me. It was you that taught me to be a Darwinist, a decent gradualist. How many times have I heard you? You can't rat on that and give all those American lunatics – and I'm quoting you – this kind of support. You can't.'

'I can,' said Rachel stubbornly.

'No, you can't. I don't mean all this, here,' she jabbed at Rachel's typescript with an irritable finger, her face looked blotchy and plainer than ever, 'this bit about your blasted reconstruction. All that's fine with me; I've known the bloody thing was wrong for ages anyway. We can take it down; we ought to take it down really. But you don't have to rush off to the other extreme. Are you crazy?'

'Clare, read it.'

'I have read it. I don't mean here, this version necessarily, but you're not the only person in the world who keeps up with the wider literature, you know. I read it all the time. And if you really want to know what I think, it's that you Cretaceous people are insanely arrogant. You can't solve one little corner, one little technical hiccup so you'll throw a hundred years of decent work out the window and replace it with sci-fi fantasies. Your time-scale is all wrong. For heaven's sake, Rachel, look at the fossil record as a whole. Not just your little bitsy corner. There's more going on than just the Cretaceous collapse. What about *arcaeopteryx*? And my therapsids? You don't have to do this.'

'But I'm going to,' said Rachel. She was too exhausted, too weary to argue it out with her now, but she was also excited. Now Clare had abandoned her respectful kindness it would be fun to fight with her.

'Look,' she said reasonably, 'you haven't even read the paper properly yet. Take it away and read it, and we'll talk it through if you are still not convinced. But I am convinced and I'm going to tell the board so today. I only wanted to tell you first so you could save yourself this sort of scene in front of them. I owed it to you.'

'Thank you,' snorted Clare in as ungrateful a manner as she could manage, swept her copy contemptuously off the desk, and stalked out of the room with a moderately successful attempt at dignity.

Rachel allowed herself a brief smile at such youthfulness. Then she sat down to write a letter to an old friend, the editor of her chosen journal. She pointed out to him the attraction of publishing so surprising a paper and urged him to do it as quickly as possible. It was a charming letter, a well-managed mixture of humility and boastfulness, and she sent it down to be typed with a feeling of smugness.

She realised that she still had fifteen minutes before the meeting was due to start and on an impulse she rang Paul. She needed someone to rejoice with her. He was out. She had neither the energy nor the time to feel irritated; instead she took out her pen again and reached for a sheet of the museum's paper.

My dear Paul, in ten minutes I am going to tell my board that I have become a convert to Catastrophe Theory. Poor dinosaurs. Now I am in urgent need of a tutor in such matters as the shadow star Nemesis, the irridium level and other such metaphysical absurdities. I hope you are up to the job. Please ring soon. Love, Rachel.

'That'll get him,' she said aloud, and grinned. Contrary to her usual habit, she rang for a motorbike messenger. She put the sheet of paper in an envelope, addressed it clearly, added the word 'Urgent' and carried it down to the office, where she left it for collection and received instead the original and the photostats of her article. Then, quite calmly, she proceeded to her meeting.

As soon as she entered the room she knew that Clare had already been telling tales; or at least complaining to her colleagues. What had she said?

'The old bag has gone completely batty.'

'Besotted by that silly queer over at Imperial.'

'How are we going to get her out of here? It's too embarrassing.'

Or even, Rachel wondered, 'You've got to say this for the old girl, she does keep on trying.'

She could sense the excitement and the nervousness, the sudden lull in the conversation as she entered. She thought someone might ask her questions, but she was saved by the arrival of their director. He was a dour middle-aged man, who feared he was a failure and compensated himself with an excessively professorial beard and a punctiliously formal manner. For nearly two hours he worked his way through his agenda, more administration and finance today than scientific exploration. He was, apparently, completely insensitive to the frisson of curiosity and tension in the younger members of his staff. Rachel relaxed, grateful, and gave her usual careful consideration to the matters before the meeting; calmly ploughing through the minutiae and bureaucratic red tape of museum management, making the sort of useful contributions that she had made at any such meeting in the last twenty years.

Finally the Director brought the whole thing to a close; he pulled his papers towards him, preparatory to getting up and said,

'Any other business?' in an off-hand and discouraging tone.

But Rachel was not discouraged. 'I have, Henry; I'm going to have to ask for a complete and urgent reorganisation of the dinosaur gallery.'

'Huh?'

'I'm afraid so. I have become convinced that our whole approach is hopelessly unscientific, in fact wrong, and particularly that my own reconstruction is so fundamentally flawed that we really don't have the right to be displaying it anywhere except in a Disneyland type of amusement park.'

'Rachel!'

'It is a bit embarrassing, isn't it? I'm sorry, Henry, but I have written a paper, which I'm planning to send to Tom Haines, which more or less says precisely this. Clare has seen it, although she probably hasn't had time to read it fully. And although she seems to disagree with its overall drift, she tells me she's in complete accord with my views on what she called my "blasted reconstruction".'

Let that be a lesson to you, Clare, she thought, to lose your temper and try me with your emotional immaturity. She was buoyed up suddenly on the wave of amazement and admiration that she could feel enveloping her from across the whole room.

She was pleased with herself and her own calm style. She had not thought she had this much spunk left in her. She smiled at them all and added,

'Clare has a copy of the paper now, and I have brought in a couple of extra copies; so perhaps the dinosaur people, at least, might like to have a look at it and see what they think. You'll probably want to talk about it without the embarrassment of having me here to listen. But don't dilly-dally for too long; once it's published we are all going to look a little risible if we have made no adjustments to what is after all known as being predominantly my own design of gallery. Also, I am a bit older than the rest of you, but you can perhaps understand that I don't want to drop dead without a proper and public recantation. Since I'm technically retired I can't say that I'll resign if you disagree with my request – and particularly that we should remove my reconstruction as quickly as is feasible, but I do feel it that strongly and I shall publish whatever you decide.'

Suddenly she wanted to put her head down on the big table and howl with misery. She pushed back her chair and stood up abruptly; she was terrified that she would sway, topple and crash to the ground. And then she heard her mother's voice. Even though she had learned so recently that this was not the authentic voice of her mother, the intellectual knowledge had changed nothing, nothing, and perhaps it never did. Now her mother's voice called to her, telling her to act like a lady. All through her childhood she had resented the voice, had resented her mother. Now she thought 'Mother' deliberately, summoning up from a deep centre the bossy voice which had haunted her and with it a sweet softness, older still and loving.

In the strength of that voice she was able to gather up her papers, push them into her satchel, and leave the room with perfect dignity. She made it back to her office and sank into her chair; but after a few minutes she sat up, combed her hair and decided to go home. Just as she was reaching for her jacket the phone rang, and without thinking she answered it.

'Hello.'

'Rachel?'

'Paul.'

'Rachel, what is all this? I get in from a dull lunch and find your urgent communication on my desk. What are you up to?'

'You can read, Paul. I suppose it was Smit and van der Kaars in the end.' And Paul himself and Maggie and Fenna, but she would not try to tell him that. 'I've written a paper; a recantation you might call it. I think Tom Haines will publish it . . . he'd be best, don't you think? I mean the whole thing is wrong, the reconstruction, the theory behind it. So I supposed I'd better tell my board about it and I did this afternoon. Clare is out for my blood of course, poor thing, but I couldn't really help that. I thought I'd better get it sorted out before I died.'

'And you just got up in front of Henry and those pipsqueaks in your department and said, "Sorry and all that, old chaps, but I've been wrong all my life and led you into error and wickedness"?'

'More or less.'

'Rachel, you are amazing. That's the bravest thing I have ever heard of. Can I come round this evening with a bottle of champagne?'

'Well, that would be very nice. Thank you. I should warn you, though, we're in a bit of chaos at home. The roof fell in last night.'

'What?'

Suddenly she could almost hear her mother giggling. She could hear her mother's distant laughter and her voice saying faintly, 'Rachel, do stop showing off.' More immediately she could hear Paul's resounding,

'What?'

'The roof, dear. You know what that is. It fell in, caved in rather. Maggie's skylight smashed. But we're all fine.'

'But Rachel, why? I mean why did it cave in or whatever.'

'Well I haven't heard the official report because I had to go to my board meeting, but if you ask me, Maggie's dragon did it.'

'Rachel, are you drunk?' There was a pause, and suddenly Paul laughed, 'Have I ever told you, Rachel, that I adore you? You are the most extraordinary and wonderful woman I have ever encountered, and I shall make it a magnum of champagne. I love you.'

When she put the phone down she felt fizzy with excitement, but with his smiling voice cut off, the feeling did not last. Instead she felt very, very tired.

Then she knew that she needed not to sneak out by the convenient back exit, but to leave through the front entrance, trusting its outrageous, ostentatious vulgarity to reassure and comfort her.

And thus it was, that February evening, that she came to be standing at the top of the monumental sweep of the staircase, under the huge doorway, pausing for a moment, offering tribute to herself and all her gods.

Meanwhile Phoebe had taken a shower, found some clean knickers, mounted her bicycle and ridden off to her appointment at the clinic. Even as she chained her bike up she noticed three different taxis drawing up and depositing their customers. Hers was the only bicycle attached to these particularly well-painted railings, and her soul cringed. Despite all her resolution, she paused outside the plate-glass doorway and looked around guiltily. The chances of any of her acquaintance passing at this moment and noting that she, Phoebe Petherington, was entering the evil portals of a private hospital, were, she admitted, so small as to be risible, but that did not allay her shame. She slunk covertly through the entrance.

Her sense of inadequacy escalated rapidly; not only was the receptionist extremely pretty, she was also immaculately dressed, well-mannered, and had perfectly clean, shell-like little fingernails.

She said, 'Can I help you?' as though she meant it.

Phoebe, on the other hand, suddenly could not remember what false name she had given when she made the appointment. She stumbled over the words, muttered and blushed, her duplicity and stupidity so abundantly clear to her that she was surprised that the charming young woman did not immediately leap to her feet, denounce her as an impostor and throw her out onto the street again. She almost wished she would.

Then the luxury of the place reached out and embraced her. It was the stuff of her darkest fantasies, her most secret longings. Well-manicured hands took her jacket respectfully, offered her a seat, brought her coffee in a china cup with a saucer. She was asked discreet questions about private health insurance and, in the face of her disclaimers, equally civil ones about her credit cards. She was led away into a crisp-looking cell where she was measured and weighed; a careful, polite pair of hands found a vein in her strong arm and removed a vial of her blood. Someone took her blood pressure and remarked on how healthy it was. She could not restrain a flash of pride in her physical fitness; all the nurses were smaller than she was and, although they were prettier, she felt her dignity and certainty returning.

She had imagined that the doctor would be male; she had looked forward to it even, a chance to pit herself against him, to resist, to overcome; but when she was finally ushered into the consulting room she was greeted by a woman younger than herself. This shocked her suddenly, shook her back into the real world and changed the entire course of the interview. It was no longer a fantasy, a ritual extension of the dark dreams of her night times, in which the doctor was to play out some version of her lost father, an ally against the demands of the women in her life. This was real; Maggie and Rachel deserved that reality. So sharp was her sense of the rules having changed that she was shocked to see the name Mary Hunter at the top of the card in the doctor's hand. Only simple embarrassment prevented her from correcting it.

'You're a remarkably fit woman, aren't you, Mrs Hunter?' said the smiling doctor. 'What do you do for a living?'

'I'm a gardener,' Phoebe said, and felt a simple pride in the fact. This proved stronger than her irritation at the surprise in the young doctor's face. Clearly well-spoken female gardeners were not the usual clientèle of this hospital.

They plodded through the whole range of routine questions. Long before they reached the relevant section, Phoebe had decided she was going to lie about the amount she drank. She had not come here for that; it was another problem that she must take on, but not now, not here.

Then, as instructed, she removed her clothes and lay out on the couch. Glancing down, her toes seemed miles away, disembodied, belonging to someone else. It was this moment that she had come for. The doctor was rubbing her hands, probably to warm them, but it looked like a gesture of glee and greed. Phoebe hated her with a brief clear flame of anger. This was the avenging angel who would steal her lover away from her. And at the same moment she had the shattering thought that perhaps she had imagined the whole thing. There would be no lump. The doctor would feel her breasts, find nothing, smile and send her off to deal with a new, an incurable bitterness.

The doctor, still chatting away, put her stethoscope in her ears and listened to Phoebe's chest and heart, then had her sit up and tapped her back. Phoebe felt the tension prickling her belly as she lay down again. The doctor, whatever her politics and morals, had lovely skilful hands, which Phoebe could not but admire. She made the vaginal examination comfortable and smooth.

'Now breasts,' she said. 'Do you do your own self-examinations?'

'Sometimes,' muttered Phoebe; she was not going to tell this woman that for the last six months she had done practically nothing else.

'You ought to, you know; I'll show you how afterwards.'

Her hands were warm and competent. Phoebe liked the sensation and was terrified. The doctor started with her right breast; circled it tenderly, skilled fingers pushing against the flesh; in some different context, Phoebe thought, it could be very sexy, this slow gentle probing, dispassionate but intimate. The doctor smiled quietly, reached for her pad and made a note; she smiled, walked round the foot of the high couch and came up towards Phoebe left-hand side.

Phoebe could feel her own heart beating. The doctor ran her hands round again, with the same disinterested precision. Phoebe knew when she had reached the lump, but the fingers went on circling, and then probing her armpit. Time slowed down, Phoebe wanted this moment to go on for ever, this calm moment before the storm. Eventually the doctor's fingers came back again, back to where the lump was. Phoebe opened her eyes and saw the abstracted professional look in the doctor's face; attentive not to Phoebe but to the lump, to the breast itself. As it should be. And then the doctor caught her eye. She began a reassuring smile and then stopped abruptly.

'You knew, didn't you?' Her eyes widened and she looked angry.

'Yes,' said Phoebe, because it was too late now for untruths or pretences.

'You must be insane.' The doctor seemed almost embarrassed by her own outburst, but Phoebe was relieved. It was a clear diagnosis, the same as Tom's. Better that than discretion and gentle kindliness. She did not want to have the news broken to her carefully.

'Go and have the mammogram and then come back and talk to me.'

In her fantasies Phoebe had somehow assumed that the mammogram would be visible. One afternoon she had lurked in the medical bookshop at the top of Gower Street and looked at glowing colour plates of carcinomas. She tried to tell herself that she had come here today to be cured, to return to the cold world of normality; but in another part of her mind she had dreamed of this meeting, the apotheosis of the love affair. She would raise her lamp and view the lover that she herself had grown, even if this meant that she must lose him for ever.

She had fantasised the meeting: she would be lying naked and on some screen in front of her she would see, pulsing and radiant, her own dark lover and his home place. There would be her breast filled with veins and glands, the source of Maggie's milk and much of her own sexual pleasure, all pink and red and living, and there, in the heart of it, would be – green and gold and sparkling – the bright egg of her dreams.

However the mammogram room was cold and scientific. There was no doctor, no magic seer to give her the golden branch and lead her into the underworld, only yet another pretty young woman, the radiological technician. Phoebe had to stand on the cold and excessively clean linoleum floor, far away from the fitted carpets and deep leather chairs of the waiting area. The radiologist apologetically but firmly positioned Phoebe in front of a ferocious-looking machine; she took Phoebe's arms and stretched them forward into an awkward position. The tie of the white gown she had been given to wear caught in her hair and pulled it. Phoebe jerked away and the radiologist only just managed to suppress her irritation.

They started the ugly dance again. Once she had got Phoebe back where she wanted her, the radiographer manhandled Phoebe's breasts, without interest, between two cold plates. These were clamped together, squashing her breasts flat, pulling at the skin of her underarms.

It hurt. It hurt, not unbearably but sharply, and under that pressure the last of Phoebe's passion was squeezed out. Under her bare toes the floor felt real and solid, and although she was lonely and sad she knew she was going to choose to return to the real and solid world.

Politeness alone made her go back to see the doctor, and listen to her almost stern advice. This was not Phoebe's place and she knew quite simply that tomorrow morning she would go to see her own GP and organize the necessary hospital visit. Maggie needed her, Rachel needed her, and she had no other choice; passion was not to be part of her calling. The old mistake made in a bathroom in Oxford twenty years before had fixed her course and all she could do was to walk it. Just before leaving the consulting room she knew that she had one thing left to do and it was important.

'There's something else I should tell you,' she said. 'I gave you a false name. I am really called Phoebe Petherington. That is my name.'

She knew the doctor thought she was a lunatic, but as she would never see her again, it did not matter now as much as the truth. She paid her bill to the efficient receptionist and left the hospital.

Leaving the clinic she realised suddenly that she wanted to go to her garden. It was an impulse she did not question. She mounted her bike and pedalled eastwards. Halfway there she remembered Maggie and stopped to telephone her. But the first kiosk only took cards, and she did not have one and the next kiosk was broken. She gave up and rode on. This was important. Maggie was safe.

But when she reached the vicinity of her garden she was seized with a sudden embarrassment. She had not even phoned them that morning to explain her absence. And she did not want to talk to anyone. Quickly she decided not to go into the garden; instead she would climb the nearby tower block and see her garden from above.

And thus it was that she came to be, that February evening, standing at the top of the tower block staircase, leaning against the wall and panting a little from her climb, pausing for a moment and thinking gloomy thoughts about life and death.

Meanwhile Maggie stayed sitting at the kitchen table. Slowly and without thinking she ate all the tuna fish and mayonnaise her mother had prepared. She also finished the loaf of bread. Later she dug about in the fridge; and although the result was depressing, she did find and consume two pots of yoghurt, a hunk of cheese and a slice of ham which had begun to curl up at its edges. She felt sick, but was relieved to feel something: the weight of the food in her stomach did something to counteract the sense of unreality that afflicted her. Her brain was foggy and muffled.

She might have sat all afternoon, nibbling and stuporous, exhausted but not sleepy; but the glazier finally came down from the upper floor, cheerfully announcing that all was now right and tight and he would be on his way. Maggie could tell that he would have liked to stop for a chat, that he felt sorry for her left on her own, but she lacked either her grandmother's grace or her mother's energy, so she did not offer him tea.

When he had gone, she dragged herself up the iron staircase to her own room. The room had lost its magic: instead of the great sheet of clear sky overhead there were subdued shadows; the polythene letting in less light than the glass. The whole place smelled of putty and turpentine, and the crash had shaken down not only stars of glass, but also dust and grime. Most of the glass had been removed, but the dirt had not, clouding the air and deadening the surfaces. Her picture and her silk quilt had been carried down below in the chaos of last night and she did not have the energy to seek them out. Phoebe had also, that morning, borne away all her bedding and some of her clothes to shake the glass out of them. The room now looked like what it was: an attic, the keeping-place for forgotten treasures, the home of the dead. It did not matter to her anyway. She tried lying down on the bare mattress, but the whole place felt cold and close.

After a bit she got up again and crept down to her mother's room. That too lacked the warmth and comfort of the morning, though her picture was still on the mantelpiece. Her stomach ached dully but distractingly.

She knew not whether from eating too much or from her period. Fenna might have given her both appetite and menstruation in his parting, but neither of them seemed as though they were worth the effort. She wanted to cry and even that did not seem worth the effort. She curled up on her mother's bed, pulled the duvet over her and lay there, inert.

She had seen and noticed this despondency, this weightedness, in her mother. Once she had assumed it was somehow her mother's fault. Out there the whole cosmos rolled and sang, out there the stars had danced and sung when Fenna called to them. On stormy nights it had been exhilarating to fly in the teeth of the wind. Hard to steer, to balance, to float, she had learned instead to consent; to cast herself onto the wind and learn the whole length and depth and height of its strength, and in perfect relaxation, the stern corseting of gravity left far below, her whole body had been open to power and loveliness. She had thought that if her mother had learned to consent, to let go, to be filled, then Phoebe's passivity and disinterest would drop off like a cloak and she too could be naked with joy and love. Now, coiled here, she thought it was not Phoebe's fault, it was the dullness of being an adult; it was the natural flavour of the world once one had said goodbye to childhood. It might be necessary but it was not fun, and nothing would ever be fun again. On a conservative reckoning she would have to live at least another fifty years in this bland and dreary universe.

She could of course, she thought with that sudden burst of adolescent enthusiasm, not live. She held the idea of death briefly between her hands; but noticed how fast her mind darted away and took up sentimental pictures of her funeral, of her mother's and grandmother's distress, of her friends. She knew she would not cheat and take that option, and she could think of no other. The swift burst of curiosity and eagerness flickered out. She just lay there, not thinking, or even feeling, anything.

The phone rang. She pulled the duvet over her head and ignored it. The phone went on ringing, and finally, irritated, she stumbled off the bed and picked up the receiver from the floor where Phoebe usually left the phone.

'Hello,' she said in what she hoped was a dignified version of annoyance.

The caller seemed oblivious.

'Maggie! how are you? Are you OK? Where have you been?'

It was Hermione, genuinely concerned because she had not been at school; someone who had missed her. Her spirits rose a little,

'I'm fine.'

'But what happened to you?'

'No, listen, this totally weird thing happened last night. There was I, sweetly asleep, and suddenly the roof collapsed on top of me.'

'What?'

'Really.'

And suddenly it could be a story, a funny story that was making Hermione laugh. Suddenly she knew how to do this, this chatting and joking and telling her life, sharing it, warming herself from the fire of affection she had lit in her friend. Distantly she remembered that she had never understood the art of it, had to work on it, conscious and struggling all the time. Now, her head emptied of Fenna, it flowed out smooth and bubbling, almost unnoticed. This was Hermione, this was her friend.

After a while she said, 'How was school, then?'

'Oh, moan.'

'No I meant really, did we get masses of homework?'

'If you came over I could give you all the assignments.'

They laughed, the transparency of their own schemes delighting them. They didn't do many subjects together and were only in the same group for French and history. Their grown-ups however, who might well, in the middle of their GCSE year, object to a Monday evening of socialising, would not know these things.

'I can't be late,' said Hermione dutifully, 'I really have got that gruesome geography project to hand in. I know what, let's do it now. I'll meet you in the park, you know the gate at the top of Gloucester Road, that's about equal for both of us. We'll hang about or something . . . my mother's out, I'll leave her a note.'

'Aye, aye, Captain,' said Maggie, 'so's mine.'

'Keep some of the broken glass for Ms Fish's break-time coffee. We can grind it during the lunch break tomorrow. See you in half an hour, then?'

Laughing, Maggie hung up.

After a moment she realised that she would have to change; there was no way she was going out to meet Hermione in her mother's elderly and considerably over-large tracksuit. As she ran up to her room she was, for the first time in her life, actively grateful to Phoebe and Rachel for their absolute laws of tidiness. Her clothes, neatly in their cupboards and drawers were not ruined or dirty after the catastrophe. If it had happened to anyone else, to any of her friends, half their garments would now be lying under glass or dust around the floor. But it could not have happened to anyone else, she was almost forgetting that this had not been exactly a freak accident in the way that everyone thought.

Not everyone. Her mother had known. Sort of. She felt a tiny moment of pride: this was an accident that her power had brought about and Phoebe knew it. Perhaps Rachel did too, or would do when she had had time to work it out. Even if it was the last thing she was ever able to do, Phoebe would have known it, and would have to notice her now. Phoebe had obviously needed her reassurance that the house was safe.

Her elation took her into her clothes, back to the kitchen to leave Phoebe a scrawled memo, and out of the front door. It carried her into the park and only wavered when she saw the playground. Then suddenly the park looked so different, filled not with dragons dancing but with ordinary people, and she was just one of them. Over the next two hundred yards she slowed down again, her misery and inertia crowding back upon her, her loneliness embracing her. Until at the top of the hill, despite spotting Hermione's black hair and bright red jacket down below her, she came to a stop.

And thus it was that she came to be, on that February evening, poised at the very crown of the hill in Kensington Gardens, looking down the hill, with her back to Bayswater and home and trembling with the fear that she had at last grown up.

Three

After a couple of minutes Phoebe recovered her breath; she pushed herself off the wall with her hands and went through the stairwell doorway into the green-painted corridor. She walked along the passage and came, as she had planned, to the window which made the end wall of that floor. She was poised now over her garden and could see the whole of it, laid out like a little world, from her great height. She had created it from the chaos, she was its God. She leaned against the window, resting her forehead on the glass, enjoying its cool smoothness.

She felt her own tiredness. And why should it hurt so much, be so unutterably wearisome, to say goodbye to death, to the dark passion that had consumed her? There was nothing left now, but to grow old, but to grow old and take on the burden of her mother growing even older. To give up the burden of Maggie getting older. To acknowledge that she could not and never would ask Maggie for the mothering that she would give to her own mother. To accept finally and irrevocably that there was no romance in her life, that romance was a deep killer, a consuming passion and that she was too tough a woman to be consumed. And there was nothing.

She leaned more heavily against the window and stared unseeing at her park below. She would offer her breast as a blood sacrifice for life and in that moment of despair she had no doubt at all but that death would accept it and she would have to live. Lopsided, belonging not to herself and her inner love, but to doctors and chemotherapy and the loss of all her hair. The tears, of self-pity and self-loss, welled in her eyes. As she raised a hand to wipe them away she noticed how deeply the dirt had eaten into her fingernails, so that they were not, and so long as she worked never would be, pink and sweet and shell-like. When she raised them the rest of the way she held them not to her streaming eyes, but to her ears, listening intently for the sound of the sea.

But she did not hear the sound of the sea, she heard instead the sound of the earth. The earth on her fingers spoke to her, spoke to her of sowing in tears and reaping with joy; of dying and growing. The earth on her fingers sung to her and she could hear the rhythm of the seasons, the wobbling journey of her planet through space, which gave the earth its sides and turns, and within that there were the smaller rhythms of her rake, of her tractor engine, of her trowel and of her brain.

Her eyes were clear of tears; she looked from a great height down into the park and saw its order and its beauty so determinedly brought forth. She saw, coming out of the hut and walking across towards the gate, Pete and Sammy, two of her youth volunteers. She could not help but pause in her misery to be proud of the fact that, without her supervision, they had been at work in the garden. As she watched, Sammy threw a casual playful punch at Pete's shoulder and, fooling, Pete fainted away and bounced back.

They were playing like children, and she could be a child too and play with them and the garden would mother her – a stern and demanding mother, but with moments of perfect attentiveness. Her park knew she was up there watching and waiting over it, and it tossed off a loving welcoming wave; it – the tractor, the boys and the bulbs in the earth – knew she had chosen for them and was coming back to them.

Of course there was still love, there was healthy, growing love and its name was called Work. She had fallen in love with it so slowly and gently and sweetly that she had never noticed it had happened. The park, unlikely though it might seem, was not a job, not a political ideology, not a way of filling in the weary hours until she was old enough to retire, not even something to spite her mother with once and for all while she accepted everything else from her. It had been all those things, it had started as all those things, but now it was work and love.

She saw her work laid out there in the garden, all the muscled cold wet harshness of it; all the labour and the ingrained resistance to working, and she thanked her mother, who had given her this thing. This knowledge that in the end everything must crumble but a woman's work is her rock and her shield, a strong fortress, a faithful lover. This enormous gift that, despite all the trying things that went with it, Phoebe had received; this capacity to look at a thing and know that, because it must be done, it is the doing of it that brings freedom and salvation.

She remembered something.

'If a woman must choose between love and work, she should never hesitate.' She could not remember where it came from, but she muttered the line to herself, and the mutter took root in her stomach, grew and blossomed into an enormous belly laugh.

Maggie saw Hermione shake exasperated shoulders and suddenly feared that she might walk away. The fear propelled her out of her stillness and she ran down the hill. It was almost like flying, this running downhill towards a friend who might vanish if she delayed. Lightness and truth came to her with the wind's speed.

'Hermione,' she said, once they had greeted each other, 'there is something I want to tell you; it is sort of a secret.'

'Oh Lord,' said Hermione grinning. 'Who is he?'

'It's not that at all,' said Maggie, but now she was nervous again. Nervous but steadfast.

'It's about what really happened to our roof last night. Let's go and sit on some bench.'

They sat on a bench in the Flower Walk, the beautifully tended beds laid out for them and all the tulips listening attentively, and Maggie broke the rule of her lifetime and told Hermione about Fenna. In the telling it became neither nightmare nor obsession, but a beautiful tale, the stuff of dreams and fairy stories, and Hermione heard it all with tenderness and pleasure while the sun set and the dusk gathered thickly around them.

Afterwards they stood up slowly, not wanting to part from such intimacy, but beginning to feel chilly now the warmth of the story was over. They looked so beautiful, together, black and gold. And then suddenly, not black and gold but gold and silver. Hermione was glowing radiant in the dusk, an intense silver light, vibrantly running in the tight curls of her hair like neon, in the soft pinker palms of her hands like candlelight, in her eyes and teeth like electricity, and across all her whole skin like fluorescence.

Maggie was almost fearful.

'It's all right,' said Hermione softly, smiling, amused. 'I'm radiant. When I was little I learned to swim in the ponds of the Romney Marshes, behind Dungeness. The water was radioactive. I'm irradiated. Whenever my atoms get excited they glow. They're glowing for you and your dragon.'

'Does it hurt?' asked Maggie, trembling with awe and joy.

Hermione grinned. 'Wait and see,' she said and to both their surprises she turned and put her arms on Maggie's shoulders. After a moment Maggie too began, faintly, pearly, to glow.

'You can give it away, magic,' said Hermione, giggling. 'If you give it away it comes back in its own good time, like that dreadful assembly hymn, you know . . . and "you end up having more".'

This is what my mother meant, thought Maggie, this is what she meant and meant to give me.

The two of them were overcome with giggles, shaken by their own senseless amusement. They were floppy with laughter, leaning against each other and passing the magic atoms backward and forwards like little kids playing clapping games in the cement playgrounds of primary schools. Maggie scraped the radiant atoms off Hermione's arms and juggled them in the air, but she was giggling too much and kept missing the rhythm.

They collapsed into each other's arms and at that moment a group of callow youths stomped past, bigger than the girls and ferocious looking.

'Well,' said one of them, 'what have we got here? Looks like a couple of little dykes to me.'

They might have been frightened, or offended, but they were laughing too much.

'Don't worry about it,' said Hermione, cheeky in her hilarity. 'It's probably just a phase we're going through.'

The boys grinned a little sheepishly, acknowledging her courage.

'It's all right,' says Maggie, perfectly clear, her bell sounding again uncracked and certain as she had feared it never would. 'My grandmother says that a normal evolutionary phase can last two hundred million years.'

Rachel was very tired and paused now on the monumental steps of her museum. She would just have to cling to her professional integrity as she had done for fifty years, and she would, as she had always tried to, make that sufficient. The pose, the swagger, the moment of pride was solitary, an indulgence for herself alone, and there would be nothing more. She would go home. And it was high time she retired.

She shook herself slightly and took a final look down the proud granite staircase towards the traffic. Then, running her eyes along the row of plane trees, she suddenly noticed, for the first time, that a medium-sized dragon was sitting in the upper branches of a particularly fine plane tree and munching a green leaf. It's back was a dull pewter colour, with a paler underbelly, but the tip of its tail was *eau de nil* and looked soft and delicate. The dragon looked directly at her. Its ancient and mischievous eyes were almost tender. The smoke furled dreamily from its navy blue nostrils and wafted gently into the evening, almost indistinguishable from the exhaust fumes of the cars below it. She had never seen a dragon before, and now she nearly exploded with joy.

For someone over seventy her descent of that great staircase was as good as a frolic; her satchel swung wildly round merrily bumping her large bottom, her sensible suede shoes skippetty-hopped like the finest quality glass slippers, while her honest tweed skirt flirted up her legs in order to give her long beige knickers their first sight of the sunshine in quarter of a century.

By the time she reached the bottom the dragon had vanished, but this, far from mattering, only added to her amusement. Quite suddenly she felt a generous relief, as though she'd given science and herself new hope of heaven, and set out through the gathering dark, home, home across the dragon-haunted park.